When I Wake Up

Anna Pickard

This book is dedicated to my beautiful family

In loving memory of my sister Tash

1

The Incident

"Who's next?"

A short woman quickly emerged from a line of waiting patients and pushed her heavy frame against the counter's edge.

"Fuck's sake!" Nancy silently sighed.

This woman was a reoccurring nightmare. Affectionately nicknamed 'The Beast' by resentful shop assistants throughout the Highstreet, she was the definition of difficult and delighted in publicly belittling Nancy. However, usually, she'd impatiently hammer on the front window, rudely bellowing insults from her mobility scooter. For her to have left her chariot in the street to make a personal appearance meant only one thing – she was up to something.

"I want my prescription!" She breathlessly demanded.

"I'll have a look now." Nancy flatly hopped up the step into the dispensary and flicked through the alphabetically filed papers. There was no sign of it, so she moved over to the computer to check her records. She'd come in too early to collect it – again.

"Here we pissing go!" Nancy thought, gently resting her head on the monitor.

To prevent patients from stockpiling medication, it was pharmacy policy for repeat prescriptions to be collected on a set date. Patients were contacted a couple of days prior as a reminder, but for some reason, this woman saw herself as an exemption. Nancy had lost count of the times she'd explained the process to her and of the fierce arguments that ensued. She stared at the screen for a few moments, searching for the right words to break the news, but she knew exactly how it was going to play out. She'd be cornered on the dispensary step, just as she'd previously been cornered against the shop's frontage, biting her tongue, while The Beast exploded into a long aimless rant.

There was no point in delaying the inevitable, she bit the bullet and peered back out into the shop. The woman now stood impatiently between the counter and dispensary step, like a little angry bollard.

"Hurry up!" She snapped, as she glimpsed Nancy's timid re-emergence.

"You're four days too early." Nancy blurted.

"No!" The woman shrieked, "It's Christmas, you'll be closed!"

"We're only closed tomorrow! Christmas Day."

If this was a reasonable person the conversation would have ended there, but this bull loved to charge.

"You're absolutely useless!" The Beast screamed, "You're telling me, that I have to come all the way back here in four days?"

"No, we can deliver it to you when it's ready."

"Deliver it? I'm not waiting around all day for it not to show up!"

"It will show up!"

"I am absolutely sick of you! There's always an issue when you're involved."

"No!" Nancy firmly protested, "*You've* come in too early for it – again."

2

"Because I basically have to do *your* job for you and remind you about it."

Nancy subtly smiled, "You honestly don't. As soon as it's available you'll receive it."

"I'm not coming all the way back here. You know full well that I struggle to walk!"

She turned to the customers behind her to encourage their support. Most avoided eye contact, but a few busy bodies in the line shook their heads and tutted in agreement.

Uncomfortable with this extra attention, Nancy tried to hop back down the step to disappear behind the counter, but The Beast shuffled forwards to stop her.

"Look, your prescription will be here in four days, other than sign you up for deliveries, there is nothing more I can do for you."

"No, I know you can't! I don't even know why you're here. I want to speak to someone else."

Nancy wanted nothing more than to palm this woman off to her manager. She never got the opportunity when she served her at the front door. She'd do shuttle runs, carrying the woman's messages of dissatisfaction to him, then return to The Beast with his blunt responses. He'd point blank refuse to get off his arse and speak to her himself – but today, he couldn't. Without hesitation Nancy looked over her shoulder into the dispensary.

"Is he there?" The Beast snapped.

"My manager?" Nancy asked, looking back at her.

The Beast slyly chuckled, "Little bit more than just your manager, isn't he?"

A rush of warm blood blew through Nancy's body. This was why the miserable cow had struggled into the shop. Nancy knew she wouldn't have made the effort just for her prescription. She'd come fishing.

"What?" Nancy smiled.

"I've been told about you two."

"Us two?" Nancy innocently pouted. She dismissed The Beast's question with a cold stare, but her heart began to race. She didn't need this today, especially not in front of such a large crowd. She needed to mute her quickly.

"Yes. Don't play coy with me, it's not really much of a secret." The Beast snorted.

"Do you want to speak to my manager or not?" Nancy impatiently huffed.

But The Beast continued, "*He's* the real reason *you're* here, isn't he?"

"Course. He hired me."

"No. I mean for him personally." The Beast turned back to her supporters, but all now looked away, uncomfortable with her bold interrogation.

"I don't know what you're implying!" Nancy seethed.

"Well, you're no good at your job. Obviously, you must be good at something else!"

Nancy's face burned. She quickly tried to think of a way to shut her up, but other than shoving the nearby pen pot in her mouth, she was out of ideas.

"You're his little side piece!"

"Excuse me!"

"I've even seen it with my own eyes, sat at the window, him putting his arms around you."

"Don't be ridiculous!"

"I'm not! No wonder you've got no time to get my prescription ready."

"That's enough now!"

"I've heard you get up to God knows what in that back room with him!"

"I said enough!"

"His girlfriend must be pretty understanding."

Nancy's audience erupted into a sea of shocked sniggers. She bit down hard on her bottom lip and tried with every ounce of her being to dispel her rage, but she couldn't control it any longer. Not only was this a very sore subject, but she'd already had the day from hell dealing with countless rude, obnoxious people. This was the cherry on top it; her anger overrode her professional composure and she unravelled, "Do me a favour, shut your mouth and fuck off on your scooter!"

Again, shocked gasps and sniggers from the audience ensued and The Beast's thin eyebrows flew up so high, they almost camouflaged themselves into her sparse, auburn hairline.

Nancy smugly basked in superiority; she'd finally silenced The Beast. She'd put up with this woman for far too long, but her sense of release was swallowed by dread, as she watched The Beast's thin lips spike into a grin; she'd just given her exactly what she'd wanted.

"Repeat what you just said to me."

Nancy silently replayed the insult in her head, but didn't speak.

"What did you just say?" The Beast screamed.

"I told you to leave." Nancy blurted.

"Oh, no, no, no, no! You said a little bit more than that, didn't you?"

Nancy shook her head.

"Get me your manager now!" She screamed.

Again, Nancy looked over her shoulder into the dispensary to signal for him. He'd sat listening to the whole commotion from his hideaway and true to form, had made no attempt to intervene. Their eyes met and he got up off his stool, flashed her his perfect, reassuring smile and rolled his eyes. His casual saunter calmed the fraught atmosphere settling Nancy's nerves. He'd defend her – or so she thought.

"Did you hear what she just said to me!" The woman squealed, wildly pointing her finger at his emergence. Her extreme exasperation now brought a tight wheeze to her voice.

"Yes madam! Unfortunately, I did." He serenely replied. His face then pulled into a concerned yet charming expression, like a male model smouldering at a photoshoot. "Her comments were completely inappropriate and uncalled for. You were simply voicing your frustrations, something you are perfectly within your rights to do."

"What!" Nancy cried.

He reluctantly glanced at her in disgust, then quickly continued, "I am personally appalled by her disgraceful comments and can assure you that she will be dealt with. In fact, I'm going to take her into the back room right now."

Nancy quickly tried to defend herself, but he held his finger up in front of her face, just millimetres away from her lips to silence her and continued. "I also apologise that unfortunately we haven't been able to provide you with your prescription today. I can't do anything about that I'm afraid, but I can assure you, that it will be here waiting for you in four days."

The Beast paused for a moment. Nancy watched her beady eyes pulse in thought, as though her mind was building another sharp comment – but unbelievably, she came back with no argument, she simply shrugged in acceptance. He had provided no alternate solution and nothing to sweeten the blow, yet she was now just going to accept the four days wait, just like that. No fuss. Regardless of his masterful dominance, it was clear to Nancy that she'd just been set up.

"It's about time she was dealt with! I don't want to see her here when I come back!" The Beast snarled.

"I don't want to be here!" Nancy childishly blurted back. The manager shook his head at her defiance and quickly jumped in front of her, taking her completely out of The Beast's sight.

The woman angrily squinted at him, but he quickly clawed her back, "I totally agree with you Mrs Jones. When you come back, you ask for me personally." Then in an attempt to close the conversation he added, "You just go and have a lovely Christmas, please don't give this unpleasantness a second thought!"

"I don't want the hassle of having to take this further!"

"You won't have to Mrs Jones, honestly, I have her in hand."

The Beast sceptically stared at him.

"We'll see you back here in four days." He nodded, breaking her stare.

She snorted in defeat, then angrily tutted. Scraping the key of her mobility scooter from the counter, she shimmied sideways along its front edge to give Nancy one final sly look. Nancy glared back; she wasn't backing down. However, The Beast now appeared content with the prospect of her losing her job, so with a raspy chuckle, pushed away from the counter and used the momentum to turn her heavy frame towards the front door.

The rush of patients had now been served and were funnelling out of the exit.

"What the hell was that?" Nancy whispered to him, "Why were you on her side?" But he ignored her and moved behind the counter to watch The Beast leave.

As the bell sounded above the door, he looked over his shoulder with a disgusting grin and loudly declared, "Strike one Nancy!" He turned fully and winked at her. Then moved closer and held his finger up in front of her face, providing her with a patronising visualisation of the number one. "You know better than to speak to a patient like that." He sniggered.

"What!" She cried, pushing his hand away, "Did you not hear what she said to me?"

Again, he held his finger up to her lips, this time gently touching them, the number one had once more become a hushing mechanism.

"Take it on the chin. I said strike one." He seductively whispered.

Nancy shook her head in angry defiance and again pushed his hand away from her face. She stepped back, to remove him from her personal space.

"Don't react in front of everyone. I don't want Lucy to get hurt." He whispered.

"Lucy! What about me? Is it okay for me to stand here and be humiliated in front of everyone?"

He grinned and discreetly squoze her bum, as he hopped back up the step past her. Clearly, that was a yes in his own arrogant language.

She looked round the shop at her colleagues for some support, but all avoided her gaze. She knew exactly which one of them would have shared the rumour with The Beast, her old high school enemy, Katie. She was a bitch when they were teenagers and unfortunately, hadn't grown out of it. She would have lit The Beast's fuse and delighted in the fireworks display, whether the rumour was true or not.

The rumour on this occasion however, was true. Despite Nancy's better judgement, she was in an ongoing on/off romantic relationship with him and she knew he wasn't single. But none of that mattered now. What mattered, was that he hadn't defended her.

Nancy turned to find him back at the dispensary counter, phone in hand using it as a mirror, fixing the stray hairs that had fallen out of place during his short journey back to his stool. She watched him for a few moments in disbelief at his nonchalance.

"His side piece?" She thought to herself. She'd basically just been called out as his whore and he didn't care. "Joel." She exhaled.

His gaze didn't leave his phone, "What now?" He sighed.

She held three fingers up in the air, mimicking his previous actions, "Count it as strike three!"

He reluctantly lifted his head to acknowledge her, "Come on Nance," he tutted, "be a bit more mature about this! You've only had a slap on the wrist". He smiled and shrugged his shoulders, as if he couldn't understand what she'd taken issue with.

His response was like a kick to her stomach. "That's it!" She cried, clenching her fists at her sides.

He shook his head and once again tutted under his breath, "Don't be so sensitive!"

"Sensitive!"

The tension between them, once so sweet, had soured over the past few weeks, as Nancy had finally reached emotional exhaustion. The little self-respect she had left, now screamed at her to explode and end it, right here, right now, but she restrained herself. She needed to regain control. The time had come to deaden the whispers and give her audience the truth from her own lips. An unhinged state of calm came over her and softly, but proudly, she addressed him, "Joel, you are the most arrogant, selfish, useless, disgusting piece of shit that I have ever shared a bed with and I'm done being your call girl."

She turned to see Katie and her other colleagues almost burst with excitement at her confession, then glared back at Joel who looked up from his phone and simply pouted. She'd struck him. His beautiful, weak, Thumbelina never spoke to him in this manner, in fact no one did. This wasn't his usual chauvinistic silence, this was he, who always had a smart answer for everything, suddenly being lost for words.

Nancy quickly walked towards him and grabbed her coat and bag from the rack. She kept her head down, to hide the angry tears that swelled in her eyes.

"That's not very professional is it Nance?" He said softly as she approached him.

She knew he'd now try to engage in a pathetic tit for tat, then play the victim to win her over, just like he'd done so many times before, but it wasn't going to work this time. She flew back out into the shop and marched swiftly for the door, hoping to escape before he retaliated with an arrogant comeback.

"I hope you all enjoyed the show!" She shouted to her colleagues, "Cat's well and truly out of the bag now!" She snorted.

Joel sprang to his feet and ran over to the opening of the dispensary, "You're such a brat Nancy!" He shouted after her, but she didn't react, so he continued, "Nance, if you go out of that door, you're not coming back!"

"Thank God for that!" She cried over her shoulder.

"I really mean it Nance!" He warned again.

"Wow. You're suddenly committing to something!" She snorted.

"Nancy, look at me!"

"Goodbye Joel!"

"Please Nancy!" He cried.

She froze in surprise. Never had she heard desperation in his voice, because he had always held the upper hand. Never had he expected her to slip through his fingers. His beautiful show piece, something nice to look at during his long boring days, or keep his bed warm when his girlfriend was working out of town – she was leaving.

"Please Nance!" He begged.

Nancy shook her head and continued for the door, tears now streaming down her face. She gripped the handle tightly, anchoring her decision to leave and the voice in her head screamed at her to pull it open and go, but his polite desperation was too uncharacteristic. She couldn't help herself; she had to look back at him.

He triumphantly perceived this as her surrender, which provoked a wide grin to spread across his face, like a wolf baring its jaws.

"Come on! Let's talk!" He pleaded. He threw his arms out, trying to reduce the distance between them and welcome her back, "There's no need to be silly! Come here."

"Silly?" She chuckled. She wiped the tears from her face with her free hand, then let go of the handle and turned to face him.

"There you go! See. You're just making a big deal of it." He sniggered, "Come on, come back up here!"

Although she knew this man was incapable of genuine emotion, she craved these small glimpses of affection from him and her relentless desire for his attention is what had trapped her.

He began to beckon her with his fingers, while mischievously pouting, to which she let out a brash cackle and apologetically threw her arms out to him.

"There you go. Don't cry Nance. Come here."

Before today she would have bolted back into his arms, but he had finally pulled the trigger on their relationship and Nancy wanted it to be put to rest. The rose-tinted veil had finally been ripped from her face. Her mind was made up.

"You have such a way with words don't you baby?" She smiled.

"Baby?" He uncomfortably grinned.

"If you want me back, then I need an apology!"

A look of disbelief struck his chiselled features. He dropped his arms and pursed his lips.

"Go on. Apologise to me!"

He looked round the shop at all the eyes on him and that sickening smile immediately crept back. He looked back over at Nancy, "For what?" He sniggered.

Nancy seethed, "Fuck off Joel!" Her tether was cut. She proudly turned her back on him, pulled open the door and stormed out, making sure the momentum of the swing slammed it shut behind her.

2

Goodnight

Nancy began her walk home. It was a cold Christmas Eve, the air was crisp and still, with the frost already glistening on the parked cars and pavement. The elf costume she was wearing wasn't the warmest of things. Joel had lied and told her that they were all going to be in fancy dress today, to get into the festive spirit. Foolishly, she'd believed him and to his and her colleague's amusement, turned up in a very flattering elf costume; this being her first humiliation of the day. She was frozen walking up the icy streets in it. She pulled her coat as tightly as she could around her shivering body and walked as quickly as her short legs would carry her.

She was a slim, petite woman, who had just turned thirty, with long dark hair, dark eyes, olive skin, plump lips and a soft, yet structured face.

The walk, although not more than 20 minutes felt like an eternity. The houses that lined the streets were festively dressed and lit brightly with a sparkling rainbow of colours, but Nancy wasn't in the mood to appreciate their beauty this evening, she kept her gaze to the ground, fixated on her mission home.

When she reached the front door of her apartment building her hands had lost all feeling, so her fingers struggled to grip the key, as she tried to turn it in the old lock. It took her about eight attempts to prise the door open. When she finally managed it, she fell through the doorway with such relief, that she landed in a small heap of cold bones at the bottom of the communal stairway. She lay still on the floor, exhausted, until, she heard a door open and the floor boards creek above her.

"Nancy is that you?" A woman shouted from the first-floor landing.

She wearily raised her head in acknowledgment and found a slim figure moving its head from side to side like a concerned pigeon. Begrudgingly, she raised her hand away from the warmth of her body and gave a half-hearted wave, "Hi Mrs Adams, I was just –"

"Shut that door, you silly girl! Its minus God knows what and you're letting all the cold in!"

Nancy tutted to herself; she knew the nosy, old cow had been waiting for her. As not only her neighbour but her landlady, she had a habit of listening for the screech of the front door to intercept her and their encounters were never pleasant. It wasn't that Nancy was a bad tenant, it was the fact that Mrs Adams was a sad, lonely, bitter, old woman, who lived in a constant cloud of cigarette smoke.

"I said close it!" She crowed again.

Nancy did as she was told. She slowly picked herself up from the ground and slammed it shut, "There! Closed!" She shouted looking back up at her.

"You'll be paying for my heating bill! You've got no regard for anyone else's wellbeing! No regard, whatsoever!" She moaned.

Nancy sighed; she wasn't in the mood for Mrs Adams. Even on a good day, she was never in the mood for Mrs Adams. She began to stumble up the stairs towards her, half listening to her pettiness and crossed her path like a zombie, wincing in the bright light of Mrs Adams' doorway.

"Are you even listening to me?" Mrs Adams snapped. Nancy squinted at her and caught her smirk as she noticed her elf outfit. She put her cigarette to her thin lips, "Where the hell have you been dressed like that? You look ridiculous!" She exhaled.

Nancy glanced down at her costume, but decided not to answer. She had no desire to converse with this woman. "Goodnight Mrs Adams." She mumbled, wafting the smoke out of her face and quickening her pace to climb the next flight of stairs.

But Mrs Adams remained on the landing beneath her and continued to ramble on, "No respect, you've just got no respect!"

"None for you!" She quietly muttered, glancing back down at her through the gap in the banister.

She reached her apartment door, pushed it open and locked it quickly behind her, shutting out Mrs Adams' droning.

"Safe at last," she sighed, as she slid down to sit on the floor.

Her attic flat was claustrophobic. The front door opened directly onto a combined kitchen and living space, with two doors on the wall to her right; her single sized bedroom through one and her miniature bathroom through the other.

She sat for a few moments and stared vacantly into the darkness, summoning the energy to move. The dim street light that shone through the far window, delicately illuminated her warm breath in the cold air. She threw her bag under the kitchen table, slid off her shoes and tossed them onto the mat next to her. Then begrudgingly, pulled off her coat and threw it over the nearest wooden chair, before using it as a climbing frame to pull herself up.

Her mind buzzed with the day's fresh criticisms; courtesy of customers, colleagues, Mrs Jones, Mrs Adams and of course Joel. She shivered towards her bathroom, flicked on the light, closed the door behind her, then fell to her knees on the bathmat and cried.

Over the last five years Nancy's life had spiralled out of her control. This wasn't through a catastrophic event or traumatic experience; it was the accumulation of life's smaller grievances continually nibbling away at her soul.

Eight years ago, she'd left university with an excellent degree, then spent the years that followed climbing the employment ladder, eventually achieving a high-flying career that provided a privileged lifestyle. She had fulfilled the dream that had always been fed to her, but was left empty rather than proud. She realised that it was never what she'd wanted, so in a brave attempt to preserve her enthusiasm for life and to the complete shock of her parents, she quit.

Professionally, she then had no direction. She had worked so hard achieving a status that society applauded, that she felt embarrassed to now be a drifter, hopping from one low paid job to the next.

Her new hollow and despondent nature also took root in the lack of belonging she felt. She didn't feel 'normal'. Observing and comparing how 'normal people' would interact with one another; finding enjoyment in boring conversations or contributing to backstabbing gossip, she found that she couldn't truthfully align with their joy or hatred.

She was an artistic eccentric, with a gentle heart that yearned for adventure and for someone to share all the beauty she saw within the world. She viewed the discontentment of poisonous people as a threat to her romantic universe, making her fearful of unlocking her cage and putting her true nature out into the world, because she knew she wasn't something that the women around her could relate to.

She learnt to mimic other women in social situations to disguise her disinterest and mirrored their cruel humour to feel accepted. However, this new false persona attracted men that were a poor match and she began settling for arrogant time-wasters because their flirtatious compliments brought a small fraction of self-love to her daily self-loathing.

Eventually, she removed herself from all of her social circles, as she felt more isolated in an alien crowd than in her own company.

She knelt upwards and pulled the tiny vanity mirror down from the windowsill. Deep black mascara and eyeliner, ran in thick tracks down her cheeks. She attempted to wipe the marks away with the back of her hand, but this only smeared the make-up, setting it deeper into her pores. She let out a long deep sigh and stared into her eyes. She was hoping to see some spark of life, some glimmer to cling to, but finally, all traces had left her.

She returned the mirror to the windowsill and crouched forwards reaching for the taps of the bath to turn on the water. She sat in silence and watched it fall, while replaying the events of the day in her head.

Although she'd never had any real feelings for Joel, she hated him the most. No one had ever made her feel so used or belittled her as often as he did. She didn't understand him, he was like Jekyll and Hyde, always luring her back to him with glimpses of a dream that she knew didn't exist. Maybe it was the dreamer in her that made his lies believable, her hope wanting to prove reality wrong. On the one hand he was always there to comfort her, not that she'd ever go to him with her problems, but during the day when they were alone, he'd almost interrogate her about what was going on in her life, or message her now and then and offer her good advice. He could appear so caring and concerned, however, on the flipside, he'd openly mock her, using snippets of the things that she'd told him in confidence to open a debate with her colleagues. Then there'd come the hug and the 'Oh, I'm only joking Nance.'

"Patronising bastard!" She huffed to herself.

When the bath was ready, she pulled herself up on its edge, stripped off her elf costume, dropped it where she'd been sat and slowly lowered herself into the boiling water. Still frozen from her walk home, when her skin submerged, she felt her limbs thaw. She took a deep breath and fully immersed herself, feeling all the cold of the outside calmly float away. She slowly resurfaced and pushed her hair back out of her face. Her mind was quickly put to rest by the heat, so she relaxed in the relief of her new silence, almost immediately falling into a sedative state, focused only on her breath and strong heartbeat.

She took another deep breath and again submerged, now blowing slow, steady bubbles into the mass of water above her face, until she ran out of air and needed to resurface.

She stared blankly at the steam rising from the water. The bathroom was a hot cloud. Her long hair tangled itself around her arms and her hands floated lifelessly on the gentle waves that her breath created.

"What next?" she asked herself, she really didn't know. She needed another job quickly; she was barely making her rent as it was and had very little savings. It also suddenly occurred to her that she'd have to face her family at Christmas dinner tomorrow. Her heart sank.

Every year her delightful uncle, step-aunt and two cousins came to her parents' house for dinner. The day would consist of a quiz about what she was going to do with her life, followed by an interrogation as to why she hadn't settled down yet. In past years, her uncle would wait until they were all sat at the dinner table, to then start his lecture on self-determination and setting goals. He wouldn't directly address Nancy, but he'd make it crystal clear that she was a disappointment, while in turn praising her cousins' achievements. Every family gathering was the same and there seemed to be so bloody many of them.

"Maybe I won't go." She thought, "It's not like they'll miss me."

She could feel her heart pumping harder now, as her body temperature rose. It was begging for her attention. She desperately needed to get out of the water, but stubbornly she refused and ignored its panic.

"Yes," she thought, "I won't go. I'll call them in the morning and say I'm sick. They'll probably be thankful. They won't have to defend me all day and might actually enjoy themselves." The tears ran down her cheeks and she closed her eyes. "That's the truth," she thought, "everyone will be better off without me."

She was exhausted, she needed a break from life, just a moment to figure everything out. She couldn't remember the last time she'd had a real, meaningful conversation with her parents. She tried to think of the last time she'd been alone with them, but they were either always busy with their restaurant or had a friend or family member visiting their home. They had grown so distant.

In a weary, dreamlike state, she tried to move her arm to reach for the cold tap, but her body had become so overwhelmed by the intense heat, that her limbs were barley responsive and her breathing had become laboured. She embraced it. There wasn't an ounce of panic in her mind or an attempt to summon the strength to fight it. She could feel herself gently slipping out of consciousness and she was happy. Her body craved sleep and she was prepared to give in to it. That's all she wanted, for her mind and her heart to be at peace. The water wrapped around her so tightly, that she enjoyed its comforting embrace and the feeling of weightlessness, as it lifted her small body gently from the floor of the bath. Despite the pain in her head, it was so calm, so quiet, so still. Second by second, she appeared to drift further and further away from reality, until finally, the rhythm of her breath no longer moved the water around her at all. The pain was numbed, her mind was silenced and she slipped under.

There was nothing but nothingness. Nothing to think or worry about, nothing to do and no one to bother her. She had been trapped by life, trapped in the monotony of something meaningless to her. She had longed to feel free and here it was, silent freedom. What more was there for her on earth? Time would march on and everyone's lives would move on. She'd be nothing more than a distant memory.

3

Suspended Reality

As she lay in limbo, the darkness and numbness became slowly replaced by a faint fluttering in the water around her arms. She'd progressed into a strange state, where her mind had awoken, but her body had not. She could hear the tick of the small clock on the windowsill, it's echo amplified under the water and despite being submerged, could somehow smell the dampness of the bathroom.

From the darkness, there then came a kaleidoscope of brilliant beams that prismed into a picture – but what she saw, she couldn't comprehend. She was a spectator, hovering above her body. She stared in disbelief at herself submerged, with her thick hair floating in a halo on the surface. Although she knew it was her, she looked different, muted against the white of the bath tub, like a shadow in the snow.

Her surroundings then began to filter out into sharp, white light. The walls disappeared, the sink and toilet fell away, even the rims of the bath began to blur, when suddenly, her body violently pushed to the surface. The bathroom surroundings snapped back into place and she watched her shoulders pull up and fall back down, then her head break the surface and slip back under. The sensation was bizarre, because although not physically connected to her body, she could slightly feel the pressure of a grip. Again, she watched as her face hit the air and could almost feel the change in temperature. Her mind began to scramble trying to understand the situation and in doing so, she realised she couldn't breathe.

She tried to put her hands up to her throat, but her arms weren't there. Other than the arms on her lifeless body, being manipulated by the invisible force below, she had none. She focused all her mental power in searching for the memory of that small, simple, unconscious rhythm that sustained life. She silently screamed in frustration, why couldn't she do it? The memory had left her; she had no mental control over it anymore. In sheer panic she somehow managed to descend and entered her rib cage like a torpedo. Her body gasped, inhaling nothing but hot water. She was back.

She could now see the hands that were desperately trying to grasp her, she could feel the water sloshing in large waves all around. Once again, she felt the pain in her head and the fingers of her rescuer tangling in the strands of her hair. Whoever this was, they didn't have the strength to pull her out alone, she needed to help them. As her head was dragged to the surface again, she felt the person catch her under her arms and there came a strong sharp tug. She used all her might to follow her mysterious aid and hauled herself up and out, over the edge, landing hard onto the floor. The pain electrified her limbs back to life. She rolled from side to side, trying to disperse it, then rolled onto her front and pulled her knees up under her body. Gasping frantically, she choked, her airways were full of water, it began falling out of her mouth in small buckets. She furiously tried to regain control. Her body screamed in agony, as the air she sucked in felt like shards of glass, splintering in her windpipe.

"Help!" she managed to whisper, but this caused her to cough so violently, that she was sick on her elf costume and the mat beneath her face. "Please!"

She faintly spluttered. She rolled on to her side, out of the sick, "Please!" She sobbed, "Help me!"

Unexpectedly, her pleas were answered by two cold hands that gripped tightly onto her side; one on her arm, the other on her hip. Immediately, their icy touch chased out the agonising fever. She took a deep breath in relief and her body went limp. She inhaled as deeply as she could, stretching her lungs to full capacity, over and over again savouring the respite from the pain, until, once again, everything faded to black and she slipped out of consciousness.

4

Who's there?

Tick tock, tick tock. The faint sound of the small clock on the windowsill echoed once more. Nancy slowly opened her eyes, as she listened to its rhythmic call. Her head pounded. She grumbled in pain as she tried to lift it up off the floor, but it was too heavy, so she remained still, resting against the radiator watching the drips of condensation, as they slid down the side of the bath panel. The smell of sick, however, soon became overwhelming and she was forced to move.

She wearily pushed herself to sit up and automatically reached for the towel from the rail above her head to wrap loosely around her shoulders.

To her delight she noticed a half empty bottle of water near her foot, that she'd possibly left there that morning or night before. She had to paw it closer, as her fingers refused to grip its slippery body. Clasping it between her palms, she used her teeth to unscrew the cap. The stale water inside felt like heaven. No matter how much it burnt her sore throat, she was too dehydrated to care. It ran down her chin and chest, as her lazy lips failed to make a seal. She drank as much as she could, then discarded it back onto the floor.

She gazed absently waiting for her mind reboot, then slowly became aware of a steady stream of drool running out of the side of her mouth. She clumsily dabbed it with the towel and lay back down, this time with her head away from the sick.

However, her slow resuscitation quickened, as she realised the bathroom door was open. She lifted her head and watched the steam billowing out into the darkness. She was confused. She always closed the door, or the fire alarm would sound, but the door had been opened and there was silence. As she watched for the little red light to flash on the alarm through the doorway, her heart froze in terror. She remembered, the door was open because she'd been saved. Her eyes widened and she swallowed hard, as she fearfully studied the dark room. "Where had they gone?" She wondered. There was no sign of any life. Her thoughts rushed to carefully plan her next move. She didn't want to shout to them because she didn't know who it was hiding out there, or if they *were* still there. Cautiously, she struggled to her feet and wrapped the towel tightly around her torso. She stepped towards the doorway and peered out, immediately flicking on the light to her kitchen/living room. The front door was closed and the room was empty. She quickly established all possible hiding places, then tiptoed into the kitchen and picked up a pan from the counter to use as a weapon. Saviour or not, it was very strange that someone would want to save her then hide. She made her way over to the sofa to check no one was hiding in the corner of the room. She slid gracefully onto the side of it and looked over the edge, but nothing, no one was there. She then made her way over to her bedroom and kicked open the door, in the hope of surprising the intruder, but again, no one was there. She crouched in the doorway to check no one was under her bed; nothing but a little dust. She put her hand to her head in confusion and walked over to her front door to check if it was still locked and it was, that was one thing she *did* remember doing and she knew the windows in each room were locked too, because she hadn't opened them in weeks due to the cold weather.

She walked back into the bathroom and sat down on the floor, with the pan in her lap. Had she hallucinated? The cold hands on her felt so real and the force that pulled her up and out of the water. She looked down at her arms to check for marks, but found nothing. Her skin was still pink from the hot water, but there were no obvious bruises where she'd been gripped. She pulled herself up to peer over the side of the bath and surprisingly, it was empty. The plug sat on the side just under the taps. "Did I pull the plug on the way out?" She pondered, "I definitely wouldn't have put it back so neatly on the side." She picked it up and studied the little black rubber disk on its chain. She couldn't remember. Her analysis, however, came to an abrupt halt as once again the smell of sick overcame her. She began to gag, so quickly contained it in the bathmat, picked up the pan in her other hand and walked back into the kitchen to bin it.

She flopped down at the kitchen table and put the pan down in front of her, then leant back in her chair to thoroughly examine the room from this vantage point. There was nothing to explain it, not a shred of evidence that someone else had been there. She rubbed her face trying to think and looked back at the locks on the front door. Her questioning was then pushed aside, as her intrusive pre-bath thoughts pulled themselves back to the forefront of her mind. Once again, she began torturing herself for her outbursts and started replaying Joels' sickly-sweet grin in her mind over and over, again and again, until she was completely consumed by him. She couldn't stop herself; she just wasn't powerful enough to shake him. She continued to wander in this agonising,

27

anxious cycle, until finally, so much time had passed that her temperature cooled and she realised how cold her apartment was. She snapped back into full consciousness.

She went into her bedroom, towel dried her hair, then threw it into her wash basket. She got dressed in her leopard print pyjama bottoms, a black t-shirt and an oversized Rocky Balboa dressing gown; a gift that she treasured from her old friend Francesco, as they shared a love of the films. She then went into the living area to turn on the heating. The small radiator hissed in disapproval at having to be put to work, which made her chuckle to herself, "I even piss you off!" She snorted.

She made herself a large mug of hot chocolate and a warm bowl of cereal. Even though her throat was still raw, she was starving. She brought them over to her grey, two-seater sofa and snuggled under a blanket on one side, while searching for a Christmas film on the TV.

It was Christmas Eve after all, so despite her lack of enthusiasm, she flicked through the channels and found *It's a Wonderful Life*. Immediately, the flood gates opened and her tears streamed into the cereal bowl that she held under her chin. This was her family's favourite Christmas film. When she was younger, she'd sit snuggled with her parents every year, all drinking hot chocolate in front of their fire, like a clip from a cosy movie in itself.

She wished she was with them now and longed so much to go back to happier times, but she couldn't tell them how she really felt. For a start, she never got the opportunity and even if she did, she didn't want them to worry about her, or alternatively tell her to stop feeling sorry for herself and *get on with it!* She was trying her best to just *get on with it,* that's what she had been doing for too long. She knew how fortunate she was, she understood how many people would die to be in her shoes, to be safe and warm, have all the opportunities available to her and to even have the safety-net of her parents, but nothing stopped her self-loathing.

She finished her cereal spiked with salty tears, put her bowl on the floor, reached up behind her to turn out the light and plumped up a flat cushion to rest her head on. She slid down onto her side and softly cried herself to sleep.

5

The Intruder

Hours passed as she lay there, a small pile of material huddled to one side of the sofa. She drifted in-between sleep and awake, as her mind wandered into nightmares then back to reality. She couldn't get the feeling of those cold hands out of her head. She kept dreaming of being in her elf costume, sitting in the bath, then The Beast exploding into her bathroom, grabbing her by the throat and pushing her under the water, her hands squeezing tighter and tighter, suffocating her. She rocked back and forth trying to free herself from the monster's imaginary grip, fighting for her life, clawing at The Beast's arms, until, thankfully, she was abruptly saved by the loud screech of a chair being pushed across her kitchen floor. Her eyes shot open and her head flew up off the cushion.

She dizzily blinked, trying to bring her vision into focus. Her eyes strained as she forced them to sleepily distinguish the dark shapes in that area of the room. She gave them a quick rub, wiping the tiredness away and looked harder, but nothing seemed to have moved. She yawned and stretched as she studied the chairs, then lay back down and turned her attention to the TV. The film was still playing, strangely, from exactly where she'd left it, George standing on the bridge wishing he'd never been born. She reached for her phone, "Twelve-fifteen?" She yawned, "It must be on repeat." She then noticed a new message, so pulled down the menu bar to preview it, but her heart stopped as she saw

Joel's name, "Na, you can fuck right off!" She hissed, leaving the message unopened and returning the phone to the floor.

She picked up the remote and pressed the power button, but the TV didn't respond, so, she pushed it again and still nothing. "Cheap pissing batteries!" She tutted, "I knew I should have gotten the other ones." She knocked it hard against the arm of the sofa a couple of times then tried the button again. This time the red light flickered, but still, the TV didn't respond. She angrily slid off her sofa in a silent tantrum and opened up the back of the remote to remove them. She reinserted them and pressed the button again, but this time the screen turned grey. She stared at it for a few seconds in confusion, then went to crawl over to turn it off manually, but something strange caught her eye.

At the bottom of one of her kitchen chairs, next to her bag she could now see a pair of shoes, a pair of black, well-worn Converse high tops in fact. The white soles and laces cut through the darkness. She did own a pair, but hers weren't under the table. She quickly looked towards the front door to find that hers were still on the mat where she kept them. She stared back at the new strange pair, harder this time, trying to comprehend their peculiar appearance, when, to her horror, one of them moved.

"What the fuck?" She squealed, dropping the remote and jumping back up onto the sofa. She could now see a young woman with a heavily shadowed face sitting at the table. Nancy quickly dove back down, snapped up the TV remote and hurled it at her uninvited guest. It flew with great force, violently tumbling like an axe through the air, but it missed and smashed against a cabinet. Nancy yelled in frustration and began a frantic back stroke to the furthest arm of the sofa, with such momentum, that she clumsily fell backwards off its edge. The impact winded her, but her adrenaline pushed her back to her feet and she stood ready to fight. Nancy heard the visitor snigger at her startled scramble and watched her piercing green eyes squint. Those eyes, Nancy knew those eyes, she was certain she did, but the rest of her face blended into the shadows behind her.

"Who are you?" Nancy demanded.

The visitor stood up out of the chair and a strong white light burst from her silhouette.

"Shit!" Nancy whimpered in terror. She quickly grabbed a cushion and threw it at her, but once again it missed and the visitor started to move around the table in the direction of the front door.

"Yeah, that's right! Get the fuck out of here!" Nancy screamed, stupidly thinking the cushion had scared her off, but the intruder paused and her light engulfed the apartment. Nancy squirmed in its power. She dropped to her knees to shield herself. With eyes shut tight, she began to frantically chant, "Wake up! Wake up! Wake up!" Which provoked a loud tut followed by a frustrated sigh from the intruder. This immediately deadened Nancy's chanting. She opened her eyes to see that the woman now stood with her hands up in surrender – and was moving closer.

Nancy crawled backwards, "Oh no! No, no, no. You stay where you are! Don't you dare come any closer to me!"

"Oh, shut up!" The intruder snorted, "It's me, you silly bitch!"

"Silly bitch?" Nancy mouthed in outrage.

"You've still got a shit aim!"

Nancy peeped through her arms to see the figure looking at the objects on the floor.

"The remote would have hurt, but the cushion was pretty pointless."

Nancy was desperately trying to figure out who this person was. The green eyes, that insulting tone, she knew them – and they clearly knew her.

"For God's sake, stop cowering like an ugly puppy, it's me!"

"You're too bright. I can't see who you are!"

"Then stop squinting at me through your arms like an idiot and just look at me properly!" The intruder came closer into the living area.

"I can't it hurts."

"Oh, pissing hell Nancy, just do it!"

Hearing her move closer, Nancy's panic overrode the pain, so she quickly did as she was told and as much as it hurt, surprisingly her eyes adjusted. "Oh my God! I knew it – Lena?"

The young woman smiled and began to do a sarcastic slow clap at Nancy's realisation.

"But – what the fuck?" Nancy whispered in awe, "Why are you glowing?"

Lena looked down at her body and shrugged, "I don't know, it literally just happened then, when I stood up, didn't' it?"

"You're like a light bulb!" Nancy gawped in astonishment, as she got to her feet. Lena smirked, but now Nancy could see her face, it was clear that her old friend had been crying. Her eyes were so red and swollen. "Oh my God! What's the matter?"

"Nothing." Lena squinted. She quickly flicked her long, dark hair from behind her ears to the sides of her face.

"No, I can see you've been crying. What's happened?"

"Nothing! Honestly!"

But Nancy suddenly stopped, "Actually, wait, no, hang on, how did you get in here?"

Lena slowly exhaled and began to uncomfortably fidget, as if searching for a believable lie. She then awkwardly looked over her shoulder to the front door and mumbled, "I just walked in."

Nancy shook her head, "No you didn't. The door was locked. I checked it!"

Lena didn't even bother to counter Nancy's challenge; her head dropped and she began to sob.

"Ah, Lena, no, don't cry. I'll call someone. Your mum? Or your dad maybe?"

"No!" Lena spluttered, "No, there's nothing anyone can do now!"

"Course they can. Whatever this is. I'll call them."

"No!" Lena cried, "They can't!"

Nancy uncomfortably ran her fingers through her hair, while she nervously examined her old friend. She didn't know what to do *or* suggest. Obviously, something terrible had happened to her, she was glowing for God's sake, never mind the tears.

Lena firmly wiped her face and cleared her throat, regaining some composure, "We need to talk Nance." She sniffed hard and motioned with her hand to the sofa for Nancy to sit.

"Talk?"

Lena nodded and pointed again to the sofa, now firmly insisting that Nancy sit.

"Oh, o-kay." Nancy uncomfortably moved to the sofa and threw the blanket out of the way for Lena to join her.

"How long has it been since we last sat together like this?" Lena croaked.

"I don't know," Nancy shrugged, "I left you so many messages with Francesco, your mum and your dad, but you never called me back."

"I got all your messages; I just really didn't want to speak about it. I was so pissed off with you!"

"I pissed you off?" Nancy cried, "Lena! Come on! *You* abandoned *me*, then replaced me with your new addict friends!"

"Abandoned you? Are you fucking joking me!" Lena protested, "And they're not addicts!"

"Oh yeah, I'm sorry, they just snort a bag of coke every night!" Nancy sarcastically grinned.

"And that is exactly why we fell out in the first place, because of you sitting on your high horse!"

Nancy tutted in annoyance, "I'm not going into all of this now. I've already had the day from hell, just tell me what's happened and why you're here?"

Lena exhaled loudly, dispersing her frustration into the room, then calmly mumbled, "Something really bad has happened Nance."

"What? Is everyone okay?"

"Yeah, yeah, they're all fine. I mean to me." She paused and once again broke down into hysterical tears, "Oh God, I don't even know how to begin!"

Nancy moved to hug her, but Lena leant away and shook her head, "You're a mess Nance!" She sniffed.

"I'm a mess?" Nancy scowled, "Look at you!"

"No! Look at you! Sitting here all by yourself, crying into a bowl of cereal."

Nancy looked down at her empty cereal bowl on the floor. "How did you know I was crying?"

"Look at the state of your face!"

Nancy quickly turned away in embarrassment and attempted to clean her face with the sleeve of her dressing gown.

"You could have at least washed your makeup off before you drowned yourself in the bath!"

Nancy's head span back to her so fast, she nearly fell off the sofa again, "Wait, you saw me in the bath?"

"It was me that pulled your lifeless arse out of it!"

Nancy sprang to her feet and stepped away from her. "No! I checked everywhere no one was here!"

"I was!"

Nancy's blood ran cold and she quickly backed away. She threw her hands to her forehead and pushed her fingers across it, trying to summon enough brainpower to make logical sense of what was happening. Was this being truly Lena? She also quickly began to doubt herself; did she imagine searching the apartment? Maybe she was still groggy after falling unconscious; but then she remembered grabbing the pan to defend herself with. She looked over to see if the pan was still on the counter or on the table where she'd left it after her search. It was on the table. She *had* definitely searched the apartment; there was her proof. She threw her arms down from her face and glared at Lena. "No! You're lying! Stop playing games with me now. How did you get in here?"

"I told you; I just walked in!"

"Bull Shit!" Nancy shouted, "Everywhere was locked!"

"Stop being a hysterical bitch!"

"You're lying though." Nancy yelled. She pointed hard at the front door, then stared at her wide eyed, beckoning the truth.

Lena casually rolled her eyes in response, "Doesn't matter really, does it? If I say I walked in, then I did."

"What?" Nancy cried at her brush off.

Lena sat back, stubbornly folded her arms and stared at the TV like a disobedient child.

This *was* Lena, or a perfect imitation of her. Nancy knew that stubborn look all too well. She was masterful in the art of the cold shoulder.

"Fine." Nancy grumbled, "If you're not going to tell me how you got in here, then at least tell me why you're glowing?"

"Oh, for God's sake Nancy!"

"You're lighting up the bloody room!"

Lena sprang to her feet, "Something really bad happened to me tonight, okay?"

"Yes, you've said that, but what? Just bloody tell me what?"

"I don't want to talk about it! Not with you!"

"Oh, fuckin' hell!" Nancy threw her head back and covered her face with her hands, but then quickly glared back at Lena, "If you don't want to talk about it with me, then why are you even here?"

Lena didn't answer, instead she quickly averted her eyes to the ground and hid once more behind her long, dark hair.

"Fuck's sake Lena!" Nancy sighed at her reaction. "Answer me this then, and I want the truth, did you honestly get me out of the bath?"

"Yes!"

"So why did you save me and then hide like a weirdo?"

Lena angrily looked back up and pointed at the kitchen table, "I didn't hide, I've been sat there this whole time."

"No!" Nancy shouted.

"I was! I wasn't hiding! You…just didn't see me."

"Oh, okay, so you were invisible sitting at the table? Is that right?" Nancy sarcastically taunted.

"I saved you Nance!"

"You're lying!"

"Look! I don't want to be here!"

"Argh!" Nancy interrupted, "Why are you then?"

Lena slumped back down onto the sofa, "Something terrible happened to me tonight." She paused again; it was evident that she couldn't actually bring herself to say what.

"Just tell me! Please!" Nancy pleaded.

"I don't know what to tell you though, that's just it."

"Well try."

"I was just told to come here."

"By who?"

"A voice."

"Oh Jesus!" Nancy rolled her eyes.

Lena ignored her reaction and continued, "It's true, the voice said I needed to help you and I thought it would be as easy as pulling you out of that stupid bath. Obviously not!"

"A voice?" Nancy grinned.

"Yes, a voice!" Lena snapped.

Nancy was lost for words, her friend was either high, having a mental breakdown, or by the looks of her, had been the victim of some awful science experiment.

"Is this a joke?"

Lena jumped to her feet again and erupted, "Look at the state of me Nancy, do you think this is funny?"

"No, of course I don't, but I don't understand."

"I'm telling you the truth."

"No, no you're not. You're being mysterious and weird."

Lena glared at her in response and silently pouted in a stale mate.

Nancy shook her head and exhaled loudly. "Look, whatever this is, I just really can't be doing with your shit tonight."

"No, you've got too much of your own shit going on, haven't you?"

"Just go home Lena. Go call a doctor or a fucking scientist."

"I can't leave!"

"Well, I'm telling you to leave."

"No, you don't understand. I have to help you!"

"And you have, you've been wonderful! Thank you so much! Go tell your voice how well you've done!"

Lena grumbled in frustration, "No, we need to go!"

"Go where?" Nancy snorted.

"You have to come with me!"

"Oh, okay, yeah, I'll just grab my coat – not! What do you mean *have* to? I don't *have* to go anywhere with you! Especially not in this state!"

Lena moved intimidatingly closer to her and whispered through gritted teeth, "Nancy! Grab – Your – Coat."

"I'm calling your mum!" Nancy dove for her phone on the floor, unlocked it, sprang back to her feet and went to dial the number, but to her horror, when she hit the call symbol, it disintegrated and the black sand slipped through her fingers into a small mound on the floor. Both women screamed and shook their hands in panic. Nancy frantically wiped the sand away on her dressing gown, while Lena mirrored her on her own clothes, clearly just as disturbed by its transformation.

"How did you do that?" Nancy cried.

"That wasn't me!" Lena trembled, still dancing up and down.

"What is happening Lena?"

"I don't know Nance; I swear! I was just told to come here and then told that we have to leave!"

"By who!"

"I don't know!" Lena shouted, "But I don't think you should piss him off!"

"Lena, you have to help me out here!"

Lena looked up to the ceiling for a moment in fear, then quickly lunged at Nancy attempting to grab her shoulders, "There's no time. You have to come with me!"

"No." Nancy screamed, dodging her, then pushing her away.

Lena fell backwards and hit the floor hard. She clutched her ribs and winced, then carefully removed her hand from her white t-shirt to show a large, fresh, red blood stain. Lena stared down at the blood in a mixture of acceptance and disappointment, then angrily looked back up at Nancy with furious tears.

"Oh shit!" Nancy shouted, "You're hurt!" she dropped to her knees and went to move Lena's hand to examine her properly.

"Don't touch me!" Lena hissed, hitting her hand away.

"Let me help you!" Nancy attempted once more to put her hand on Lena's.

"No! I said don't touch me!"

"Who did this to you?"

"None of your concern."

"It is my concern! We have to get you to a hospital!"

"No! It's too late Nance!" She began to cry once more, "It's too late!"

"Tell me who did it!"

"It doesn't matter." Lena spluttered.

"Is it the same people that made you glow?"

Lena angrily pushed Nancy away and got to her feet. "It had to be you Nance! It just had to be you! Out of everyone I could have been sent to, it had to be you!"

"What's wrong with me?"

"You're a fucking nightmare!"

Nancy angrily huffed and got to her feet.

"I'm here not only glowing, but bleeding in your living room, asking you to help me and all you're interested in, is asking stupid pointless questions."

"Did you not hear what you just said?" Nancy scoffed, "Not only are you bleeding in my living room, you're fucking glowing! And you won't tell me how, or why or anything!"

Lena didn't retaliate; she put both her hands behind the back of her neck and closed her eyes.

Nancy suspiciously watched on. "Lena?" she prompted after a few moments, breaking the silence.

But Lena simply said, "Shush." Then after a few seconds more, she opened her eyes with a mischievous pout. Nancy was unsettled by this sudden emotional turnaround.

"Fine," Lena shrugged, "it's fine that you don't want to come with me; *but*, if you're not going to come with me, *or* help me, then the least you can do is give me a hug goodbye."

Nancy hesitated, extremely uneasy with her request. This was completely out of character. "You don't do hugs Lena! Especially not with me!"

"I do today. Come on Nance, give me a hug!"

"No - I'm not hugging you!"

"Look at me! I really just need a hug. Please, come on!" She opened her arms and moved closer.

"No!"

"Just give me a fucking hug Nancy!" Lena shrieked in frustration.

Nancy defiantly shook her head, bent her arms defensively in front of her body and quickly stepped back, but Lena pounced and grabbed her. The immediate pain of the cold was horrendous, the same cold as the icy hands of her saviour, but this time it caused her pain, instead of chasing it away. She tried to scream, but the arctic blast took her breath away.

She broke Lena's grip, by furiously pushing at her shoulders. "What the fuck was that?" Nancy screamed.

"What?"

"You, you just did something to me!"

"I didn't do anything to you!"

"You did; it was like ice shooting through my body. Lena, what did this person ask you to do to me?"

"What?" Lena's mouth dropped open in astonishment. It was clear that the very notion that she would hurt Nancy infuriated her, "Do you honestly think I'd do something bad to you Nance?"

Nancy didn't answer and continued to angrily glare at her.

"Oh my God. You do!" Lena choked, "You really believe I'd hurt you?"

Once again Nancy said nothing.

"Oh, fuck off Nancy!" Lena cried, shoulder barging her out of her way. "You're such a horrible bitch!"

Nancy didn't know how to respond; she was too conflicted. Her adrenaline had her poised in fight mode to protect herself from this strange being, while conversely, she loved Lena. Despite the glowing and freezing touch, "Who else could this be, but Lena?" She asked herself. She had no clue, so on the assumption this *was* her, she turned to apologise, "I'm so –" She stopped as the room behind her had now opened up onto the dark street below. She quickly turned back expecting to find the safety of her living room, but it had now been replaced by the front door of her building and she was standing on the doorstep locked outside of it.

"No!" Nancy screamed. She quickly turned to Lena, "How did you do that?" She shouted after her, but Lena didn't respond, she didn't even look behind her, she just continued to walk away.

"Lena!" Nancy screamed after her. It was too dark and too open out here. She turned back to the door and began frantically banging on it, shouting for Mrs Adams, "Mrs Adams! Mrs Adams! Come on!" She screamed through the letter box, "Help me, you miserable old cow!" She tried the old intercom system to her side, but it was dead.

"She's not there Nance!" Lena shouted from the distance.

"What do you mean she's not there? She's always there! Mrs Adams!"

"It's just me and you!"

"You stay away from me, you! Mrs Adams! Please!" She dropped to her knees in front of the door and sobbed, while continuing to bang on it as hard as she could, "Please help me!"

"Nancy, look at me!" Lena growled.

"No!" Nancy screamed. "You go away!"

"Nancy, look at me now!" She demanded.

Nancy reluctantly peeped at her luminous friend, who was a spotlight in the dark. She was, in fact, the only glimmer of light in existence.

"Nancy, I've already saved you once tonight. If I wanted to hurt you, wouldn't I have just let you die in the bath?"

"Die?" Nancy hissed.

"Yes! You were gone Nance! Dead!"

44

Nancy shuddered, as that word settled in her mind. "Dead?" She whispered to herself. She did believe that Lena had saved her from the bath, because she had the same icy touch as her saviour, but how could she be dead, if she'd woke up?

"Am I dead now?" She breathlessly trembled.

"I don't know." Lena shrugged.

"Are you?"

Lena shrugged again, but a little weaker than before.

"Who sent you?" Nancy shouted, "Tell me now!"

"I don't know! I told you, it was just a bright light and a voice, next thing I knew I was in your bathroom. Now just stop being pathetic for once in your life and come with me!" Lena pleaded, "I just want to go home! That is all I want! But I need your cooperation."

Nancy looked back at the door. What was this hell? Had she really died? She had so many questions and couldn't process any of them. She shakily got to her feet and looked up and down the street. There was nothing but the dark. She looked up at her building, but that too stood the same, shrouded in darkness. There wasn't even a star in the sky. Lena wasn't lying, there was no one else here and nowhere to go. Her only option *was* to follow her friend, she couldn't think of any other escape route.

"Come on Nancy!" Lena shouted, "You can't get back in there."

"Where are we going?" Nancy asked, but there came no response from Lena, instead she silently beckoned with her hand for her to follow.

Nancy admitted defeat; she wiped her tired eyes, pushed her long hair from her face and stepped away from the door, when bizarrely, the cold concrete beneath her feet suddenly warmed. She looked down to find her Converse high-tops on her feet, the ones that sat on her mat by her front door, the same as Lena's, although Nancy's were in a little better shape. "What the f —!" Nancy whispered to herself. She slowly picked up one foot and then the other, analysing them. "How?" She thought.

"What are you doing?" Lena moaned.

She looked back up at her, seeing her now stood hands on hips, pouting impatiently. "I have my shoes on." Nancy quietly grimaced in confusion.

"What?" Lena snapped.

"I don't have a choice, do I?" Nancy asked.

"Neither of us do!" Lena groaned, sticking out her tongue in sarcastic disgust.

Nancy sighed and tutted, then sulkily began walking to join her.

6

The Storm

As they walked together, again Nancy tried her best to spot some signs of life, but the streets were truly deserted. "Where is everyone?" She asked, but Lena didn't reply, instead she quickened her pace to ensure she stayed ahead, demonstrating that she was still annoyed with her.

There remained an awkward silence between the two for the duration of the walk. Nancy tried to pull her dressing gown up around her chin; her hands and face were frozen. It didn't help that the wind had now picked up and the cold blasts felt like knives against her bare skin. Peculiarly, Lena didn't seem to be affected, she walked proudly in just her t-shirt and black jeans, her head held high to the elements, as though the cold torrent was nothing more than background noise. Nancy on the other hand began trying to shield her face with her arm as it intensified.

Eventually, they came to a crossroads, where Lena stopped. Nancy timidly peered out at her friend for her next cue, but Lena didn't turn to her.

"Why have we stopped?" Nancy yelled over the wind, but again her question received no response, Lena simply glanced over her shoulder. Nancy assumed by this that Lena was awaiting her other worldly instructions, so she looked round to figure out where they were herself. She recognised nothing, they were surrounded by unfamiliar buildings and the roads to her sides, ahead and behind were all lost in darkness.

Nancy fought to ask again, "Where are we?" But this time her voice became lost in the wind and it began spiralling around them with such strength, that they became encased in a great tube. Nancy tried to fight, but she was quickly overcome, being pushed and pulled in every direction as it whipped and curled. She fell flat to the floor to stop herself from being swept away, then dragged herself along the ground to grab hold of Lena's ankles. Lena stood unaffected in the hurricane, so Nancy closed her eyes tightly and clung to her anchor for dear life.

It was relentless and Nancy grew impatient. She let go of Lena and fiercely pushed herself up onto her hands and knees in an attempt to save herself, but was ferociously knocked away from her friend and pushed back to the ground with such force, that her skull bounced off the concrete. She became instantly numb; her ears rang and everything around her began to move in slow motion. She made a drunken attempt to crawl back to Lena, but she didn't have the strength, her fight had deserted her. With her head on her hands in defeat, she stayed obediently pinned to the floor and waited out the storm.

Eventually, the great force that held her in place began to ease and cautiously she opened her eyes. She gingerly rolled on to her back to find great chunks of concrete, still being ripped from the ground by the wind and tossed into the air. Their destiny completely taken out of their hands and manipulated onto a collision course with fate. They smashed into one another like meteorites, exploding on impact and strangely, being the deep thinker that she was, she began to sympathise with them. She passively went along with other's wishes and in doing so, had smashed herself to pieces. She sat up and looked down to see her hands painted with blood. She moved her fingers to her forehead and found a large gash. The blood began to run down into her eye, but there was no pain. She wiped it with her dressing gown, then looked up, out of the top of the great funnel to the dark sky. This was the prison she had created for herself, she thought and she was trapped.

Lena moved to her side and gently kicked her in the arm. Nancy looked up at her and Lena moved away. Nancy could still see the angry frustration on her face, so she didn't bother to speak, or ask for help getting to her feet. She rose silently, continuing to wipe the blood from her eye and looked out ahead, past Lena and the thick walls of wind.

In the distance she could just make out two chairs. She stepped forward and the hurricane came to an abrupt halt. Both women froze.

"Why did it stop?" Nancy trembled, but as soon as the words left her mouth, the ground began to quake. She screamed and once again clung to Lena. The concrete broke beneath them. It began tearing itself apart, revealing great shoots of tall grass. Nancy scrambled onto Lena's back in panic. The buildings surrounding them crumbled to the floor. They watched in terror as the ground thunderously swallowed the rubble, until, finally, in all directions there was nothing more than a luscious green meadow and the two chairs.

"Oh God, please tell me that's it!" Nancy nervously whispered; her arms clamped tightly around Lena's neck.

Lena forcefully pulled Nancy's arms from her throat and lent sharply to the side to throw her off her back. She landed hard on the grass, but again felt nothing.

"You nearly choked me out, you silly bitch!" Lena scolded, rubbing her neck with her hand.

"Did you not just see what happened?" Nancy cried, "There was no need to throw me off like that!"

Lena didn't acknowledge her response and once again avoided eye contact.

"Help me up!" Nancy insisted, stretching out her hand.

Lena shook her head and walked towards the chairs.

Nancy scrambled to her feet and followed quickly after her. "Lena! What's happening?"

As they got closer, Nancy realised that the two chairs were from her kitchen, but they were now teetering on the edge of what looked to be a very tall cliff.

"Oh shit!" She cried, stopping a few paces away from the edge. "We're not going to sit there, are we?"

"I don't know." Lena shrugged. The two studied the chairs from a safe distance, until Lena said, "Look." She pointed to a small, cream envelope on one of the chairs.

"Get it!" Nancy commanded.

"Why don't you get it!" Lena snapped.

"Because you seem to be in partnership with whoever built this nightmare, so I think I have much more to lose than you!" Nancy hissed.

Lena rolled her eyes, then cautiously moved and plucked the envelope from the seat.

"Open it then!" Nancy impatiently instructed.

"Give me a second!" Lena growled, as she fumbled to tear it open. She pulled out a folded piece of paper.

"Read it out loud."

Lena tutted, "I'm not going to read it in my head, am I?"

"Well, you don't seem to be sharing any other information with me!"

Lena huffed, then swiftly unfolded the paper. "Oh!" She smirked, looking down at it, while turning away from Nancy.

"What? What does it say?" Nancy tried to look over Lena's shoulder, but Lena span round to face her and hid it behind her back.

"It says that before I read it to you, you have to take a seat."

"Fuck off!"

"No, really it does!"

"Let me see!" Nancy tried to wrestle the paper from her, but Lena pushed her away. "No. Stop messing about. Just sit down!" Lena gestured with her head to one of the chairs.

"Show me!"

"No! Just do as you're told and sit there! Come on!"

Nancy gave up and reluctantly grabbed the back of one of the chairs. She tried hard to pull it towards her, but it was fixed to the ground.

"Stop wasting time and just sit in it where it is!" Lena ordered.

Nancy looked back at her with uncertainty, but Lena pointed firmly at the seat, hurrying her. Nancy took a deep breath, stepped carefully to the side of it and clung to its back as she slid onto the seat.

"Oh my God Lena, I can't look!"

"There's nothing much to look at!" Lena chuckled.

"Lena!" Nancy screamed.

"Sit in it properly! You have to put your feet over the edge!"

"Why?"

"Just do it!" Lena cried.

Nancy closed her eyes and trembled as she slid her body ninety degrees to let her legs hang free.

"We're so high up Nance!"

"Shut up!"

Lena erupted into laughter.

"Just read the stupid paper!" Nancy screamed.

"Okay, okay!" Lena cleared her throat and began, "Imagine there are three states of being, past, present and future. Every moment of our lives is captured in time, carved into the stone of time. If I moved into the past, I couldn't change it because it's nothing more than a memory, a shadow of time. If I moved into the future, I still couldn't change it, because the stones of the present are continually being laid. So, it is right here and only here in the present that I can make change. The past shapes us, but it can't dictate the future. It offers only an advisory notice. Therefore, you shouldn't fear the future, because right here in the present is where we are in control of our universe."

Lena paused in silence for a few moments deciphering the message.

"Is that it?" Nancy asked.

"Yeah." Lena snorted, "What a load of shit!"

"Well, what now?"

"Sitting where you are right now Nance, do you feel in control of your universe?"

"Not particularly no! Just get on with it!"

"That's it!"

"What do you mean that's it?"

"That's it! I was just meant to read it to you, then ask you that question."

"Give it here!" Nancy demanded.

Lena held out the paper and Nancy snatched it from her, "It doesn't say I have to sit here!" She cried.

Lena erupted into loud laughter.

Nancy flew out of the chair and back to safety, well away from the edge. "Are you insane, what if I fell?"

"Oh, don't be dramatic, the chair was fixed, you felt it!"

"It's on a bloody cliff edge!"

"How do you know it's a cliff? It's that dark it could just be a step."

"But you don't know that!"

"Then jump and find out!"

"Jump? What is wrong with you?"

Lena laughed back at the question, then quickly changed to a more serious tone, "That *was* a genuine question Nance, do you feel in control of your universe?"

"What do you mean?"

"Down there is your universe, apparently." She pointed down into the void, "You heard what I read, are you going to control it?"

Nancy looked back at the paper in her hands and took a few moments to analyse the passage. "Well, no, like I said, I don't feel in control at the moment. I've just been abducted by you and pinned to the floor by a hurricane."

"Then there's no hope!" Lena exhaled in frustration.

"Why isn't there?"

"Because, we are stuck here until you are in control."

Lena moved and sat in one of the chairs. She playfully swung her legs out over the edge without a shred of fear and examined the deep pit. She sighed angrily to herself, "I'm now meant to ask you why, but to be honest Nance, I really can't be bothered sitting here, listening to you whine on about why you don't. I honestly, really couldn't give a shit."

"Why are you being so horrible with me?"

"Because I just want to go home! Like I said before, I thought pulling your pathetic arse out of that bath would have been it, but no, we now have to do a deep dive into what's wrong with you."

"What is wrong with me?"

"What's ever right with you? Oh, poor me! Why me? So, you've had shitty things happen to you, haven't we all?"

"Oh, coming from you!"

"What about me?" Lena glared back over her shoulder.

"You'll cling to any arsehole you see! Where were you tonight? It's Christmas Eve and I know for a fact you weren't at home! What piece of shit were you chasing tonight?"

Lena went quiet.

"Oh. Stuck a cord there, haven't I? I'm right."

Lena remained silent, she had no witty comeback or defence. She returned to staring down into the abyss and Nancy watched as she moved her hand to the blood stain on her t-shirt to gently cradle her wound. Her contemplative silence was then quickly overwhelmed by a torrent of tears.

Nancy's anger immediately dissipated, "No. Don't cry. I'm sorry Lena." She paused, "Who you were with tonight hurt you, didn't he?"

Lena wiped her eyes and nose with the back of her hand. "He did!" She whispered. "Nance, I just want to go home, please try, so I can go home. I need to be *there*, not here with you." Lena looked back over her shoulder; her face was dewy with snot and tears.

Nancy folded up the piece of paper, put it into her dressing gown pocket, then walked over to her friend and put her hand on her shoulder. "I'm sorry Lena. Really, I am. What did he do to you?"

Lena shook her head in response; she obviously still wasn't going to tell.

Nancy bravely looked out over the edge. The two women had been friends since birth, they were more like sisters than friends, however, in recent years they had distanced themselves from one another, as both had become too wrapped up in their own dramas and both were too stubborn to apologise for it. While Nancy's heart broke to see her friend in this state, it also infuriated her. Nancy knew it had been coming, as Lena had a habit of playing with fire. It was ironic that they should be standing on a cliff edge, because that's how Lena lived her life. She went down a list of men in her head, possible suspects that could have hurt her friend. There were too many to choose from. For someone so beautiful and intelligent she had always had the worst taste in men. The last boyfriend that Nancy had met couldn't even string a sentence together; he'd arrogantly grunt one-word responses to anyone who tried to interact with him and she never saw a beer bottle leave his hand. All that to one side though, her friend was now sitting in front of her upset and from what she could see, hurt badly. Nancy wasn't used to seeing Lena so fragile and helpless. She was the feisty warrior of the duo, Nancy's bodyguard.

She looked to the sky. The dark veil was now bejewelled with thousands of beautiful stars. She closed her eyes and inhaled the fresh night air. Born into a catholic household, she had been strongly religious growing up, but had rapidly lost her faith as she spiralled. In this moment, however, she felt the need to pray. She desperately needed courage. She looked back at Lena and gently moved her long hair from her face, fixed it behind her ear, then put her hand back on her shoulder. "I could sit here all night and ask you millions of questions," Nancy began, "but you're obviously not going to tell me anything, especially not the truth!" Even when Lena was in a good mood, she wasn't one for question time. "But I'll do this for you!"

"Thank you!" Lena whispered, moving her hand to hold her friends.

Nancy then slowly removed her hand and shuffled to the edge, "Oh, God if you're listening to me, please don't let me die! – Again!"

"Wait. What are you doing?" Lena scowled.

"Jumping!"

"What! No! Don't jump! We'll look for a way down!"

"You said we're short on time!"

Lena swivelled in her chair and grabbed Nancy's arm with both hands, "Yes, but don't jump!"

Nancy exhaled slowly, then span to face her and quickly grabbed onto her arm with her free hand, "Too late!" She nervously braced as she pushed out over the edge, dragging Lena out of the chair down into the darkness with her.

7

His House

Both women hysterically screamed as they fell. Nancy's stomach churned, she held her breath and gritted her teeth hard; even though she couldn't feel much, the falling sensation definitely hadn't left her. She couldn't see anything; it was like falling into oblivion. They tumbled violently, continuing to accelerate, with all sense of direction lost, clinging to each other for dear life, while woefully anticipating the bottom. But they fell for that long Nancy eventually became desensitised to the fear, at which point an invisible force began to break their fall. This new strange feeling was inexplainable. A gradual deceleration, with the density of the air steadily increasing, until its sponginess became a brake and they came to a complete stop.

"Thank God for –" Lena began to breathlessly exhale, but before she could even finish the sentence, they were swiftly pulled sideways, as though a pair of giant, invisible hands had clasped them tightly. Nancy tried to move her limbs against the pressure, but the current was too fast and too strong.

"You have to control it Nance." Lena shouted.

"What do you mean?"

"This is your universe. Think about how we get out of here and land?"

"I don't know."

"Just bloody think of something!"

"Okay, okay! How do we land, how do we land?" Nancy mumbled to herself.

"Nancy! Quick!"

"We slow down!" She shouted.

Instantly both women felt themselves slow, but the air became increasingly oppressive.

"Where are we going?" Nancy struggled to shout.

"I don't know!" Lena yelled back, "But it's crushing me!"

A rush of thoughts filled Nancy's head and a road lined with unlit street lights suddenly appeared ahead of them.

"Okay!" Nancy shouted, "Look at the road, treat it like a runway, we'll land like planes."

"What? How the fuck are we meant to land like planes?"

Before Nancy could answer, both were spat out of the strange portal. They hit the ground hard and tumbled a few meters across the concrete.

Nancy fought to calm herself and clung to the ground in relief. The gravel stuck to the side of her bloodied face, hugging her back. Slowly, she rolled over and brushed it off. She took a few deep breaths, then dizzily sat up and looked over at Lena, who still lay flat on her face.

Nancy panicked, "Lena are you okay?"

"No, you crazy bitch! I am not okay!" She groaned, pushing herself up onto her knees, "Land like a fucking plane?"

"We're fine, aren't we?"

"Are we?" Lena looked up, wide-eyed and shook her head in disapproval, as Nancy grinned at her. "What were you thinking, jumping off a cliff?"

"I did it for you!"

Lena immediately looked away and tutted under her breath, as she rose to her feet. Nancy watched, hoping for a delayed 'thank you', but it never came.

"Well don't just sit there staring at me, let's get moving!" Lena snapped, glaring down at her.

Nancy tutted at her cold response. She obviously still wasn't ready to be friends again, so deflated by her lack of gratitude, she got up and turned her attention to their new surroundings.

It took Nancy less than a second to realise where they were and on cue the street lights came on, illuminating the large, expensive houses that stood behind them. The well-manicured front gardens, in obvious competition with their neighbours framed the wealth of the street. This was somewhere she had known very well. She stumbled towards Lena who was now standing at the foot of a driveway, with a wicked grin on her face. "Who lives here Nance?" She asked playfully.

"A prick!" Nancy sighed.

Lena erupted into loud laughter, "Oh, this is going to be so good!" She began to practically dance up the driveway, while Nancy sluggishly followed.

"Wait, Lena! Why do we have to go in there?"

"I don't know, I was just told who lives here and told to go in."

Nancy squirmed and caught her hand to stop her, "Do we really need to though?"

"Apparently so." Lena frowned, pulling her hand free.

Nancy looked at the sportscar resting in the driveway and cringed at it in disgust.

"Come on Nance, hurry up!" Lena shouted over her shoulder, continuing for the door.

"I am, I am!" Nancy moaned.

Lena stood in front of the entrance and impatiently gestured for Nancy to hurry and join her.

"Oh, I hate this already!" Nancy grumbled.

Lena bared her teeth in excitement.

"What if he's in there?"

"He can't see us!" Lena shouted, cupping her mouth to amplify the sound.

Nancy winced at the loud echo that bounced back from the empty street, "I hope he can't bloody hear us!"

Lena sniggered, then while facing Nancy, held her arms out at her sides and jumped backwards, disappearing through the closed front door.

In any other circumstance Lena's disappearance through a closed door would have amazed Nancy, but not only did this type of thing now seem to be the norm, her sense of dread overrode her awe. Her stomach tied itself in knots as she reflected on her last shameful visit to this residence and after today, she wanted nothing more to do with him. She stood outside for a few moments, puzzling what to do. She couldn't stay outside, she knew that. She had to go in for Lena's sake (even if she was being a brat), but could she handle seeing him again so soon. It was such a hard decision, but helping her friend eventually swayed her, it was the right thing to do. Lena needed her to do it. She gathered her courage, threw her arms up in front of her face and ran towards the closed front door bracing herself for the impact. To her amazement she too slipped straight through it and was now standing in his dark hallway.

She looked round and silently scrutinised the minimalist décor. It had always felt cold and exclusive; it had no heart. Even though she'd been personally invited here, on numerous occasions, she never truly felt welcome. As she looked down, she noticed his white, new trainers with the key to his sports car thrown inside of them. She also noticed that they were next to a pair of beautifully delicate women's heels. Her heart sank in reminiscence. Nothing had changed, not the décor, not the feeling of unease, not the stupid place he'd keep his car key, nothing – except for the heels.

"Where are you?" Lena shouted.

"Here!" Nancy whispered back. She followed Lena's voice and walked slowly into the living room. It was lit by the light of a huge TV mounted on the wall and there in the flesh was the arsehole himself, Joel. He sat snuggled on his large, beige, suede corner sofa with a new mystery girl nestled romantically under his arm.

"Decided to join me then?" Lena beamed.

Nancy responded with a sarcastic glare.

"What did you see in this guy?" She cackled.

Nancy didn't know how to answer. She wasn't proud of her affiliation with this man.

Lena walked over to get a closer look at him. "Look at these eyebrows for God's sake!" She ran her finger along them, then glanced over at Nancy, "I've never seen sharper angles."

She then inspected the rest of his face while chuckling to herself, "Does he ask the mirror who's the fairest of them all?"

Nancy flatly shrugged, unamused by her jokes.

"I'm serious, he actually looks like he's made of Lego!"

Nancy couldn't find any comedic value in how he looked; he made her feel nothing but physically sick. "I don't want to be here!" She mumbled.

"I know." Lena smiled, "But now I've been told a little bit about your situation, I think it's important that you are."

"It's really not the time to be mysterious now Lena! Just tell me what I need to do, so we can leave!"

Lena sat on the arm of the sofa, put her arm around Joel's shoulders and leant into him, to rest her head on his.

"Tell me the Nancy and Joel story, I want to know what happened."

"You know what happened! You just said you did!"

"No, all I know is he's now the ex. I want you to tell me everything."

"No!" Nancy defiantly shook her head, "You won't tell me what happened to you tonight; so why should I tell you anything?"

"Suit yourself!" Lena grinned, "But you're not going to like the alternative."

Nancy scowled in confusion as Lena pointed at the enormous TV. It began to hiss wildly with static, as if trying to tune in to some remote broadcasting. A picture then began to slowly appear through the grey haze, until finally, it beamed in full colour. Nancy was on the screen; this was the first meeting of the two.

Nancy turned away, "Oh my God, I can't watch this! Please! He makes my skin crawl."

"Oh, don't be so bloody dramatic!" Lena snorted. She had now moved to sit next to the mystery girl and pinched the bowl of popcorn from her lap.

Upon hearing her crunch, Nancy turned to look. "Seriously?" She frowned, "You're eating their popcorn?"

Lena shrugged as if to say 'why not' and patted the seat next to her. Nancy sighed and joined her. There was no point in arguing, where else would she go? She grabbed one of the many plump cushions that sat near them and held it in front of her, to use as a shield.

"I'm not watching it all!" She warned.

Lena snorted again, "Don't worry, I don't want to watch it all either! There are things that I really don't need to see." She filled her mouth full of popcorn and mumbled, "We'll just watch the appropriate bits! Now shut up, so I can listen!"

The two looked up at the screen and the story began to play.

Nancy was out with friends at a local bar. "Oh, I love that bar!" Lena interrupted.

"If I'm going to sit here, I don't want a running commentary from you!" Nancy warned.

"I'm just saying it's a nice bar!" Lena huffed.

They were all sat round a table sipping cocktails, laughing and telling stories. Nancy appeared to glow with happiness on the screen, her confidence radiated through her beauty.

"Where are these people now?" Lena asked.

"Gone!" Nancy mumbled, "I'm still sort of friends with maybe one or two, but the rest were more acquaintances."

"You look happy though!"

Nancy flared her nostrils, raised her eyebrows and pursed her lips in response, while she gave a faint shrug.

"You weren't happy there then?" Lena deciphered from her response.

Nancy didn't answer, she just looked ahead and continued to watch on.

The group talked jovially, with many of the males surrounding Nancy trying their best to impress her with witty conversation and the offer of countless drink refills.

"They seem nice! Why didn't you go on a date with any of them?"

"I went on a date with all of them!" Nancy grimaced.

"Of course you did!" Lena laughed.

"Why ask when you already know!"

"Just getting my facts straight! So, what was wrong with them?"

"They're all the same!" Nancy moaned, "There's no real conversation in any of them. We weren't into the same things."

"I suppose that made you feel lonely then?"

"It did. You had abandoned me and I didn't have anyone else."

Lena ignored her abandonment comment and interrupted, "Oh, wait, what about him?" Lena pointed to the screen, as a tall, brown-haired man in a blue, plaid shirt came over to the table. "I remember him!"

"Yes!" Nancy cried, "Ah, he was such a beautiful person!" Her eyes began to fill with tears in reminiscence, "I did love him. But I just wasn't in love with him, if you know what I mean."

"Poor guy! I remember you dragging him along. Just like Joel dragged you along really."

"What?" Nancy furiously glared at her, "No I did not!"

"You broke his heart Nance! He told me you did!"

Nancy buried her face into the cushion.

"I told him he shouldn't have gone anywhere near you. He was too nice. He did so much for you and all you did was take, take, take!"

"It wasn't like that at all!" Nancy snapped, lifting her head.

"It was from where I was sat."

"You haven't got a fucking clue." Nancy erupted, "I had no one Lena, no one. I was having a full bloody mental breakdown and he was there. He was the only one that was there. He had such a beautiful heart!" She paused, took a breath, wiped her eyes, then continued in a calmer tone, "I tried to love him, I did, I really, really did, but I just couldn't. Something was missing. Don't you think I know how much I hurt him?"

Lena shrugged.

"Do you really think I'd purposefully do that to someone?" Nancy shouted.

Lena smiled slyly.

"All I was to Joel was an ego boost, you have no idea what happened between me and him, so don't you dare compare me to Joel. You don't know anything!"

"I do. It sounds to me like you just used that poor guy because you were lonely."

"How dare you!" Nancy fumed.

"That is basically what you just said to me though Nance! You said you had no one, so you strung him along."

"No, I did not! I loved him, I just told you I did! Just not how he wanted me to!"

"Then you should have told him that sooner!"

"I-I, well, I – tried." Nancy sighed in reflection, "When I eventually realised how much I was hurting him, I did."

"Then what?"

"I never heard from him again obviously." Nancy watched in sadness, as she laughed with the blue shirted man on the screen. "I saw him a few years later from a distance and I was actually going to go over and apologise, but the people I was with at the time warned me against it. I'd still like to apologise and give him an explanation."

"I don't think he needs your apology. Last I heard he's happily married. I think he dodged the Nancy bullet to be honest."

"Why are you trying to make me feel like shit?"

"Well, he's off enjoying life and you've just killed yourself in the bath. I think he's won there, don't you?"

"I didn't kill myself; it was an accident!" Nancy snapped.

Lena huffed in disagreement and directed Nancy's attention back to the screen, "Shut up now and watch the rest of it." She instructed.

"Oh God. Here we go!" Nancy began to sob. There, now in full luminescence, stood Joel. He greeted his friends, who then swiftly introduced him to Nancy. His charisma burst from the screen and filled the room.

Nancy grumbled in disgust, "I can't watch this!"

Lena let out a loud giggle, her eyes were transfixed. She clearly enjoyed every moment of Nancy's relationship drama, whereas Nancy once again hid.

The two strangers on the screen began to talk, share commonalities, ambitions for the future and past adventures, until, the Nancy of the past had been magnetised. Lena prodded her in her side to encourage her to look, but she continued to cower behind the cushion.

"Okay fine, let's just skip it to the good part then."

"Skip it to the end!" Nancy shouted into the cushion.

Lena swiped her hand to the right through the air and the film pushed forward.

"Oh God! Even worse!" Nancy recoiled, as she snook a peek.

The onscreen couple were now both sat in his living room, on his sofa, just as the mystery girl now sat with him, but the pair were kissing and affectionately cuddling, barely paying any attention to the TV. Then Joel put his hand beneath Nancy's chin, gazed into her eyes for a few moments and said, "You're like an exotic flower!"

Lena quickly paused the video and fell to the floor creased with laughter. Popcorn flew everywhere. She rolled back and forth holding her stomach, crushing the stray pieces into the carpet. She looked in pain she was laughing that hard. "This guy can't be for real!" She giggled.

Nancy cringed, she could feel the knots in her stomach tighten and her face burned. She wanted to be sick; she couldn't understand Lena's amusement with the situation.

"Oh God!" Lena cried, "This guy is just too much." She lay on her back and looked upside down at the screen, swiping her hand through the air to replay it, making her break out onto a higher-level of hysterics. She then rolled onto her knees and looked at Nancy, who met her gaze with a sombre scowl. She quickly realised that she was the only one to find it amusing, so reluctantly pulled herself back on to the sofa and tried her best to recompose herself. "I'm sorry, I know you feel bad, but this idiot, he's just too much!"

"We don't need to see anymore!" Nancy seethed, gritting her teeth.

"Oh, we really do!" Lena smiled, wiggling back into a comfortable spot beside her.

"Why are you enjoying embarrassing me?"

"You embarrassed yourself!"

Nancy angrily shook her head, stood up, threw the cushion at Lena and walked towards the door to leave.

Lena quickly skipped the story on to get her attention. "This is the bit you need to see," she shouted, "turn and watch."

As Nancy's back was turned, she heard herself saying goodbye to him. She dropped her shoulders and sighed. She begrudged still helping Lena after her laughing fit and cruel perspective of her playing with the blue shirted man's heart, but she selfishly wanted out of this nightmare too, so she glanced back over her shoulder at the screen.

The two had said goodbye, Joel walked back into his living room, sat down and pulled his phone out from the crease in the sofa. He then dialled a number and waited on the line, while he flicked through TV channels.

"Who's he calling?" Nancy asked.

"Shush! Just watch!" Lena whispered.

The call was answered, "Hey Babe!"

"Hey Babe!" Nancy repeated in confusion.

"I said shush! Just listen!"

Joel continued, "Yeah, just had a boring day really. Missing you. What time are you back tonight?" The voice on the other end responded and Joel smirked, as he listened, "Can't wait, I'll come pick you up. We'll get a takeaway on the way." The conversation went on, but Nancy had now zoned out. She was beyond furious. She did, however, hear him end the call by saying, "See you soon beautiful, I love you!" Which completely winded her.

Lena stopped the video and stared at Nancy waiting for her response, but she stood in a trance, wrestling with her impulse to smash every window and piece of furniture in his house.

"Are you okay Nance?" Lena asked awkwardly.

"I hate him!" Nancy seethed. "I just hate him!"

She marched over to Joel, pulled the cushion out from under his arm and hit him hard in the face, three or four times. He obviously didn't flinch.

"I hate you!" She screamed in his face. "I hate you so much!" She dropped to her knees in front of him in tears.

"I thought you knew?" Lena sniped.

"At that point no, I didn't! Oh God what an idiot!" Nancy held her face in her hands, "How could I have been so stupid?"

"So, why do you hate him?" Lena asked calmly, still munching on popcorn.

Nancy threw her hands down, "Are you serious? What the fuck is wrong with you tonight?"

"I'm just trying to get through this as quickly as possible. I know why you hate him, but I'm asking why you still hate him. This happened a while ago?"

"Are you winding me up? You've just seen with your own eyes that he's an arsehole! He used me! You're meant to be my friend!"

"I am your friend, but *you* were the other woman and what I'm trying to say is that you really need to let it go. It's weird that you're holding on to it so much."

"What is your problem?" Nancy snarled.

"Because I know you keep playing it out in your head. What happened, all the things he did and how things ended today. You literally analyse every minute detail of all the times that you could have saved face, but you didn't. You had multiple chances to walk away, you knew it wasn't right, but you stayed. All you did was keep his bed warm when he was lonely, you were nothing more than his cheap electric blanket."

"That's not true!" Nancy cut in.

"Yes, it is!" Lena furiously argued, "This is not the Nancy I know, so it makes no sense to me, you are not that person! What confuses me the most though and what I'll really never understand, is why after everything, you even went to the arsehole for a job! Like, what the fuck? Who does that? He treated you like shit and you let him. He's nothing more than a complete prick and he always will be!"

Nancy looked away like a spoilt child that had just been told off. Lena spoke sense, it was not only the truth, but the tough love she had desperately needed, no matter how cruel it felt. She had been taken advantage of by this selfish man, because she'd let him. She knew how arrogant and manipulative he was, so why did she crave his attention so much? That was the bit that she couldn't understand about herself.

"I honestly didn't know he had a girlfriend to begin with, then he told me he'd left her, but that was just another lie. When I started working with him, I had it confirmed that they were still together, but you're right, it still didn't stop me. I don't know why." She sighed as she looked back at Lena; her eyes glazed with shame. "He hurt me though Lena. He'd hurt me all the time, so much and he wouldn't care! Maybe I just wanted to make him care!"

"He will never care about you. He only cares about himself!"

Nancy threw her head back and shrieked in frustration, "How am I supposed to control the present, when I get sucked in by people like him?"

"Experience," Lena replied, jumping to her feet. "You've gained experience. You put an end to it today, because finally you realised your self-worth. Now you know the warning signs, you won't let it happen again."

Nancy shook her head.

"You have to leave all this in the past now Nance! Stop criticising yourself, you weren't in the right frame of mind, you're still not for God's sake. Joel preyed on that; he seized the opportunity to sink his fangs into you!"

"I'm so angry with him though!"

"No!" Lena corrected her, "You're angry with yourself!"

"What are you asking me to do exactly? Every shitty thing that happens I'm just supposed to take it on the chin? Put it down as experience." Nancy mimicked quotation marks with her fingers as she said 'experience' to sarcastically mock Lena or whoever it was talking through her (she had never been this wise before).

"No. That's not what I'm saying at all! I'm trying to tell you that you're too hard on yourself! Why torture yourself over the past? It can't be changed. Did you not understand the passage in the envelope?"

"Yes!" Nancy snapped, "But don't think for one minute that a silly little paragraph is going to help me!"

"Don't be like that Nance."

"No, I am going to be like that. I'm done! I'm not playing this weird little game with you anymore!"

Lena flared her nostrils in frustration, "Don't be ungrateful!" She warned.

"Ungrateful? For what? Falling off a cliff and being dragged here by you?" Nancy looked up and shouted, "Yeah, amazing effort, thanks very much."

"Stop!" Lena cried, "Don't take the piss!"

"Oh, shut up Lena! Why don't you just disappear back off to fairyland and leave me alone!"

There suddenly came a great rumble of thunder from the ceiling. Both women cowered to the floor and cautiously looked above them as it began to crack. The white plaster crumbled and fell like snow to the floor. Both women shrieked in fear and quickly looked down to protect their eyes.

"What are you doing?" Nancy screamed in terror.

"It's not me. It's you!"

Great, grey clouds filled the void above them, followed by lightning that cut down into the room, setting it ablaze. Strong winds rose from the ground and began to swirl. Nancy was thrown up against a wall and once again pinned in place by the strength of the gale.

Joel and the mystery girl remained completely oblivious to what appeared to be Armageddon. They appeared to be in an invisible bubble of protection, as the tornado of fire ripped and curled in a great tube around the four souls.

"Make it stop! Now!" Nancy screamed.

"You're doing it! Not me!" Lena angrily screamed back.

Nancy trembled with fear as the flames licked her skin, "Please, stop this now! I want to go home!" She squinted at Lena across the room, but to her horror, she found that her angelic aura had turned red and her eyes now burned like molten gold. This wasn't Lena.

Her voice cut through the room, sending shockwaves into the chaos. "You want to go home?" She boomed, "To what? What have you got to go home to? To sit there, examining your pitiful excuse of a life? I have a daughter Nancy, a beautiful little girl, remember her? She needs me to come home and you've spat your dummy out at the first hurdle? How can anyone help you, when you won't help yourself?" She clenched her hands into fists and hammered the air at her sides, "The past does not matter anymore!" Then pointing at Joel in fury, she spat "He doesn't matter anymore!"

"Okay!" Nancy cried, "Okay, I'm sorry. Please just stop!"

"Are you wasting my time Nancy?"

"No! I'm grateful for your time! I swear!"

"You're lying!"

"No! The truth is hard to hear! Please Lena, or whoever you are!"

"Don't lie to me!"

"I'm not lying, I promise. I'm begging you, make it stop!"

Lena scowled dubiously at her.

"Please!" Nancy begged again, "I'm sorry!"

But Lena continued to stare sharply in silence. It was as if she was looking deep into Nancy's soul, determining whether this mere mortal was worth saving.

"I swear! I'm sorry!" Nancy shouted again. Her helpless, frightened face now illustrated her deep remorse. She looked like a small deer, caught in a hunters' snare. "You're right, I don't have anything to go home to. I don't want to go back to that. I do need help! Please, I want to be helped!"

"Like I said, *you* are doing this! This is *your* universe! Help yourself!"

Nancy hesitated; all she could think about was the heat from the flames.

"Make it stop!" Lena boomed, "Prove to me that you care about something more than yourself!"

Nancy panicked; she was too crippled with fear. How could she control this other worldly storm. She didn't know where to begin.

"Tick, tock Nancy!" Lena taunted.

Nancy closed her eyes to think. She needed to tune everything out and focus. She tried to think of happier times. Things that made her feel safe. Something calm – Her dad. He was her rock. His dark humour got her through the saddest of times. She should have reached out to him for help long ago, but she didn't want to disappoint him. How would he feel now knowing his daughter was gone? The thought broke her heart and she immediately fell from the wall to her knees.

As she hit the floor, the room returned to normal in a cloud of hot ash. Maybe her focus had become so insular over the years that she was the real problem, not the outside world, but her mindset. She beckoned misfortune, to strengthen her argument for hating the world. Wrapped in sadness, everyone had left her alone, because she'd wanted to be alone. She bowed her head to the ground in awe of this reawakening.

"I'm so sorry!" She whispered, "I'm so sorry for everything!"

Lena now thankfully back to her angelic self, walked over to help her to her feet. Nancy flinched in terror at her offer of assistance, but Lena insisted, so Nancy cautiously accepted. Lena looked at her sternly, "No one wants to hurt you here. You only hurt yourself. Do you understand that?"

Nancy nodded, "I am sorry Lena! I've been a little self- absorbed, haven't I? Lena nodded.

"There have been so many times when I've been a real selfish bitch, especially to you."

"We're both selfish bitches," Lena exhaled, "that's why we're here together." Nancy tried to smile.

"I am your friend Nancy, but I don't like this version of you. I want the Nancy I love back. I want *my* Nancy back, not this person. I have no time for this silly bitch!"

Nancy hugged her tightly, but Lena didn't reciprocate, so she awkwardly let go.

"Well, this visit turned into more than I expected." Lena huffed.

Nancy timidly nodded.

"I think it's safe to say we're done here. Do you agree?"

Once again Nancy nodded. "Can we at least shave his eyebrows?" She joked, trying to provoke a smile from her friend.

Lena didn't smile, "No. Unfortunately, not!" She replied flatly.

Nancy looked back at Joel's face in disappointment, then grinned back at Lena in another attempt to crack her serious composure, but still, she was not amused, she simply motioned with her head for them to leave and led the way back out of the house in silence.

Leaving through the front door, Nancy asked, "Can we not do anything to help that girl he was with? She only looks like she's in her early twenties; it doesn't feel right leaving her here with him."

Lena did smile at this question, "I'm being told that life will catch up with Joel, so we don't need to worry!"

"Hm." Nancy sarcastically huffed.

"Maybe she'll be his kick in the balls!" Lena smiled.

Nancy broke out into laughter. "Yeah." She chuckled, "He definitely deserves it!"

She then took one last look at the house to silently bid it good riddance, "I want to leave this version of myself here. I don't want to carry her with me anymore."

Lena nodded in agreement, "It's for the best Nance."

Nancy closed her eyes for a moment and replayed all the painful memories in her head. All the emotions she'd been avoiding swelled in an estuary of despair. She sat on the ground and cried.

Lena knelt beside her and nudged her, "We can talk about it if you like?"

"No." Nancy spluttered, "No, thank you. It needs to be forgotten."

"That will take time Nance."

Nancy sighed. "I don't know how I let myself get here. Why did I –"

"STOP!" Lena interrupted, "Just stop, you're already trying to find answers and reasons. This obsession with analysing yourself. You're too critical! Just stop. It happened. It was unfortunate. Now let it go."

Nancy nodded, wiped her eyes, then looked at Lena and said, "He'd always make out that everything was my fault, because he'd say that I didn't know what

I wanted. Like, he'd go through periods where he'd seem really frustrated and he'd want me there, but I couldn't do anything right; he'd be horrible and call me some horrendous things. He'd also say that I was pretty but not what anyone would ever call beautiful."

"You are beautiful Nance! He's a monster!"

Nancy faintly smiled, "Whenever I tried to distance myself from him, he'd hound me, until I gave in and went back to him." She closed her eyes, "You said I was like him, because of how I treated that poor guy, but I was never like that!"

"No, I know you weren't. You were selfish and should have put him out of his misery a lot sooner, but I know how much you cared for that guy and were scared of hurting him. You're nothing like Joel."

Nancy looked out onto the dark street. She suddenly felt a little lighter, as if she had shaken a heavy weight from her back.

Lena smirked as she watched her silent breakthrough,

"Come on. Lot's more to get through." She got up and Nancy followed back down the driveway out onto the street.

8

The Wolf

Having just witnessed her friend as an angry possessed puppet, Nancy now felt even more uncomfortable in Lena's presence and wary of completely trusting her. This universe also now terrified her, because she *was* in control and she didn't trust herself.

"I'm actually looking forward to what's next and I think you'll be really pleased too." Lena reassured her, seeing her unease.

"Can't wait!" Nancy mumbled nervously.

"No, it's actually something really nice, so don't worry."

"Anything's got to be better than that!"

"We're addressing your issues!"

"It's going to be a bloody long night then!" Nancy grumbled.

Lena began to laugh loudly, but her laughter was unexpectedly cut short. "Stop!" She commanded. She threw her arm out across the front of Nancy to guard her and her light sparked into a brighter beam. She stood still like a rabbit that had just sensed the presence of a fox.

"What is it?" Nancy whispered.

Lena closed her eyes and tilted her head, as if trying to listen out for something.

Nancy watched, but her patience quickly waned, "What can you hear?"

"Just hush for a minute, something's there."

Nancy fell silent and frantically scanned the darkness ahead of them, then Lena opened her eyes and angrily tutted as she looked out ahead.

"What's the matter?" Nancy asked.

"It's you, you idiot. Stop feeling scared!"

"You're the one that's making me feel scared!"

Lena's eyes suddenly widened and the blood drained from her face. She had obviously just caught sight of what hid in the darkness ahead.

"Oh my God Lena, what's there?" Nancy spoke like a ventriloquist, as her body tightened with fear.

"Think of something happy quick!" Lena whispered.

"I can't. You're freaking me out!" Nancy hissed.

Lena grabbed hold of Nancy's arm and pulled her close to her side, into her light.

Nancy gazed at her in panic, "What's there Lena?"

"Just think of something bloody happy! Stop being scared!"

"I can't help it! You're frightening me!"

"Fine. Fine." Lena whispered, "Then just stay calm, close your eyes and brace yourself."

"Brace myself?"

"Close your eyes and stay calm," Lena snapped, as she tightened her grip on Nancy's arm.

Nancy winced, "You're hurting me!"

Slowly, the street lights began to flicker all around them.

"What's happening?" Nancy panted.

POP! POP! in the far distance, one by one the lights began to blow. Something dark was moving closer.

"Oh my God. What's happening?" Nancy's eyes flooded with terrified tears.

"It's your fear!" Lena hissed.

"What do you mean?" Nancy quivered.

"For your own sake Nancy, you need to calm down."

"I can't. Just tell me what it is!"

"It's a fucking wolf!"

"A wolf!" Nancy exclaimed, "What do you mean a wolf?"

"Nancy whatever you do, don't run!"

"Don't run?" Nancy hissed.

"Listen to me! I'm telling you now, it's literally the scariest thing I've ever seen in my life! When you see it, don't you dare move!"

"Oh fuck!" Nancy squeaked. She shut her eyes tightly, but couldn't resist peeping as a strong, low snarl echoed from the darkness. The anticipation was killing her; she needed the night to give up the monster hiding in it. Suddenly, she noticed two golden orbs floating high in the black. She opened her eyes properly and blinked a few times, trying to focus in on them. They appeared to glow, then simultaneously flicker, then glow again in a repeated pattern.

"What are they?" Nancy whispered.

"I don't know!" Lena lied.

"Oh, shit!" Nancy whimpered, as she quickly realised, "They're it's eyes!" Its long snout then emerged, "It's a fucking monster!"

Lena gawped in awe at the scale of the beast, "Just, don't move."

"We're going to die!" Nancy squeaked.

80

"We're not!" Lena cautioned, "You're in control remember!"

The beast fully emerged in to the dim flickering light. It was truly a thing of nightmares. Standing around ten feet tall, with jet black, shaggy fur and those golden eyes, no pupils, just balls of solid gold. The two women could see great beads of saliva sliding down its enormous, sharp fangs and dripping out of its muscular jaws.

"What the fuck!" Nancy whined, now seeing it in all its glory.

"Trust me! Just, stay calm and don't move."

The wolf lowered its head to the ground and resumed its approach causing the street lights on either side to continue to explode in its presence.

"Just stay still," Lena continued to reassure her, "I won't let it hurt you!"

The ground vibrated with its steps and its thick, hot breath floated in the cold air around its head. Closer and closer it crept; its demon gaze fixed on Nancy. Her heart screamed with adrenaline, she had to run, she could feel her pulse pounding wildly in her head, she needed to run or she was going to faint. She started trying to pull out of Lena's grip, to slowly edge backwards, but Lena held her tighter.

"Stay still!" Lena warned sharply, "Nancy, don't look at it, either close your eyes or look at me!"

"I-I-I – I can't!" She screamed and fiercely pulled her arm free. She leapt into action and the monster threw its head high into the sky, letting out a deafening howl. The chase was on. It leapt through the air, furiously bouncing up the concrete after her. Nancy ran wildly, screaming as loudly as she could. The beast too let out a spectacular roar gaining on her in the darkness. Her body also screamed with pain; she was running faster than her legs had ever carried her in her life. She clawed at the air in front of her, willing it to pull her along, but nothing was working. Her heart sang, electrified by the vibrations of the monster's thundering footsteps. She frantically scanned the street, looking for some sign of escape. There was none, no glimmer of light, no dark corner to duck into, no hope, nothing but darkness. Even the moon and stars were hidden behind thick cloud. She knew she couldn't outrun it, twenty of her paces equalled one small stride of the monster's, this was the end, but she didn't want to die.

"I want to live!" She screamed, "Please, whoever you are, I want to live!"

She suddenly felt its warm breath on the back of her neck. It was too late. She had realised how much she wanted to live when it was too late! Crying hysterically, she braced herself for her impending doom. She heard its teeth slide apart and pictured her death inside its hideous jaws.

"Please!" She desperately screamed again, "I'm begging you please!"

Snap! Its jaws slammed shut and she felt a hard, blunt blow to her side. Her body flew through the air and smashed through some kind of hard surface, which is when she realised, her feeling had returned. She lay lifeless, she was too terrified to open her eyes and see what had happened or the state she was in. She decided to play dead, until a cold hand gently tapped the side of her face, encouraging her consciousness. She carefully peeped and found Lena kneeling over her; her glowing face rattled with concern.

"Thank God you're okay!" She smiled down in relief, watching Nancy open her eyes.

Nancy didn't move; she stared in bewilderment at her friend.

"That was a close one Nance!"

Disorientated, she closed her eyes and covered her face with her hands. "Am I dead?" She trembled, "It got us, didn't it?"

Lena chuckled, "No! It didn't."

Nancy peered cautiously from her hands.

"Are you okay?" Lena smiled.

"No!" Nancy whispered.

"You're safe here!" Lena reassured her, grabbing her hand to help her upright, "I promise."

"What the hell was that!" Nancy whispered.

"I told you, your fear." Lena sat on the floor.

"What do you mean my fear though?"

"We all have fear don't we," Lena began, "but we control it by establishing what's logical and illogical. We use it to our advantage, use it to protect us, not to restrict us. This is your universe remember and *your* fear is running wild within it. It has become a monster with no master. You've given it such power that it overpowers you. That's why in life you're so stagnant, your fear is basically running wild."

Nancy took a few moments to digest this, she didn't know what shocked her more, the monster or Lena being profound. "That beast is mine?"

"Yes, your fear manifests itself in the form of what you fear the most. Apparently, yours is an angry wolf." Lena appeared quite in awe of this fact, she hunched her shoulders, raised her eyebrows and pushed out her bottom lip, pondering why Nancy's worst fear was a wolf.

"Did you know it was coming?" Nancy cut in.

Lena rocked back, "No! Honestly that shocked me as much as it did you! I mean shit Nancy, that was disturbing! I told you not to run though and you didn't listen! Why didn't you listen to me?"

Nancy pushed herself up off the floor to sit straighter. "What did you want me to do?" She asked, "Wait for it to come close enough to rub its belly? I'd be rubbing it from the inside if I'd have stayed still!"

"Actually no." Lena corrected her, holding her index finger up in the air. "The only way to conquer your fear is to face it. You did the stupidest thing; you tried to run from it. You can't outrun it."

"You would have done the exact same thing! Don't act like you weren't scared!"

Lena let out a quiet chuckle, "Honestly, I have never been so scared in my entire life! How does your mind even work to create something that horrible?"

Nancy shrugged.

"That's pretty dark Nance, even by your standards."

"We're safe in here, aren't we?"

"We're safe in here." Lena nodded

"But, how? If this is my universe and it's running wild, how are we safe here?"

"Because there are protected places and this thank God is one of them. You've always been safe here."

"Can you make the wolf go away?"

"No, I'm not your fairy godmother! You have to deal with your own scary shit!"

Nancy sighed, "I think I would have preferred a fairy godmother."

"Why?" Lena asked as she helped her to her feet.

"She wouldn't have rugby tackled me through a brick wall!"

"I saved you, didn't I?" Lena snapped defensively.

"Yeah, I suppose, that's twice now, isn't it?"

The women smiled at each other, but Nancy winced as the cut on her forehead suddenly became tighter. She moved her hand to gently touch it.

"That's a nasty cut." Lena frowned, moving closer to examine it.

"You didn't even ask me if I was okay when I did it!" Nancy snapped.

"Because I was pissed off at you then and you got up and were moving about, so I assumed you were fine!"

Nancy rolled her eyes and tutted at her lack of sympathy, then turned her head to their new surroundings, "So, where are we now anyway?"

9

Francesco

The décor was dated, but it was welcoming and homely, while also spotlessly clean. Religious Christmas decorations adorned the walls and in the corner of the room a large, beautifully dressed Christmas tree stood proudly. The smell of the fresh pine filled the air and the fire blazed. Nancy felt a great warmth in her heart, as though she'd just been invited home.

"Your house!" She beamed as she looked at Lena. She walked over to the middle of the room to admire the Christmas tree.

"I told you that you were going to like our next stop." Lena moved to stand next to her, "If you'd have just trusted me, we would've avoided the wolf!"

"I couldn't help it. You really scared me back at Joel's."

"That was for you own good, but as you just said, I've saved you twice now, you need to start trusting me!"

Nancy shrugged, "You're just a little spooky."

Lena chuckled, "Coming from the woman that's just dreamt up the monster wolf. It's me that should be scared of you!"

Nancy snorted then turned to find two people sitting at either end of a small, old-fashioned sofa. "Oh my God!" Nancy exclaimed bursting into happy tears, "It's them! They're here!" It was Lena's mother and her brother Francesco, who was five years older than Nancy and Lena.

Nancy's parents had been friends with Lena's since the women were born. Lena's parents were the main supplier for Nancy's parents' restaurant and over the years their friendship had grown to the point that they now treated each other like family.

When Nancy was growing up her grandmother would look after her while her parents worked, but when she died shortly after Nancy started high school, she began spending most of her time at Lena's house and her parents loved her like their own. She'd go straight there after school and dinner would be ready on the table. The two girls would eat, tell Lena's mother all the gossip of the day, then do their homework together. It was beautiful, the house was always loud and full of chaos, Nancy loved being there. Francesco always kept out of their way; he was pleasant but distant, as he was always busy with other things.

Around seven o'clock Nancy's mum would come to pick her up and drop her off back at home, before returning to the restaurant. Nancy would then spend the rest of the evening alone, then get up at 5.30am the next morning to see her parents for a few minutes before they'd rush back off to work. Maybe that's why she found it so difficult to open up to her parents, because as much as she loved them and felt loved by them, they were strangers to her. She was grateful for all their hard work in providing her with such a comfortable life, but if it wasn't for Lena and her family, she would have been lonely.

After Nancy quit her big city job, she briefly worked at the restaurant, which is when she got to know Francesco. He worked as a delivery driver for a while, so the two saw each other most days and this was when she fell in love with him. She loved everything about him and for a short period, the two would spend a lot of time together. To Nancy's disappointment, however, what they shared remained platonic, but it didn't matter to her too much, she'd rather have spent time with him as friends than not at all. Unfortunately, their friendship eventually fizzled out, as Francesco became busy with renovating a house he'd bought and Nancy attracted the attention of Joel, but she was overjoyed to now be standing in front of him.

He was in his mid-thirties; his dark, brown hair fell messily on his head and his piercing, blue eyes sparkled in the light of the Christmas tree. He was a little over six feet tall, with a muscular build; a short beard framed his strong, square jaw line and he had beautiful, full lips. He also had a darker complexion than Lena, possibly from the years spent out in the sun, playing sports and building things.

"I haven't seen him in so long!" Nancy's voice broke with excitement, as she admired him. She knelt down on the floor in front of him, as he stared straight through her. "He looks so beautiful!" She declared, with a wide smile. "Oh God. I've missed him so much!"

"You're making me feel sick!" Lena frowned in disgust.

"Don't be like that! How is he? He still lives here, right?"

"He does, he's still renovating his place at the minute and I actually don't know how he is; we don't speak."

"You live in the same house!"

"Yeah, I know, we just don't though."

"That's sad."

"He's as self-righteous as you are!"

Nancy sighed, "He just cares about you Lena! *We*, just care about you!"

"Care about me?" Lena snorted, "All you do is pick fault!"

88

"That's not true!"

"You always have something to say about how I live my life!"

"Like when?"

"Remember what you said when I told you I was pregnant."

Nancy quickly looked at the ground. She did remember! She could in fact photographically recall every frame of the argument, she regretted it that much. "No. What did I say?" She sheepishly asked, looking back up at her.

"You, said I wasn't fit to have a child Nance. You called me a train wreck. You said that I'd be selfish to bring a child into my world *and* that the father would leave me before the baby was even born."

Nancy put her hand to her mouth and uneasily rubbed her lips, "I did, but I told you I was sorry and you proved me wrong, you've always gone out of your way to prove me wrong."

Lena tutted in annoyance and shook her head.

"You're a great mother!"

"How do you know?" Lena sarcastically snorted, "You haven't been there!"

"No, no I haven't."

"You hurt me so much Nance. I needed you!"

"I know. I shouldn't have said any of those things and I regret them so much. I've honestly thought about that moment a lot, but I think I was just scared."

"*You* were scared?" Lena snapped.

"Yes, I didn't want anything to change. A baby is a huge deal and nothing would have been the same. I didn't want to lose you."

"You did though."

"I know. I just didn't want you to leave me behind. You were moving on with your life and I – well, I still haven't."

Lena turned away to look into the fire.

"I'm so sorry Lena. I swear I am."

Lena didn't respond.

"I know how much you needed me, but all I could think about was myself. I was such a cold bitch, but that's me and you of all people know that."

Lena glared at her over her shoulder.

"That's not what you needed though." Nancy exhaled.

"No, it wasn't." Lena mumbled.

"I should have been the person you needed."

Lena nodded.

"I've met Evangeline a few times, when she's been out with your parents in town. She's so beautiful. It broke my heart every time, because I'd been so cruel and missed out on such an important part of both your lives. I sent her presents and messaged you on her birthdays and every Christmas. You know I care!"

Again, Lena didn't answer, she turned and stared at her mother as she wiped tears from her face.

"Lena, please! Please forgive me. I came to apologise properly just before she was born, remember? You screamed at me to leave when I was standing on the doorstep."

"I was so angry."

"I know and you had every right to be. You still do."

"No, I was angry because you were right. You're always fucking right Nance."

"What do you mean?"

"I thought having a baby would help me sort my life out. I wanted so much to change. I was bored of our routine, going out Thursday to Monday, seeing different guys, I just wanted something more. But not everyone was as excited about the baby as me – including the father." She looked up at the ceiling trying to balance the tears in her eyes, "He left me two weeks before she was born."

Nancy didn't know what to say, she knew he'd left her, but not just before the birth. She tried to think of a generic comforting line that people would usually use in a situation such as this, but quickly gave up, "I don't know what to say Lena. I really don't, other than I'm sorry."

"No, I know you are." Lena smiled, as she plucked a tissue from a box on the small table next to her mother. "I forgave you a long time ago to be honest. I knew exactly what you meant and I know how you go cold when you can't deal with things. You've never been able to cope with change. Remember when they stopped making your olive shampoo? Jesus!"

Nancy laughed, "That was a really hard time!"

Lena nodded, "I've missed you so bloody much Nance."

Nancy got to her feet and hugged her friend tightly. This time Lena reciprocated and they wept in each other's arms.

"Oh God, I'm going to get snot in your hair!" Lena laughed. She quickly let go of Nancy to grab another tissue.

But Nancy caught her hand as she pulled away, "I actually don't care. I'm so happy to see you. Even if all of this isn't real, it's amazing just to be with you again."

Lena squoze Nancy's hand in agreement, "We're both going to go home with a story to tell. Okay?"

Nancy nodded, "I promise to be different."

Lena smiled in acknowledgment.

"Friends?" Nancy grinned.

"Friends!" Lena confirmed. "Now talk about something else to stop me crying!"

"Well, what are we doing here?" Nancy asked, looking back at Francesco.

Lena paused for a few moments, waiting for her orders, then also looked at Francesco, but in disgust.

Nancy laughed glancing back at her face. "What's the matter?"

"My brother - he likes you!"

"What?" Nancy exclaimed.

Lena nodded in confirmation; her face then contorted into disappointment.

"I wondered if he liked me." Nancy went on, "He never made it clear though! We went out so many times, but he never asked me out on a proper date."

"Maybe because he still lives with his parents?" Lena slyly responded.

Nancy shot her a quick unamused glare, then gazed admiringly back at him. "Well, I would have said yes!" She confirmed.

"I know you would have said yes! I think we established at Joel's house that you'll say yes to anyone!"

"Cheeky bitch!"

"And, you said you went out with all those other guys on screen too."

"Yeah, on a date, nothing more!"

Lena looked sceptically at her friend.

"Nothing more!" Nancy sharply reiterated.

"I knew he liked you!" Lena went on, "After we'd go out together, he'd ask me like a million questions about who you were with and all that."

"Why didn't you tell me?"

"You didn't need to know!"

"Why not?"

"Because you'd break his heart Nance!"

Nancy's face dropped in astonishment, "I would never do that to him!"

"You can't say that, how do you know that you wouldn't?"

"I just know! How do you know that I would?"

"Because I've seen you do it! You've got a pretty good track record."

Nancy frowned and shook her head in disapproval, "This is different!"

"Why?"

"Because I love him!"

Lena rolled her eyes, "Seriously?"

"Yes! I do! I really do! I have for years. My heart beats really fast when he talks to me and I get lost for words."

"That happens to you when you order a takeaway, because you feel like you're on a timer."

Nancy laughed, "That's true. But no honestly, other than ordering Chinese food, I've never felt like this before."

"Well, if it's not love, you do know you'd have her to deal with." Lena pointed to her mother. She was a small, Italian woman in her sixties, with dyed, light brown hair and the remnants of her youthful beauty still subtly beaming from her soft, kind face.

"Your mum loves me!"

"Not if you hurt her son she wouldn't."

"Well, like I said, I wouldn't hurt him!"

"He's taken anyway."

"What? No! Who?"

"This girl called Grace. You don't know her. He met her at the gym."

Nancy frowned in disgust, "Er, the gym?"

Lena laughed, "Yes, the gym. Somewhere you've never been!"

"Is she one of them? Full of herself?"

"No, she's really lovely actually. Well, maybe she's a little snobby and she looks like Barbie, but she's an amazing cook and I'm sure she's an accountant or something like that."

Nancy rolled her eyes. "She sounds amazing!"

"Yeah, I think my parents really like her too."

Nancy sighed. "Oh well, I'm glad he's happy."

"But that's just it." Lena smiled, "He's not!"

"What do you mean?"

"He sometimes seems, like a bit distant with her. You know when we're at family gatherings and things, you can just read him. They don't look natural together." Lena watched a sly smile creep onto Nancy's face. "Oh God! Here we go!"

"Do you think he'd pick me over Barbie?" Nancy asked, studying Francesco.

"Probably, which makes absolutely no sense to me, but then again, I don't understand my brother! I'd choose Barbie any day!"

"I'd choose Barbie over me too, to be fair," then Nancy mischievously grinned, "but you can't argue with what the heart wants."

"Oh God! Anyway," Lena said grimacing back at her, "I'm being told that when you'd help out at the restaurant, you'd draw a little doodle every week for him?"

Nancy smiled, "Yeah, I did."

"He kept them all!" Lena pulled a face and stuck out her tongue in sickening disapproval, "Apparently he has a little scrapbook."

"Honestly?"

Lena sighed and nodded.

"Where?" Nancy shrieked excitedly.

"Come with me." She groaned flatly and led the way out of the room. Both women ran up the bright staircase, and across the landing's varnished, creaky floor boards to the entrance of his room. The door was left open, with a thick, blue dressing gown thrown over the top of it. As Nancy peered round it, she was struck by how neat and tidy it was, everything was in its place. It was however, in desperate need of a good hoovering and dusting, but Nancy admired that. With the rest of the house being so spotlessly clean, it was a sign that Francesco was his own man, he didn't have his mother still cleaning his room for him.

Lena sat on his bed and made herself comfortable, crossing her legs under her.

"Where is it?" Nancy asked impatiently.

Lena reached over to a small chest of draws next to his bed and pulled out the top drawer. Nancy sat beside her, as she wiggled it fully open.

"Here!" She pulled out a little, blue photo album and handed it to Nancy.

Nancy carefully opened it, then proceeded to slowly turn through the shiny wallets. There they were, all the drawings she'd given to him, perfectly preserved between the plastic pages. She had always been quite the artist and sat doodling whenever there was a pen in her hand. The fact that he'd kept them all safe, made her love him even more. That was Francesco though, he was so caring and thoughtful, but what Nancy really admired the most about him, was how strong and logical he was. He was truly a guy that had his shit together (in stark contrast with her). She was such a dreamer, while he was motivated, he didn't sit still, if he had an idea, he made it happen.

"What's with all the sketches?" Lena frowned.

"I was just doodling one day while I was on hold in the restaurant, ordering new cutlery, I think. Francesco came in and saw me doing it, he said it was amazing, so asked if he could keep it. Then he just started requesting random things."

"What a weirdo!"

"It's not weird, it's really sweet!" Nancy snapped.

Lena frowned, but Nancy ignored her and continued to look through. At the very back of the album was a picture of herself and Francesco, smiling arm in arm, with cake frosting all around their mouths.

"Look! This was my birthday." She tilted the album to show the photograph to Lena, "He bought me a giant cupcake with a candle in it and walked in singing happy birthday. He pushed my face into the frosting when I went to blow out the candle, so I smeared it all around his mouth."

"I just don't get it Nance. If you loved him so much, why didn't you make it happen? It's not like you're shy. You literally flirt with everyone!" Lena smiled.

Nancy scowled at her, "I was waiting on him!"

"*You* should have made it happen, never mind waiting on him."

Nancy shrugged, then fell into Lena, resting her head on her shoulder. "I was just scared he'd say no."

Lena laughed, "I've never seen anyone say no to you Nance."

Nancy joined in her laughter, "He's different though! Like, he's never tried to kiss me or anything, so I assumed he just wanted to be friends."

"You were dating every other man under the sun though. Maybe that put him off!"

Nancy sat back straight in protest, "Oh my God, drop it now. I wasn't. I literally went for a drink or maybe to the cinema once with those other guys and pretty much all of them tried to put their hand on my thigh after the first thirty minutes."

"My brother isn't like that." She smiled proudly.

"I know, he's perfect!"

"Well, I wouldn't go that far, but I know he's a good guy."

Nancy flicked back through the wallets in thought, "If he ever did break up with Barbie, do I have your blessing?"

Lena paused for a few moments and smirked, while pretending to think.

"Oh, bloody hell Lena, you don't have to think that hard about it!"

Lena laughed. "I'm joking! I'm joking. You have my blessing." She whispered begrudgingly.

"Yes!" Nancy beamed.

"But you have to promise me Nance, that you won't mess him around!"

"Why are you painting me out to be some man-eating monster! You know I'm not like that!"

"No, I know, I know. I was only joking before, but I know you like attention that's all and he's a busy guy!"

"Excuse me!"

"Don't get defensive about it! That's just you!"

"It is not!"

"Nance, I'm not even going to argue with you. You go to a bar with some guy and you're giving another your phone number, while the first one is buying you a drink, even if you don't like him."

Nancy stayed quiet, this was true, but with Francesco it would be different. She knew it would be. "But I love him!" She reconfirmed.

"Or so you keep saying."

"Don't be like that!"

Lena got up off the bed, "Come on, put it back in the drawer. Time to go."

"Oh my God Lena, don't be like that with me!"

"I just want you to be sure and promise me!"

"Of course, I promise you. I do really love him!"

Lena sighed, "Okay, I believe you, but if you —"

Nancy quickly cut her off, "I won't! I'm too scared of your mother!"

"Good!" Lena smiled, "You should be!"

Nancy got up off the bed. "I'm actually really excited to go back home now."

Lena rolled her eyes, "There's a bit more to go yet unfortunately."

"Oh God, yeah, that pissing wolf!"

Lena chuckled, "Yes! Come on." She turned and left the room.

Nancy left the book on the bed and followed her. "In all seriousness though, how am I actually supposed to fight it?"

"A spear apparently."

"What?" Nancy cried, the worry in her brows pulled new wrinkles to the surface of her bloodied forehead.

Lena's serious face cracked with laughter, "I'm joking, I think you just have to stand up to it."

"You think?" Nancy huffed.

"Well, I don't know, do I?" Lena continued, "It's your fear, not mine!"

Nancy shook her head in disappointment.

"I won't let it kill you, put it that way!" Lena added turning to Nancy with a bright toothy smile.

The two suddenly stopped in their tracks, as they simultaneously spotted Evangeline standing in the doorway at the end of the landing. Her face beamed with happiness and she sprinted out of her room; arms open wide to hug Lena. She was the image of her mother.

Lena dropped to her knees to embrace her, "Evangeline!" She held her tightly and burst into tears.

Nancy stood back and observed in confusion, wondering how Evangeline could see them.

"Oh, my baby!" Lena cried.

The little girl stood out of her mother's embrace, "Why are you crying!" She asked.

"Because I just love you so much, my little bear!"

"Where have you been?"

"I just went to check something with Santa, he —"

"You've been gone ages." She interrupted, rubbing her little tired eyes, "I've been waiting up for you!"

"Ah, I'm sorry my baby, we spoke for a while." Lena smiled, "But, never mind waiting up for me, you need to go to sleep!"

"Oh no, Mum!" A look of horror spread over Evangeline's face, as she pointed to the blood stain on Lena's top.

Lena quickly clasped her hands around her daughter's and smiled. "It's nothing my angel, silly mum slipped on the ice outside. The same as Nancy here, look at her head!"

"It looks big Mum!"

"No, it's not, I promise it's nothing at all. I'm going to just nip out with Nancy now to buy some plasters. It's only small."

"No, stay here. Please don't go out again!" The child lunged at her mother and cuddled her neck tightly.

Lena couldn't speak; she appeared choked with sadness. Nancy felt disgusted with herself, now witnessing the love this child had for her mother, after the vile things Nancy had said. She had projected her own fears onto the situation, instead of being the pillar of support that Lena needed.

Lena pulled away from Evangeline's embrace and held her beautiful, little face between her hands. She smiled with such joy as she studied every freckle.

It appeared to Nancy as if she was holding her face for the last time, trying to create a lasting mental image, memorising it down to the tiniest of details. This glimpse of defeat, struck Nancy to her core.

"You will be back tonight won't you Mum?" Evangeline asked, as she wiped tears from her mother's face with her small fingers.

"I love you, Evangeline. I love you more than you'll ever know. You know that don't you?" Lena whispered.

The little girl nodded and smiled.

"I'm sorry I went out tonight. I'm sorry I always go out!"

"It's okay Mum!"

Lena burst into tears and pulled Evangeline back into her for another hug. "No, it's not my angel!" She whispered. She shut her eyes tightly, appreciating every second of their embrace.

Evangeline pushed her away giggling, "You're holding me too tight!"

Lena smiled, "I just wanted a big snuggle before I go." She wiped the new tears from her eyes and cleared her throat, "Now come on, get back into bed. Santa will be here soon." The little girl held her mother's hand and pulled her along the landing into her room.

"Go on jump into bed." Lena said softly. Nancy peered round the door to see Evangeline hop up into her bed and Lena pull the covers over her. Lena placed her hand on her daughter's head and stroked it with her thumb. "Now, you be good for Uncle Frank, Nonna and Grampy. You promise?"

"I promise! You won't be long though will you Mum?"

Lena leant down and kissed Evangeline's cheek. "I love you so, so much! In the whole wide world."

"I love you too!"

"You sleep tight now my angel!"

"Okay, I'll wake you up when Santa's been!"

Lena faintly nodded, while trying desperately to keep her composure, "Goodnight my baby!" She pushed away from the bed and watched as Evangeline closed her eyes. She then walked silently towards the doorway; but stepped back to take one last look at her child. "I'm so sorry!" She mouthed, then turned with her shoulders now drooped in mourning and ushered Nancy back out onto the landing. She looked up at Nancy with furious tears in her eyes, "I have to get home to her Nance! Even if I have to stitch up this hole in my side and rip that wolf's fucking head off. I have to get back to her!"

Nancy silently nodded.

Lena pushed past her and flew down the stairs, "Let's go and find that big bad bastard!"

The stairs creaked and squeaked loudly as they walked down and upon reaching the bottom to their surprise, they heard a voice shout, "Evangeline, why are you out of bed?"

They both froze. "Oh shit!" Lena whispered.

Nancy's eyes widened in panic.

"Hide!" Lena motioned with her hands for Nancy to run back up the stairs.

"Oh Shit, oh shit, oh shit!" Nancy mumbled. She flew back up to the landing and quickly darted into Francesco's room. Lena followed quickly behind her.

The voice belonged to Francesco. Nancy heard him slowly climb the stairs then go into Evangeline's room.

"Hey spud." Nancy heard him say, "Santa won't come until you go to sleep you know."

"I was just talking to Mum." The little girl replied.

"She's not back yet silly, she's still out drinking yucky wine!"

"No. She was just here."

"I think you must have dreamt it sleepy head. Listen, I'm just going to see Grace, then pick Grampy up from the pub. If you're still awake when I get back, I'll read you a story okay?"

"Okay!" Evangeline agreed.

"Please though, just try and go to sleep now!"

"Okay."

"I love you!"

"Love you!" She replied.

"I'll be back soon, I promise!"

Listening from his bedroom, Nancy breathed a sigh of relief, as she thought he'd go straight back down the stairs, but he didn't. He walked across the landing, came into his room and flicked on the light. Nancy was hiding down the crack in between his bed and the wall. She tried her hardest not to breathe. Had he heard her sigh while on the landing? If he found her, how could she explain being in her pyjamas, covered in blood, hiding in his room?

"What's this doing out?" She heard him say.

She winced as she realised, she hadn't put the photo album back in his drawer. She listened attentively, as he appeared to put it back in its place. She silently prayed for him to leave, but his footsteps then started to come closer. She squirmed as he stopped right in front of her. Shutting her eyes tightly, she listened to what sounded like him pulling his coat down from over the top of his wardrobe door. She couldn't bear to look, her heart pounded and she began to sweat, but he said nothing and then thankfully walked away, oblivious to his intruder. The bedroom light went out and he ran back down the stairs.

Lena poked her head over the side of the bed to look at Nancy lying on the floor. She could see Nancy's face contort with worry in the dim light coming from the landing and erupted into a fit of laughter, that threw her backwards on the bed.

Nancy slowly climbed out of the gap to look at her, "What's so funny?" She whispered.

"Your face!" Lena replied holding her stomach.

"Why am I funny?" Nancy hissed.

"He can't see us!"

Nancy looked confused.

"He can't see us! I was told when we hid that he couldn't!"

"But Evangeline?"

"That was a brief exception! Oh my God! Your face is hilarious!"

Nancy didn't find an ounce of humour in Lena's prank, "What is wrong with you?" She climbed over the bed past her and marched out of the room.

Lena scrambled after her, "Wait!" She shouted, "It was just a joke! Don't be like that."

Nancy paused on the landing and turned to her, "There's something seriously wrong with you!"

"Come on. Old Nancy would have found that hilarious!"

"Well new Nancy doesn't!"

104

"When did you become so serious!"

"This is a serious situation!" She whispered.

"Why are you still whispering?" Lena laughed.

Nancy glared at her, then dramatically turned.

"Aw. Don't be like that Nance! I just really, really needed to lighten the mood. Please!"

Nancy paused by Evangeline's door at the top of the stairs. "Are you going in to see her again before we go?"

Lena's silliness quickly dissolved into a sombre scowl and she shook her head.

Nancy paused for a moment; she had lots of questions for her friend. Not once did she confirm to Evangeline that she'd be back home tonight and why did she have a hole in her side? She knew now wasn't the time to ask though, just in case Evangeline could still hear them, she'd save her questioning for when they were back outside. She silently descended the stairs, then marched out through the closed front door.

10

The Truth

"Tell me now how you got that hole in your side!" Nancy demanded, turning to Lena as soon as they were out on the street.

Lena huffed awkwardly and looked away.

"Just tell me for God's sake!"

"I got skewered with a tree branch." Lena mumbled.

"What?"

"A tree branch went through my side." Lena said a little louder.

"Oh my God! How?"

Lena heavily exhaled and her face tightened, as if she was reliving the pain.

Seeing her anguish, Nancy didn't wait for an answer, "How big was it?" She continued.

"Big enough!"

"Well did it just pierce or more?"

Lena flared her nostrils in frustration, "What part of skewered don't you understand? Of course, it went straight through!" She then quickly walked ahead, trying to end the conversation.

"Wait!" Nancy cried, catching up to her.

"No!"

"We need to find help!"

"No one can help me, not now."

"Surely there's something someone can do? It doesn't look like it's bothering you that much!"

Lena silently looked Nancy dead in her eyes, then through gritted teeth, firmly growled, "There's not anything anyone can do for me now! So, drop it!"

The frustration Nancy felt was intolerable. Why wouldn't Lena just let her help? She didn't understand. She watched, while Lena walked a few more paces ahead, then threw her head back and screamed at the heavens. She started angrily muttering to the darkness. Nancy remained patiently silent as her mutterings escalated into a ferocious one-sided argument, but she had no idea what her friend was saying, she was speaking in some strange, made-up language. The verbal war continued until, Lena ended it with a shrill scream of frustration.

"Are you okay?" Nancy nervously whispered.

"No, not really!" She furiously marched back past Nancy. "Just start walking!"

"Where are we going now?

"Your house!"

"Oh, okay."

Lena stopped and span back to look at her, "Aren't you going to ask why, or moan about it?" She snapped.

"No." Nancy shrugged, taken back by her anger. She attempted to calm her friend by reaching for her hand, "I'm going to get you back to Evangeline. I swear!"

Lena dropped to her knees and burst into tears.

"Oh my God, Lena!"

She snorted hard between sobs, as she wiped her nose on her t-shirt. "I just want to hold my baby Nance. I want to be there tomorrow to hold my baby!" She croaked.

"You will. I'll make it happen. I promise!"

Lena shook her head.

"Come on! Don't give up." Nancy said, pulling her back to her feet.

Lena couldn't respond. Seeing Evangeline had obviously broken her. Her head hung and she gripped Nancy's hand tightly. It was as if she was trying with every ounce of her being to carry on, when she just wanted to crumble.

"We're going to get back!" Nancy smiled, "That's what you told me. You said we'll go back with a story to tell. Don't stop now."

But again, Lena shook her head and defeatedly closed her eyes.

"Don't give up. We can do this!"

"Just walk!" Lena spluttered, using Nancy to steady her.

Clearly there were no words that could console her, how could there be in this situation. Nancy continued to hold onto her hand and did as she instructed. Lena kept her head down and continued to sob as they walked. Her aura seemed to flicker as she sniffed and Nancy felt useless, she didn't know how to help.

As they neared the end of the street, Lena gently pulled Nancy towards a dark alley at their side.

"This isn't the way!" Nancy frowned.

"Don't be paranoid!" Lena hissed. "It's a short cut!"

Nancy stopped still. The corridor held too many shadows to be safe.

"Nancy, I'm not in the mood. If you start feeling scared, that wolf is going to show up. Just contain it, please!"

"Promise me no surprises!"

The spine-tingling howl of the wolf split the distant night.

"Nancy, I am going to slap you silly if that wolf gets into this alley. Now get a grip!"

"I'm sorry!" Nancy trembled. She closed her eyes and took a deep breath, trying to calm her nerves.

"Oh shit!" Lena cried, shaking her head.

What?" Nancy whimpered.

"It's here."

Another long sharp howl announced its entrance, as the two women stood in awe of the monster behind them.

"Oh my God, we're going to die." Nancy whined.

"Fucking hell Nancy!" Lena shouted, "Run!"

The two women darted out of the street, through the small corridor. Lena leading and Nancy behind.

The wolf jumped up onto the building, running alongside them. Debris snowed from above, as the creature stalked them.

"How much further?" Nancy cried.

"Not much, just don't slow down."

Nancy noticed a multicoloured glow in the distance, the light flickered between Lena's wild limbs.

The alley opened up into a small, beautiful courtyard, decorated brightly with Christmas splendour and in the centre stood a beautifully painted, red front door, hovering a few centimetres above the ground. Its brassy coloured number 50 centred above a large door knocker.

"This is my mum and dad's front door!" Nancy cried in relief.

"Get in!" Lena yelled, quickly slipping through it.

There was no time to admire its magical presence, Nancy threw herself out of the dark.

As she passed through the doorway, a bright, white light surrounded her. Her fear became immediately dissolved by the warm embrace of home. She closed her eyes and took a moment to enjoy this alien contentment, the feeling of weightless safety.

She opened her eyes to find herself standing in the hallway of her parents' home, with Lena looking unamused sitting at the bottom of the stairs to her left.

"What are you doing?" She sniped.

"Did you not feel that?" Nancy looked behind her at the door.

"Feel what?"

"I can't really describe it. It was just a really nice feeling."

"No. To be honest I've been losing more and more feeling all night. Haven't you?"

It was the opposite for Nancy, she had begun to feel more as the night had unfolded, but she didn't want to worry Lena, so nodded in agreement. "Did you feel Evangeline hug you?" Nancy asked.

"It was strange really. I knew she was in my arms and I knew I was hugging her, but I couldn't feel her warmth or smell her strawberry shampoo. It's like my senses are disappearing."

"Oh!" Nancy didn't know what to say.

"When you just held my hand walking here, it was like I knew it was in yours, but it was numb."

"Honestly?"

"Yeah! Aren't you the same?"

"Yeah!" Nancy grinned, unconvincingly.

"Strange, isn't it?" Lena pouted. She pulled herself up on the banister and joined Nancy in the spacious hallway. "I've missed being here with you all." Lena said, as she snooped through the dark doorways that connected to the hall.

Nancy's attention, however, was firmly on the photographs of herself that adorned the four walls. They showed a timeline of her life, from her first years, to her university graduation ceremony, all neatly displayed in all sizes. It felt as though someone had just punched her in her heart. All these happy memories that her parents obviously treasured and she'd just thrown a future with them away, however, her contemplative mood suddenly lightened and she chuckled, as she picked up a framed picture of herself and Francesco from the side table.

"What are you sniggering at?" Lena asked, walking over to her.

Nancy held the picture up.

"Oh God!" Lena laughed. "Look at his hair?"

"Look at both of our hair!"

In the picture a twenty something year old Francesco stood with his arm around Nancy. He had a short, buzz cut and Nancy had shoulder length, platinum-blonde, pin-up curls.

"I don't even remember this being taken. Where were we?"

"I have no idea." Lena replied. "I think it's hilarious that your mum has it framed though."

"Why?"

"She's living in hope!"

"Shut up!" Nancy smiled, as she put the picture back in its place.

A strong smell of cooking filled the air.

"How amazing does that smell?"

"I can't smell anything." Lena frowned.

Nancy motioned with her head for Lena to follow her into the kitchen and they found her mum busily preparing food for tomorrow's Christmas feast.

Her mother was glamourous. She was in her early sixties with dark, brown hair pulled up neatly on top of her head and her glasses perched on the end of her nose. She was hunched over the kitchen table squinting at a recipe in her cook book.

"If you survive the wolf, are you coming here tomorrow?" Lena sniggered.

Nancy nervously laughed "I'm supposed to be. I was going to call them in the morning to cancel though."

"Why?" Lena cried; her face twisted in disgust at the thought of Nancy turning down the opportunity to eat all the wonderful food.

"I really can't be bothered to be honest."

"Wait, wait, wait! Your mum is going to all this trouble and you can't be bothered?"

"No. It's not like that. I just can't be bothered with the rest of the family."

"Why not?"

"Because they just ask too many questions and then there's the lecture from my uncle."

"Uncle Pete?"

Nancy confirmed with a faint nod.

"I've never liked Pete, he's a prick!"

"Exactly! All he does is boast about what his family have got, or how well his children are doing! I can't be arsed with it."

"No, I agree, but you can't not see your mum and dad, just because of Pete the prick!"

Nancy laughed. "It mustn't be nice for them though, having to defend me all day."

"Hm. Up to you." Lena shrugged and walked back out the room.

Nancy followed her into the living room. They found her dad sat watching TV, reclined in his seat on the farthest end of the sofa, with a box of Maltesers skilfully balanced on his prominent stomach. He was a tall, thick framed man and despite his age, still had a full head of grey hair that he slicked back. Nancy sat down next to him and Lena sat on the grey, single seater to the side of the pair.

Lena reclined her chair and made herself comfortable. "Why didn't you spend the evening here?" She asked.

"I didn't want to." Nancy shrugged.

"You wanted to cry by yourself into a soggy bowl of cereal instead?"

"I'm a grown woman!" Nancy cried, "I'm not going to go running back to my mummy and daddy every time I have a bad day."

"No, it's Christmas Eve and instead of spending it with the people who love you, you decided to have a solo pity party! Why are you too proud to come home Nancy?"

"I'm not too proud to come home!" Nancy snapped, "I just don't want them to worry about me! I don't want them to think that I'm not capable!"

"They're your two biggest fans! I mean look at all of these photographs. You have to be one of the ugliest looking kids I've ever seen and still they've decorated their walls with your face!"

Nancy smiled. "I just don't want them to worry!" She rested her head on her dad's shoulder.

"But they do worry! They don't know what's going on in your head, because you don't talk to them. They would move heaven and earth to make you happy!"

"I know!" Nancy snapped. "And that is exactly what I don't want them to do! I don't want to be a burden."

"They love you! You need to talk to them!"

Nancy sighed. "I'm a disappointment."

Lena shook her head. "You're anything but that! I wish I could talk to my parents again."

Nancy sat up and looked hard at Lena in confusion, as her luminous face suddenly appeared to dim.

"What happened to you tonight? And not the condensed version about you talking to some light. How did that tree branch go through your side?"

Lena fixed the chair back straight, stood up and walked over to stand in front of the open fire. She looked at her face in the mirror that hung above it, then slowly raised her hands to stare at the glow that radiated from them. She silently studied the magic of their luminance, then sat down on the floor and gazed into the flames, with her back to Nancy.

"I put Evangeline to bed, then I got a message from Si Davidson."

"Oh Lena! Not him!" Nancy cried in disappointment.

"Yes. Him!" Lena's head fell forward, "I've kind of been seeing him for a while. He asked if I wanted to go for a Christmas drink and I said yes!" She paused and looked up at the ceiling trying to hold the tears in her eyes and compose herself to continue.

"Then what?"

"He picked me up," She smacked her lips, "and, he was drunk. I knew he was when I got into the car with him. Let's face it, when have either of us ever seen him sober?" She glanced over her shoulder at Nancy, who shrugged in agreeance. "I mean, if it wasn't drink, it was coke and I don't even think he has a license!" She turned back to the fire, "Anyways, he drove like a bat out of hell down Hillside Way, I told him to slow down, but he just laughed and thought it was funny to go faster, then he clipped the curb and lost control near the cut through to Sandy Lane." She paused and once again, tried to regain control of her emotions. "Argh!" She exhaled in frustration. "We flew off the road into the trees!" She paused again, "I didn't feel the pain at first just a hard blow to my side, then, before I blacked out, I watched him get out of the car."

"What did he do?" Nancy cut in.

"Nothing! He did nothing!" Lena sobbed, "And I couldn't move, I saw him on his phone to someone, I thought he'd called an ambulance, but then his friend turned up. He walked towards the car and I heard him say, 'It's too late for her now mate, let's just get out of here'. I screamed! I pleaded with them not to go, but they just walked away, so I screamed and I screamed and I screamed, until I blacked out again."

Lena stopped, waiting for Nancy to ask another question, but she didn't. She remained silent, digesting the tragedy.

Lena sniffed, swallowed hard and continued, "When I woke up, I tried to move, but noticed a tree branch had gone right through me, into the seat, so I was pinned there. It felt like I lay there for hours. The pain was horrific and then gradually it wasn't. I just sat and watched the blood run down my side into the footwell, until everything went hazy and I felt nothing at all."

"Then the light?" Nancy whispered

"Next thing I knew, I was being pulled from the wreckage, but it was weird because my body stayed behind. It was honestly the strangest thing. I just stood for a few moments looking at myself, I didn't cry or scream or anything, I just couldn't comprehend what I was actually looking at."

This immediately registered with Nancy. She too had been a spectator, watching herself lying lifeless in the bath. "What happened then?" She whispered.

"Then there was a huge beam of bright white light behind me."

"The voice?" Nancy asked.

"Yeah, The voice." Lena sarcastically snorted, "We just sat and talked, it felt like we talked for an eternity, we spoke about everything, until, I was told to come and find you!" Lena turned to look at Nancy, whose face was now soggy with tears. Lena, however, now appeared almost emotionless. There was a strange, false sense of acceptance in the way she told the end of the story, as though she was trying hard to pretend that she had already made peace with her fate.

Nancy cleared her throat and whispered, "When you say help you to get home, you don't mean your family home do you?"

Lena shook her head and forced a half smile, "I did, but now I mean our final home." She whispered and turned back to the fire.

Nancy got up and walked over to her friend, she fell to her knees and embraced her from behind, hugging her as tightly as she could.

Lena put her hands on Nancy's arms and squoze them gently to comfort her. "It's shit Nance." She sniffed. "But it's my own fault. I shouldn't have got into that stupid car with *him*."

"I can't believe he left you! Maybe you could have been saved."

"He shouldn't have left me, but no, no one could have done anything to save me."

"Is that it then?"

"At the beginning of the night, when I came to you, I was told if I helped you, I could go back home, but after we saw Evangeline, when we were hiding in Francesco's room, I was told that," She paused and her voice crumbled into tears, "I was told that, that was my goodbye!"

"No Lena!" Nancy cried.

"Yes, that's why I didn't tell you straight away that he couldn't see us and why I was smiling like a fool when I came over to where you were hiding. I just couldn't process it, I couldn't accept that, that was it. That I'd never hold my baby again." Lena threw her head into her hands and snarled in frustration. "I'm a fucking idiot Nance, an absolute fucking idiot."

Nancy dropped her hands, "You weren't to know."

"Of course I was. What the fuck was I doing with him anyway. Fuck, sake!"

Nancy averted her gaze into the fire.

"You know I even took Evangeline out in that car with him a few days ago. That's me, mother of the year! What if something had happened to her?" Lena got to her feet, pointed to her blood stain and screamed, "What if this had happened to her Nance?"

Nancy jumped to her feet, pulled her in hard and held her tightly. Lena's body went limp and again, she broke down.

"It didn't though Lena. Evangeline is safe."

Lena pushed Nancy away and shook her head. "I've ruined Christmas for her. Selfish bitch that I am. She's going to wake up and realise I'm not home. Then realise I'm never coming home and every year, she'll relive it. All because her mother was a stupid, selfish bitch!"

"No," Nancy sobbed, "You can't torture yourself like that."

"I can!" Lena shouted, "I can and I will. I've ruined my little girl's life and you knew I would."

Nancy took a step back and shook her head.

"Yes, you were right. You're always right."

"I'm not! We can change it; there must be a way!"

"There's not!" Lena snapped.

"If you love her as much as you say you do, then why have you given up!" Nancy cried.

"Because, honestly, I don't know whether she's better off without me!" Lena blurted, "I put her in harm's way! I happily put her in that car. What was I thinking even letting her be anywhere near someone like Si?"

"I don't know." Nancy exhaled, "You shut me out years ago remember. Why were you even going out on Christmas Eve?"

"Because I can't stay in that house. All my parents and Francesco do is pick at me all the time. Why aren't I doing this? Why have I done that? Nothing is ever good enough!" She paused and looked at the floor, "I'm not good enough." She mumbled.

"Don't be stupid! They love you! Have you ever told them how you feel?"

Lena shook her head. "I've felt so low since Evangeline was born. I love her to bits and she's my little pal, but other than her, I'm lonely. Her dad was a waste of space; when I got pregnant, I knew I wasn't in the best place and that I was going to be raising her alone, but selfishly I wanted her so bad. I thought I'd finally be able to prove myself, prove that I'm capable, that I could do something good." She sighed, "Everyone knew better."

Nancy shook her head. "That's not true! But I still don't understand, why Si? You weren't doing drugs too, were you?"

"No." She snorted, "No, I wasn't. He was just funny and a good time. He doesn't live in the real world, so being with him was like escaping. No responsibilities, no one looking down their nose at me. All he and his friends care about is getting wasted and having fun."

"I wish you'd have come to me!"

"You're just as bad as the rest of them though, sorry Nance. I was too proud to come to you, just like you're too proud to talk to your parents."

Nancy turned and sat down in the single grey arm chair behind her. She slumped to the side, rested her elbow on the arm and held her head in her hand. Lena sat back down in front of the fire and once again began watching the TV.

Nancy looked across the room at her dad, who still sat oblivious to the invisible turmoil in the room. Lena was right, Nancy was too proud to ask for help. She'd always been, but to her own detriment and here she was now, knocking at deaths door, realising what an idiot she'd been. Not only could she not help herself, but when her friend had so desperately needed her, she couldn't be relied upon. The guilt tore through her heart like a knife. What had she done? Had she really helped sentence her friend to death? Si may have driven the car, but had Nancy helped her into the passenger seat?

It was true that all those that loved Lena, fiercely tried to change her with their own pig-headed illusions of how she should live her life. Not one of them ever stopped to actually listen to her. Nancy had grown up watching it. Lena had such a fire for life, with her excitement for experience making the silence of the mundane too loud for her to bare.

"Are you okay?" Lena eventually whispered.

Nancy shook her head and glanced over at her. "I should have been there for you. You needed me and I just, wasn't!"

"No one was Nance." Lena grinned, "But like I said, it's my own fault, I let my pride get in the way. I was too proud to let anyone in."

Nancy closed her eyes and rubbed her forehead, trying to keep her composure. "I'm sorry Lena. I really am." She whimpered.

Lena got to her feet and held out her hand to pull Nancy up, "It's not too late for you." She whispered.

"We can switch places, you go back to Evangeline and I'll go, well I don't know, wherever I'm meant to."

Lena shook her head. "No. Thank you though." She hugged her tightly.

"It can't be too late. Surely there's something we can do." Nancy protested, pulling out of her embrace.

"There's not, it's done! We just need to get you home."

"That's not fair though."

"I don't think fairness comes into it." Lena frowned.

"Go on, just tell whoever that I'll switch places with you."

"We can't!" Lena exhaled firmly, "Just drop it now, please. I'm really grateful that you'd do that for me, but it just can't be done."

Nancy erupted into tears and clung to her, "It can't end like this though Lena, I can't go home knowing that I left you behind."

Lena pushed Nancy away and put her hands on her shoulders. "It's done! It's out of your hands, it's not on you, it was my fault."

"No, it was that fucking prick! I swear when I see that bastard –"

Lena quickly cut her off, "Please, Nance, enough." She wiped her friends face with her palm, "No more tears. Let's just make the most of the time we have left together. Okay?"

"But –"

"But nothing." Lena grinned, struggling to keep it together. "There's nothing more to say!" She turned and made a quick exit back into the hallway and out of the front door, but this time Nancy didn't follow. Instead, she fell to her knees and cried.

She couldn't leave her behind. Why did she deserve a second chance and Lena didn't? There wasn't a single reason she could think of. It just wasn't fair.

She looked over at her dad, then moved to sit next to him. She hugged his arm tightly and once again rested her head on his shoulder. If only she'd gone straight to her parents' house after work and Lena had stayed home, none of this would have happened.

"Me and Lena are in so much trouble Dad!" She whimpered, tightening her hold and sobbing sharply, "So much trouble!" She then lifted her head to look at his face, as he remained silently engrossed in his film. "You'd know what to do!" She sniffed and kissed his cheek, "You'd know exactly what to do!" She spluttered.

She took a deep breath trying to calm herself and stared into the fire. Small embers spat out onto the stone hearth and for some reason it suddenly reminded her of the great chunks of concrete at the mercy of the storm. She quickly sobered herself. This was her universe, she thought, so why did she have to accept Lena's fate? She didn't, she wouldn't. She had to keep going, maybe she could do something, she at least had to try. She let go of her dad's arm and jumped out of the chair to leave the room, but briefly paused by the door to look back at him, "I love you, Dad! See you tomorrow!" She whispered.

She then walked into the kitchen to find her mother still busy, wooden spoon in hand, cream all over the kitchen table, glasses now teetering to the point that the smallest of movements would send them tumbling off into the bowl below. She wiped her tears and chuckled to herself; this was the perfect snapshot of her mum. If someone asked Nancy to describe her, this would be the image that would come to her mind. Her beautiful, loving mum. She walked over and stood by her side, just observing her for a few moments, "I'm so sorry Mum. I love you so much!" She whispered, while kissing her cheek.

She walked back into the hallway and did a slow three-sixty, taking in all the photographs of her life spread across the walls. "This isn't it!" She sobbed, wiping her nose on the sleeve of her dressing gown. She knew there was more to add to her timeline. She then clocked a picture of her and Lena and her sadness ignited into angry determination. She walked over to it. They must have been about ten years old and were pulling silly faces. A bonfire exploded inside her heart and its tall flames pushed new strength into her arteries. She wasn't going to let her down – not again. She threw her head back and yelled at the ceiling, "I'm going back home and I'm taking her back with me! You hear me!" She gritted her teeth and stamped her foot, "I'm taking her home!" She glared at the front door, "No more running." She hissed, she had a fight on her hands, a fight for both of their lives. She took a deep breath, summoned her courage and shook the furious tears from her face. "I need her!" She screamed and launched her attack, sprinting back out into the night.

11

Anything for You

As she emerged back into the courtyard, she found Lena at the mouth of the alleyway leaning against a wall, looking to the sky. Nancy thundered towards her and without a word grabbed her hand as she passed, to pull her fiercely down the dark corridor.

"Let's go and find that big bad bastard!" She insisted as she looked over her shoulder and flashed Lena a dark mischievous smile. Lena attempted to smile back, though failed and gave more of a numb grin, but joined in Nancy's sprint and both ran hand in hand out of the darkness on to a new, loud, illuminated street.

"Oh my God! Where are we?" Nancy yelled over the noise.

"I have no idea." Lena replied, looking round at the buildings.

The street was adorned with inflatable snowmen, Santa's, flashing reindeer, snowflake projectors and an array of lighting. Moulded festive figurines guarded every front garden, even the bare branches of the trees were dressed with all manner of baubles, bows and stars. It straddled the line between spectacular and grotesque. There was no order, or theme, everything was everywhere, it was chaos. There was also a deafening scramble of festive songs being played together, creating so much noise that neither could bear it.

"What's going on?" Nancy shouted, holding her hands over her ears.

"It's you! Your mind is racing!" Lena shouted back, "You need to calm down!"

This was the perfect opportunity for Nancy to practice her control in preparation for the monster. She closed her eyes, ignored the chaos and simply focused on her steady breath, eventually falling into an almost meditative state. She felt her chest rising and falling, as her lungs expanded and deflated, and smiled as a strong sense of contentment washed over her again. The warmth of a full heart. Her surroundings were immediately silenced.

She opened her eyes to find everything back in darkness, everything that is, except for Lena.

"You did it!" Lena frowned in surprise, "Bloody hell Nance!"

Nancy pouted and shrugged; she couldn't believe it herself.

"Let's see if it works on the wolf!"

"Oh God. I bloody hope so!" Nancy groaned.

Lena held out her hand and Nancy held it tightly.

They began to walk again, with neither knowing what to say to the other, but the heavy atmosphere lightened, as Nancy decided to talk about their past escapades. "Remember when we forgot, that we promised your Nonna that we'd walk her to midnight mass." Nancy sniggered.

"Oh my God. Ha. Yes." Lena laughed. "We were so drunk and you started singing *We Wish You a Merry Christmas* to that old man handing out prayer books by the entrance!"

Nancy broke out into hysterical laughter, "Oh my God, he didn't know what to do, bless him! His face! He just stood there and listened to the entire song smiling."

Lena snorted. "That was honestly one of the funniest moments of my life! The crowd clapping for you when you finished. My Nonna loved it!"

"I can't believe they all listened to the whole thing!"

"I nearly peed myself laughing. I had to use those horrible toilets in that pub across from the church because the priest wouldn't let me in."

Nancy winced, "Oh, they were vile! I remember your Nonna telling him off."

Lena grimaced. "Do you remember when we sent that fake Valentine's Day card to Francesco?"

Nancy burst into laughter again. "He didn't realise for ages. He was so pissed off at us when he found out! He thought it was from that girl he liked in his year. What was her name?"

"I can't even remember. I know who you mean though."

"Remember when we hid all his golf stuff because we wanted him to drive us to that festival thing?"

"Yes! And it turned out to be shit."

"It was pretty shit to be fair! He missed his tournament taking us there too."

"We used to really terrorise him, didn't we?"

"I think that's why he stayed out of our way so much." They both looked at each other and sniggered.

As they finally reached the street corner, they realised they were back in familiar territory. Nancy's apartment was about a fifteen-minute walk away.

"Yes. We're not lost anymore!"

"No, we're not." Lena smiled.

Nancy began to walk in the direction of her apartment, pulling Lena along behind her, but Lena grabbed her arm to stop her. "You can't go back yet remember. You're forgetting something."

"Ah fuck!" Nancy exhaled.

"Are you ready?"

"No, but let's just do it!"

Lena broke out into loud whistling, calling for the beast, "Wolfy!" She shouted, "Here Wolfy!"

Nancy once more became overcome with fear, "Wait stop!" She whispered.

Wide-eyed, Lena pursed her lips and shook her head. She threw her head back and howled at the top of her lungs.

"Stop!" Nancy hissed trying to jump on her back to cover her mouth. They began wrestling with each other, until, boom! The ground shook and both women froze. Boom! It shook again. Harder.

"Oh God!" Nancy whimpered, "I just needed a minute to ask you what I needed to do!"

Boom! It shook again.

"I have no clue! In this moment though, I'm actually glad I'm already dead." She pointed for Nancy to look behind her. Terrified, Nancy turned and there once more in the distance stood the great beast. It slowly moved closer, just as before, head to the ground, ready to attack.

Nancy started edging backwards, but Lena quickly scrambled to grab her arm.

"No running!" She ordered.

"No. No running!" Nancy whispered, trying her best to remember how to slip into that meditative state. "Any heavenly advice?"

Lena paused, then looked blankly at her, "Radio silence I'm afraid."

"Well, that's helpful!" Nancy sarcastically growled.

The wolf continued moving closer; Nancy could feel Lena's grip tighten on her arm; she needed to protect her frightened friend. She closed her eyes and tried to focus on her breathing, but her fear overruled her intention, the creature was getting too close. She couldn't calm herself, so did the only other thing that she could think of, she threw open her eyes and with an, "Ah, fuck it!" charged at it like some crazed animal.

The wolf let out a long low growl and hurtled on a collision course towards her. Nancy angrily screamed and bared her teeth; in her mind she was a fierce warrior, battle hardened and brave, fearless and skilful. To Lena watching from the side-lines, she looked like she'd finally lost her mind. The beast, now just meters away, fiercely roared back at the crazed woman, obliterating Nancy's nerve and it used its head like a battering ram, which sent her flying clear across the street, onto the pavement at the other end. The pain was excruciating; she screamed as she rolled from one side to the other trying to disperse the agony, when suddenly, she felt those familiar cold hands on her side, Lena numbing the fires of her distress.

"Open your eyes, Nancy!" She yelled, "Nancy, open your eyes!"

Nancy groaned and wearily looked up at her.

"Face your fear!" Lena commanded.

"Is it still there?"

"Yes!"

"Fuck's sake!" Nancy cried in defeat, "I don't know what to do!"

"Come on, don't let it win!"

"But –" Nancy's face dropped in horror, as the beasts' head rose up behind Lena. It tilted to the side, paused for a brief second as if revelling in its power, then lunged down and snapped Lena up into its jaws.

"No!" Nancy screamed. The wolf danced about as it shook her like a rag doll, then flung her through the air behind it. Nancy jumped to her feet and attempted to run to her aid, but the wolf blocked her path.

Nancy had finally had enough. Enough of being a victim, enough of being pushed around, enough of having no control. "Stop!" she screamed, "Just stop!" The wolf paid no attention to her command and began its advancement. Nancy quickly looked at Lena lying motionless on the floor in the distance. She had to get to her. "I said stop!" She furiously repeated, while pointing sharply at it. The beast let out a low grunt and halted. Nancy marched towards it, fury burning in her eyes. The beast began to growl and lower its head.

"You fucking horrible – thing!" She screamed. She noticed Lena roll on to her back and her march turned into a jog. The beast began to growl louder, but this didn't deter her. Lena was her priority, it didn't matter what the wolf did to her, she needed to save her friend. Her jog then became a sprint, until, Nancy stopped in touching distance of its snout. She said nothing and the wolf fell silent and shut its mouth. Both glared into each other's eyes, daring the other to blink.

"This ends now!" Nancy whispered. She gritted her teeth and sharply broke eye contact, as she side stepped the monster. It barked violently at her and the soundwaves pushed her body to the floor, but she scrambled back upright and ignored it, keeping her focus ahead, on Lena. The wolf snapped its jaws at her back, engulfing her in its hot breath, but still, she held her nerve. She had to ignore the threatening steam of its desperation. She had to refuse it the attention it desired. Finally, she reached Lena and as she knelt down to assess the damage, the wolf completely left her mind. Thankfully, other than the blood stain from her previous wound there wasn't a mark on her, in fact, she lay there smiling.

"Are you okay?" Nancy asked frantically.

"What do you bloody think!"

"It tossed you like a ragdoll!"

"Don't I know! Thank God I can't feel anything!"

Nancy sat down next to her on the ground. "You didn't feel it? Honestly?"

"Not a thing!" She said holding onto Nancy's hand, "It bloody scared the shit out of me though!"

"It scared you! Oh my God, the pain when it hit me! I thought I was going to die!"

"But you didn't Nance and you did it."

"I, did it?"

"You faced your fear, look behind you, the big bad bastard has gone! Just like that!"

Nancy cautiously looked back to where the wolf had stood. It was gone. The street was empty.

"Where did it go?"

"Nowhere. It will always be with you, but you took away its power, by refusing to give it the attention it craved." She held her arm up and pointed to Nancy's head, "You put it back in its cage."

Nancy sighed in relief and lay down next to her friend, "I'd say I felt good about it, but that was horrific!"

The two women laughed.

"Who dreams up a ten-foot wolf! I think you need to control you imagination next."

"I hope this is all in my imagination and you're still alive when I wake up!" Nancy glanced at Lena lying next to her.

"I'd love that Nance!" Lena sighed, squeezing her hand.

The two lay in silence for a few moments looking up at the sky. Lena appeared to be in a peaceful contemplative state, while Nancy continually sniffed, trying hard not to cry.

"Stop bloody sniffing, you're driving me mad!" Lena quipped.

Nancy snorted and wiped her nose, as she sat back up, "What am I going to do without you?" She frowned.

Lena sat up and sniggered, "I honestly don't know, it's evident that you need me."

Nancy looked at the ground and desperately tried to hold back her tears.

Lena put her arm around her shoulders, "You're going to be okay Nance. I promise. You're a lot stronger than you think."

"I just don't want you to go!" Nancy broke down.

"Nancy, look at me!"

Nancy reluctantly raised her head.

"I love you Nancy, I love you so much and I know you love me!" Lena spluttered, "I mean, you just side-stepped a monster for me!" She gently rocked

Nancy trying to encourage a smile, "We're sisters, you and I. I might not be around like before, but nothing, not even death can pull us apart!"

Both women closed their eyes and fell into each other crying. They let the minutes tick by, neither wanting to let go of the other, neither wanting to say goodbye.

12

Time to Go

Time passed and Lena began to sense something change in their surroundings. She curiously opened her eyes to find a small, old man in a brown trench coat perched on the railings by the doorway of one of the buildings. "Holy shit!" She shouted, pushing out of Nancy's embrace and jumping to her feet.

"What?" Nancy asked, copying and scrambling upright.

Lena pointed at the man and Nancy turned to look.

He smiled, jumped down, then walked towards them. The two women stepped backwards; his youthful movements didn't match his appearance. He looked ancient and frail, wearing worn, brown, sensible shoes, grey socks, an oversized trench coat and it didn't look like much else. The women stared at each other in confusion, then looked back at him. The old man reached into his pocket and pulled out an old, silver hip flask, put it to his lips and took a big swig of its contents, while grinning at the pair. "I'm here to see you both!" He slurred.

He was clearly drunk; he swayed softly from side to side and stumbled as he moved closer. Nancy looked at Lena for guidance, but Lena shrugged, she was just as surprised by his appearance.

"I need you to see something!" He spluttered.

"O-kay." Lena replied hesitantly.

He placed his hip flask back into his pocket and began to undo the knot in the belt of his coat.

"Oh wow!" Nancy sniggered.

"Hey Mr! We don't need to see anything like that, thank you very much!" Lena said angrily. They looked at each other in disgust, but the man ignored this and carried on.

"Hey, weirdo! Stop!" Lena shouted, but again, this was ignored.

"You dirty old creep! Don't you dare!" Nancy angrily shouted.

The man then threw open either side of his coat, causing the two women to quickly avert their eyes.

"Look sicko! I said —" Lena stopped mid-sentence, as she noticed the bright light coming from the old man's direction. She cautiously turned to him.

"Nance." She whispered, motioning with her head for Nancy to look. Nancy turned, now seeing that under his coat, he was actually wearing an old stained vest; a pair of cotton shorts and glowing like Lena.

Seeing that he now had their attention he softly smiled and from either side of his coat, he threw out two gigantic film reels. They rolled down the street, unravelling, as far as the eye could see, then came alive. The light from them illuminated not only the street but the sky, it was so powerful, that it hurt Nancy's eyes, but she couldn't stop looking.

"What is it?" She whispered to Lena.

"I don't know." Lena shrugged.

They both stood in awe, trying to make sense of the video clips hanging in the air. The people in the videos on the right appeared to be upset, in mourning, while the people in the videos on the left, appeared to be in a state of sloth, with some surrounded by dirt and clutter. The two women focused intently, until all of a sudden, a boom of sound cut through the air. The women fell to their knees and covered their ears. The chaotic sounds deafened them. Every voice from the videos on the right cried out into the night, begging the master of the universe for more time, whereas the videos on the left of the lazy and discontented stayed silent. They were overcome at what they were witnessing. The sights, the sounds, the intense brightness, Nancy fell on to her hands and was sick.

"Are you okay?" Lena asked, putting her hand on her back.

"It's too much!" Nancy choked.

Lena looked up and shouted to the old man, "Hey, you, enough now!" But apart from his hands gently trembling from his alcohol consumption, he was statuesque. Lena looked back up at the reels and one video in particular suddenly caught her attention.

"Oh no!" She whimpered, "Please, no!" Lena crawled forwards in tears; it was of her mother. She was pleading with God for more time with her daughter, begging him to bring her back. Lena stopped just underneath it and numbly watched as it replayed, over and over and over again. Her mother sat in her bedroom, holding a rosary, sobbing, "Bring back my baby, please bring back my baby." Lena slumped to the floor riddled with guilt, as her voice pierced her.

"I'm sorry." Nancy saw her mouth, "I'm so, so, sorry, Mum!"

At this point, the old man shut his coat, forcing the reels to burst into golden sparks, that dissipated into the night sky. The street returned to dark silence.

He tied his belt tightly, then reached into his coat pocket for his flask and took a bigger swig of whatever was in it. Neither Lena or Nancy spoke a word.

"I'm sorry!" He slurred. "But I was told to show you."

The two women still didn't speak.

"Please, Lena. I *am* so sorry!" He apologised.

Lena didn't respond.

Nancy, still on all fours, sluggishly pushed herself to her feet and wobbled over to Lena, where she dropped to her knees and gently put her arm around her shoulders.

"Look what I did to my mum Nance!" She whispered.

Nancy pulled her in closer and kissed her head, "I know."

The old man walked closer to them. They could hear him slurping on his drink, taking larger and larger gulps, watching them sorrowfully digest the sad truth of the turmoil that Lena would leave in the wake of her death.

As usual, Nancy didn't know what to say, there were no words of comfort she could offer. She couldn't say, 'Oh, don't worry it will be alright,' because it wouldn't. She turned to the old man and asked, "Can this be changed?"

He shook his head and the kind wrinkles on his face slumped into apologetic disappointment.

"Who are you?"

"I'm a time keeper." He began, "One of many. I wasted my life, so, now I carry the sadness of those who begged for more time." He sighed in reflection and took another large swig. "All this sadness!" His voice cracked, "I must carry!" He paused for a moment, looked down at his flask, then back at Nancy and mumbled, "Don't waste your precious time on your own self-pity Nancy."

Nancy nervously nodded in agreement, but Lena still faced the ground.

"Oh, I am so sorry Lena." He sobbed. "Truly I am, it kills me every time – but, that's another reason I'm here. Nancy, I'm afraid it's time."

"Time for what?" Nancy murmured.

"Time for Lena to come home!"

Nancy scowled at the old man, "No, not yet!"

But he lightly nodded in insistence. "It is time!"

Nancy turned back to Lena and whispered into her hair. "You don't have to go Lena! We'll figure something out."

Lena said nothing, but gently shook her head and obediently rose to her feet. She didn't look at Nancy, she couldn't, she was truly broken. She clung to Nancy's arm and encouraged her to start walking with her. Nancy quickly looked back to her side for some help or guidance from the old man, but he had vanished, there was no sign of him anywhere. They were once more the only two souls in existence.

13

Don't Leave Me

Lena was in a trance. Seeing her mother so heartbroken appeared to have cut her deeper than the tree branch. Nancy, obviously, was also fraught with sadness, as she was now walking her friend to her final place of rest. She had been there at the start of her journey, walked with her through life and now here she was at the end. She couldn't comprehend what was happening, this bizarre twist of fate that had befallen them. She thought Lena would live forever, she had that sort of legendary aura about her, that false bravado that would allow her to clumsily cheat death until she was old and frail. It wasn't supposed to end like this.

All of their precious memories filled her mind. Learning to ride bikes together, their obsession with the Spice Girls, going on family holidays; Lena wasn't just a friend; she was her sister. What an honour it had been, she thought, to have had the privilege of such a special bond. This person who was always there, she couldn't think of many moments where Lena hadn't been! Even for the duration of the school holidays; Lena's parents would blow up an air mattress to put in Lena's room, for Nancy to stay. They were inseparable.

"I don't want you to go!" Nancy choked.

Lena simply responded by holding her arm tighter.

They walked and walked, navigating the familiar streets, walking past where they'd shop, eat and drink together. How could it all go on without Lena? How could everything go on the same, when nothing would be?

They walked past her parents' restaurant and she thought about the times they'd play hide and seek in there, when they were young. Then they walked past their old high school, where they got up to most of their mischief. Nancy thought about the boyfriends they'd had, sitting in the park with them, sneaking to parties and all of their petty relationship dramas. Then Nancy smiled, as she suddenly remembered a time at school when Lena had quite literally come running to her defence. Katie (the woman Nancy had worked with in the pharmacy) had brought Nancy to tears with some vicious gossip she'd spread (the bitch hadn't changed) and was verbally ripping Nancy apart in front of a growing crowd on the yard after school, when Lena barged through the crowd and told Katie to shut her mouth. Katie spat some disgusting smart-arse comment back, so Lena punched her in it. Obviously, they got into a lot of trouble, but she wished Lena had been there today when she was getting grilled by The Beast. Nancy would've had to of held Lena back. It was horrific to see someone so strong and fierce now look so scared and defeated.

They reached the top of the street where Lena lived and began to walk towards her house. Nancy slowed their pace, doing everything she could to savour the memory of the final time she'd ever walk her sister home. She recorded the feeling of her holding her arm and put her head to the side so it touched Lena's. She felt so foolish for drifting from her, but never in her wildest dreams had she foreseen this outcome. All that time they could have spent together – wasted.

The street lights began to fade. All except one. One that stood like a spotlight, at the end of Lena's driveway, guiding the wounded party home. They approached it and as its beam touched their skin, Lena's light went out. That beautiful aura radiating from her silhouette, disappeared. Nancy watched as she studied her hands, then looked at her dark house; the street light went out above them and the front door opened flooding the night with a warm, welcoming beam.

Lena let go of Nancy's arm and turned to face her. She stared hard into Nancy's eyes, "I'm really scared Nance!" She trembled.

Nancy threw her arms tightly around her, "You don't have to go!"

"I don't want to! I really don't, but it's too late." Lena cried.

"This can't be it." Nancy spluttered. Both held each other and gasped for air in between loud sharp sobs. "You can't go like this!" Nancy wailed.

"I have to!" Lena sobbed, "It's my time." She gently pulled out of Nancy's embrace and held both of her hands. "I'll never leave you! You know that don't you?"

Nancy shook her head, continuing to cry, "You are leaving me though."

"Not because I want to!"

Nancy clung to her.

"Please tell everyone how much I love them! Especially, Evangeline. You'll tell her that for me won't you! Swear to me you will!"

"I swear!" Nancy whispered, "But, please, stay!" She whimpered.

"Oh Nance. I wish I'd have just called you!"

"I wish you had too."

Lena pushed out of her grip and looked nervously at the doorway. She swallowed hard, then looked back at Nancy, "Promise me Nance, you'll sort yourself out. Evangeline needs you now!"

"She doesn't need someone like me!" Nancy sobbed.

"She does!" Lena spat, "She needs someone exactly like you! You know me better than anyone and you can tell her all of our stories!"

"Stay and tell her yourself!"

Lena closed her eyes tightly, "I wish I could."

Nancy dove back in for another hug, "It should be you going back, not me."

Lena once again, gently pushed her away and wiped her tears with her hand.

"No. This is how it's meant to be." She sniffed, "I love you Nancy, you're such a bloody pain in the arse, but I love you so much!".

Nancy snorted, "I love you too. So much!"

Lena held her hand up in front of her and Nancy gripped it, then they pulled each other in close, resting each other's fists on their hearts, "Sisters?" Lena whispered.

"Forever!" Nancy sobbed.

Lena kissed Nancy hard on her cheek. "Don't forget me!"

"Never!" Nancy mumbled.

Lena took a deep breath and exhaled loudly, while letting go of Nancy. She then turned to the house, "I can do this!" She breathed, "It's time."

She briskly walked up the driveway, while Nancy frantically tried to reach out and grab her to pull her back, but she slipped from her hands and continued ahead. Lena bent her head low, as she approached the doorway, as if in honour of some greater power. Nancy shielded her eyes as the light became brighter, but peeped between her arms desperately watching every last second. As Lena reached the doorway, her silhouette paused and she turned back, "Goodbye Nance!" She shouted, but before Nancy could respond, she was gone.

Nancy fell to her knees in hysterical tears. She had failed.

"No!" She screamed, "No! You bring her back! You bring her back right now!" She hammered the ground with her fists, "She needs to go home, please! Let her go home!" She lay face down on the cold concrete in a puddle of slobber and tears. "You don't need her, I do, so you bring her back, or I'll –" She stopped and lifted her head, as she suddenly had an idea. "Or I'll come and get her." She whispered.

She threw herself forwards on all fours, then pushed herself to her feet and desperately rushed up the driveway, like a spider making a break for a dark cupboard. Launching herself head first into the light, she screamed in pain, as the heat from its power burnt her skin. She writhed in agony, suspended in the dense fire, until thankfully, the pain was numbed by a rush of cold air and she began to drift.

It was as if she was performing some great acrobatic feat, corkscrewing further and further into the house, again she was sick with disorientation. All she could see was light and all she could feel was the rush of cold air, when abruptly, she fell hard onto a surface.

She lay on her back, freezing cold, with her head pounding from the bizarre spiralling. She squirmed, like an upside-down tortoise, rocking from side to side trying to roll onto her front, but try as she may, she couldn't roll over. She squinted back out into her bright surroundings, but there was nothing but her hot breath in the damp air.

14

On the Run

She couldn't summon enough brain power to think of what to do next, she felt exhausted in both body and mind. She craved sleep, but it was too cold and she didn't have the power to curl up into a warmer ball. She began softly whimpering as she shivered, when suddenly a loud voice echoed around her, "Nancy. Nancy. Can you hear me?"

Her heart sang; someone was there. Dazed and confused she tried to look out to see where it was coming from.

"Nancy?" The voice called again.

It wasn't Lena's voice. It was female, but it definitely wasn't Lena's or any voice familiar to her.

"Nancy?" The voice said again, "I think she's coming round."

Nancy squinted once more, then tried to open her eyes wider, straining desperately to see who this person was. She hazily made out the silhouette of a woman, crouching over her. She appeared to be holding a bright light to her face.

"Can you hear me, Nancy?" The woman asked again.

Nancy fiercely wanted to respond, but she couldn't. She tried with all her might and just managed to let out a small groan. The light dropped out of her face and the woman knelt beside her; she had brown, tight, afro hair, with a light behind her creating the illusion of a halo around her head. Nancy tried desperately to focus on her, when another figure suddenly caught her eye. There was a man there too, stood at Nancy's feet, his thick frame filled the doorway and his bald head glistened in the dewy steam of the room.

"Paul, go get Jack and the stretcher please." She heard the woman say.

Nancy closed her eyes tightly and reopened them a few times, trying to clear her vision. It was a torch the woman was holding; she could see it now, a small metal torch.

"Nancy, can you hear me?" She asked once more, gently pulling down on Nancy's eyelids to study her pupils.

"Where's Lena?" Nancy managed to whisper. To her it sounded coherent, but she watched the woman's face twist in confusion.

"What was that?" She asked.

Nancy took a deep breath and slurred louder, "Lena?"

The woman politely smiled; she clearly didn't understand. "You've had a nasty fall. We're going to take you to hospital, okay?"

"We?" Nancy mumbled.

"Yes, my colleagues are getting the stretcher."

Nancy twitched in an attempt to roll onto her side, but again, her body didn't respond.

"No, don't try to move!" The woman instructed, "It's really important that you stay still, okay?"

Nancy stared back at her blankly.

"Nancy, have you taken any medication or consumed any alcohol?"

Again, Nancy just stared at her.

"Are you in pain anywhere?"

"Everywhere." Nancy thought, but remained silent.

"Are you in pain Nancy?"

"Yes." She softly groaned.

The woman again removed the torch light from Nancy's face and Nancy suddenly realised where she was. She recognised the dark light fitting on the ceiling, a plain circular disk, she was back on the floor of her bathroom. She studied it, as there were three new burn marks on the casing, like all the bulbs had blown at once. The woman slowly got to her feet and Nancy watched her smile reassuringly, but Nancy didn't smile back, she couldn't, it was as if her mind was getting reacquainted with her body and she hadn't figured out how to control it yet.

She then watched as two men appeared back in the doorway now holding a stretcher. She watched as the woman removed the towels from her body and slid her arms into a hospital gown, then watched all three carefully manipulate her onto the stretcher. She listened to their warm reassurances, marvelled at how they achieved it in her tiny bathroom and finally, as she left over the threshold of her front door, felt a sense of relief. She had been rescued. She admired the clear night sky, as they carefully loaded her into the back of the ambulance and was overcome with a strong sense of humbleness.

"Just a few more steps to go. Are you okay?" The woman asked.

"No." Nancy mouthed.

"Are you in pain Nancy?"

"Yes." She groaned.

The woman again smiled down at her. "We'll be in the warm ambulance in a few seconds."

The paramedics secured her into position, lay a blanket over her and the woman sat down in the seat next to her, with the two men leaving to sit in the front seats. They set off on their way. Nancy felt the sway of the bed as the ambulance sped over the worn roads.

"Okay, Nancy, my name is Monique. I'm just going to take a little blood, okay? You'll just feel a little pin prick."

"Yes." Nancy slurred.

Nancy watched as the woman readied the needle. She had no inclination to object; she was happy to serenely follow instructions, that is, until the needle pierced her skin. Immediately, she was awoken; her body and mind synchronised, she pulled the syringe from her arm and threw the blanket from her body.

"No, no, no!" She cried, staring in terror at a shocked Monique, "Lena! I have to save Lena!"

She didn't even give Monique a second to reply, nor did she register her reaction. She lunged for the ambulance doors, pulled the lever and they flew open. Monique screamed for her colleagues to stop and Nancy fell back onto the bed as it came to a sharp halt. She rocked back up onto her feet and flew out of the doors, running as fast as her legs would carry her.

Luckily, they hadn't made it out of town and she wasn't too far from Lena's house, but even if it was hundreds of miles away, she'd have run it. The cold air stung in her throat, her lungs felt as if she was inhaling gravel and her hospital gown tangled in between her legs, but she couldn't let anything slow her down. If she fell, she fell, she'd get back up and carry on. She was so determined, so focused, so driven, that she'd failed to realise that she was still naked from the bath and her gown hadn't been tied around her back. She was unknowingly flashing her backside to the world, running through street, after street, after street of evening dog walkers and fellow joggers.

Finally, she neared her destination, the houses beamed with coloured lights and there it was, just ahead, Lena's house. She could faintly see someone in the driveway.

"Lena!" She screamed, "Lena!"

The dark shape halted upon hearing her screams and walked towards her. Nancy quickly realised there were two people standing there, a man and a woman. "Lena!" She screamed again, but as she got closer, she realised it wasn't her. It was in fact, Francesco and his girlfriend Grace. He opened his arms to her and she fell hard into his chest, nearly knocking him off his feet.

"Oh my God. Nancy!" He gasped from the impact, then held her tightly, "What's happened?"

Nancy tried to regain control of her breathing, but she couldn't. Panting wildly, she did her best to say, "Lena, we have to save Lena!"

"Save her?" Francesco squinted in confusion.

"Yes! We have to find her!" Nancy exhaled.

She looked sternly into his calm, blue eyes.

"She's in the house." He smiled.

Nancy looked at the house, then back up at him, "In the house?"

"She's just got back; I've literally just seen her run up the stairs."

"She's, okay?" Nancy panted.

"She's fine!"

Nancy broke down in tears, "She's fine?"

"Ah Nance, what's the matter?"

"Are you sure she's fine?" She sobbed.

"I'm sure! But what the hell has happened to you?" He studied the wound above her eye.

Nancy pushed herself away from him and wiped her tears, steadying herself back on her own two feet. She then noticed his girlfriend standing behind him, with her face a mix of bewilderment and concern. Nancy jealously looked her up and down, then looked back at Francesco. "You promise me that Lena is safe?"

"Nancy, I swear. You, clearly are not though."

But before Nancy could explain, the ambulance came hurtling down the road towards them, then came to a sharp stop. All three watched as the doors flew open and the three paramedics ran towards Nancy.

"Oh shit!" Nancy cried, scrambling past Francesco and his girlfriend. She attempted to make a break for the house, but was swiftly apprehended only a few paces up the driveway.

"I just need to see my friend!" She yelled at the paramedics, struggling to free herself from their guard.

"What's happened to her?" Francesco asked them.

"She's injured her head; we were on our way to the hospital when she bolted! Are you family?"

"No. I'm her friend." Francesco replied.

"I need to see Lena!" Nancy shouted still struggling.

Francesco tried to calm her, "Nance, she's fine! Honestly, I swear. That's a really nasty cut you have though, you need to go and get that looked at."

Nancy paused and looked back at the house. "But Lena, I —"

Francesco smiled and cut her off, "Nancy, you need to go with the paramedics!"

Nancy looked at the unamused faces of her rescuers.

"Come on Nancy!" Francesco insisted, "Don't waste these people's time." He grabbed hold of her hand and clasped it between his.

"Waste time." She muttered. She'd been told not to waste time.

"Yes." He reiterated, "Don't waste their time."

She looked hard at Francesco's hand, in a slightly unhinged manner, then looked him in the eye, winked and obediently nodded. The paramedics watched her closely, as she removed her hand and began to slowly walk to the ambulance.

To her audience, she appeared lost inside her own world, mumbling to herself, her gaze fixed to the floor. They remained close at her sides, anticipating another manic episode, but she remained calm.

"Is she going to be okay?" Francesco asked.

"I don't know. We've just picked her up. That cut on her head looks quite deep." Monique replied.

"Is she usually this erratic?" One of the male paramedics asked.

"No. I've known her since she was born, she's not like this."

"Hm." The male paramedic grunted in response.

Nancy's mind was in overdrive. She couldn't put the puzzle pieces together. "Francesco," She mumbled to herself, "Fran —" Her daze broke. She suddenly realised she'd just seen Francesco. Not only had she just seen him, she had clumsily fallen into his arms. She winced in embarrassment, then looked over her shoulder, peeping past the paramedic behind her to see Grace pull at his arm, encouraging him to move away, but he stood firm; his beautiful face tight with worry. Her heart smiled as she noticed this, "Maybe he does love me!" She thought.

As they reached the ambulance, the male paramedic standing behind her moved to get into the front seat and she heard Francesco quietly snigger. Again, she looked back to now find him with his hand over his mouth, concealing an obvious smirk. She didn't understand what was so amusing, but Monique responded by gently closing the back of her gown and holding it in place. Nancy immediately caught on. She cheekily grinned at him, then watched as Grace hit him hard in his arm, clearly disgusted by his immaturity. Monique motioned for Nancy to continue to the back of the vehicle, but she silently refused and her heart began to race. The two paramedics grabbed hold of her arms, making sure she didn't run again, which made her chuckle. She flashed Francesco a mischievous pout. He smiled, but shook his head and motioned with his arms to encourage her to go.

"Nance, go on!" He insisted.

She shook her head.

"What's the matter Nance?" He asked.

"I don't have time to waste. So, I need to tell you, that I love you!"

A beautiful smile beamed from his strong face, "I know you love me! We've known each other forever!"

"No." She said, "You don't understand. I'm *in* love with you, Francesco!"

The two stared adoringly at one another. Nancy tried to pull her hands free, she wanted to run back over and jump on him, but Monique awkwardly cleared her throat, quickly bringing her back to reality. She looked wide eyed at Nancy and motioned with her head for her to get back into the ambulance.

"You go to the hospital Nance." Francesco advised, "I'll drive up soon to see you, okay?"

Nancy smiled and nodded. She turned and the paramedics let go of her arms, but she couldn't help herself and quickly blew him a kiss goodbye, before disappearing into the ambulance.

15

Ambulance Ride

Once inside, Nancy slid back onto the bed, Monique closed the doors and again, they sped away.

Monique turned to Nancy, but the soft concerned face that she had previously woken to, had now been replaced with a stern frustrated glare.

"What the hell was that?" Monique snapped.

"I love him!" Nancy replied.

"So, you ran all that way, to tell him that you love him?"

"Oh no. I ran to save Lena?"

"The girl he was with?"

"No. That's his girlfriend!" Nancy pulled a face of disgust.

Monique shook her head, "You just confessed your love for him, in front of his girlfriend?"

"I had to!"

"Are you having an affair?"

"No. Oh God no!" Nancy blurted, "Well, not with him."

Monique stared at her in bewilderment, "With who?"

"That doesn't matter. It's just that Lena told me, that guy we just saw, Francesco, he loves me!"

"Who's Lena?"

"His sister."

"Why did you need to save her?"

"She died in a car accident tonight!"

"I just heard him say she was okay."

"Yes, but –" Nancy paused. Lena was okay. She looked down at her hands to study her skin and at the freckles on her arms; each mark was as she remembered it. She wiggled her fingers and looked at her painted festive nails, everything was just as it should be. She gently pinched her skin, to see if she could feel the pain. "Ow." She winced. She was real; she was alive.

"Did I die?" Nancy asked looking back at Monique.

Monique gave a nervous smile and shook her head, "I don't think so."

Nancy could see her demeanour beginning to soften again, but there was still a subtle look of alarm on her face.

"It was all so real!" Nancy whispered, looking back down at her hands.

Monique put her hand on Nancy's shoulder, "It sounds like you've had quite a night."

Nancy didn't respond, instead she dropped her head into her hands and burst into hysterical tears. "She's okay!" She cried, "She's okay!" She then began to chuckle wildly with happy relief between sobs. Monique removed her hand and uncomfortably watched on in silence, a little afraid of Nancy's erratic and apparent delusional behaviour. Nancy fell back onto the bed and looked up at the ceiling. "Thank you! Thank you so much!" She sobbed, wiping the tears from her cheeks and the snot from her nose.

"Nancy, are you okay?" Monique asked, cautiously standing out of her chair.

"I am now." She spluttered. She then began nodding in gratitude and mumbling as if some invisible person was hovering above her.

Monique glanced up at the ceiling, then back at the crazed woman on the bed, "Nancy, can you look at me for a second please?"

Nancy immediately turned and halted her tears.

"Oh shit!" Her sudden change of emotion startled Monique, "Okay, I need you to be totally honest with me. Can you do that for me?"

Nancy squinted at her, anticipating her question.

"Have you taken any drugs today?"

"No!" Nancy frowned.

"Are you sure? It's very important that you tell me!"

"I swear! Check my blood if you don't believe me."

"We'll do all that when we get you to the hospital." Monique put her gloved fingers onto Nancy's forehead, to examine her wound, "It is a hell of a gash, which may explain your delirium."

"Delirium?" Nancy chuckled.

"Yes!" Monique grinned, "So, I just need you to lay back and relax."

Nancy nodded.

"Okay. Good! Try not to go to sleep, just lay back and we'll be there soon."

16

Hospital Visits

Beep. Beep. Beep. Nancy could hear an electronic sound close to her head. She gently opened her eyes and found, to her left, up a tall metal rod, a cream plastic box, with an LED display. She stared at it for a few moments, then realised it was a heart rate monitor. She watched the green line jump to the gentle rhythm of her pulse, then, with her eyes, followed the wire attached to it all the way back down to her bed, until it disappeared under the sheets wrapped over her body. She was obviously now in hospital and surrounded on all four sides by walls of drawn blue curtains. She looked down to her left to see a worn pink padded chair; the plastic patterned material on its back shone in the light of the lamp above her head. As she looked to her right, she found a tall cupboard and could just see what looked like a grey remote sitting on top of it. It was connected to a long wire that disappeared down the crack between the cupboard and the bed. The head of the bed had been positioned up high, so she was able to shuffle a little higher to see what the remote was for. The top row of buttons were bed controls, but the bottom green button had 'Assistance' written below it. She reached out and pawed it towards her, just managing to grab it properly before it fell down the gap. She pressed the assistance button and watched as a small, green light to the side of it illuminated, then began to flicker. After about two or three minutes the curtains at the foot of her bed twitched and the head of a nurse popped through them.

"You're awake!" The nurse joyfully smiled.

Nancy didn't respond immediately, she just stared at this new strange woman.

The nurse slid through the curtains and stood at the side of her bed, looking down at her smiling incessantly.

"What am I doing here?" Nancy mumbled.

"You hurt your head doll."

Nancy stared at her in bewilderment.

"Don't you remember?"

Nancy slightly shook her head in response.

"It looks like you hit it on the radiator in your bathroom. We think you slipped getting out of the bath. It's a nasty gash, but it's all stitched up now."

Nancy still stared vacantly at her. She was trying her best to take in what she was being told, while also trying to remember what had happened.

"I'm Kim." The nurse said, interrupting Nancy's trance.

"How did I get here Kim?"

Kim chuckled, "You were brought here in an ambulance."

"Why is that amusing?" Nancy asked.

"I'm sorry, it's just that you gave our ambulance staff quite a memorable night."

"Why?"

"You bolted out of the ambulance and went on the run with your gown untied."

Nancy slouched down in the bed. "Oh shit!" She mumbled, covering her face with her hands. She winced in pain, as she accidently touched the cut on her head.

"Do you remember now?" The nurse asked.

"Not really!" Nancy murmured, squinting with her left eye, to feel the tightness of the stitches above it. "Can I have a mirror to see it please."

"Yes, I'll go get one now. Would you like a drink?"

"Yes. Water please."

The nurse nodded, "Your parents are on their way. I'll send them through when they arrive."

"Thank you."

Nancy stared at the ceiling, moving her eyebrow up and down, feeling the tension of the tight stitches and the pain of the wound. She didn't remember falling out of the bath. She remembered getting home and running it, then the warmth of the water, but – she sprang upright, "Oh shit!" She cried. She remembered everything. The cliff, Joel, the wolf, Francesco, Evangeline, the old man, but most of all, Lena. She had to help Lena!

She tried to detach herself from the heart rate monitor so she could make a break for it, when, once again, a thin break in the curtains appeared and in stepped her parents followed by Kim. Her parents rushed to either side of her and Nancy immediately began to sob with relief. They'd know what to do, she thought. She hugged them both tightly while Kim watched on at the foot of the bed, holding a mirror under her arm, a jug of water in one hand and a cup in the other.

"Oh, my beautiful girl!" Her mum wept, as she held her.

"You're such a clumsy sod Nance!" Her dad scolded.

"You're really hurting my head, Mum." Nancy mumbled, as her mum held her cheek to Nancy's forehead.

"Ah, sorry my darling." They both quickly let go of her and sat on the bed at her sides, each holding her hand tightly.

"Mrs Adams said you were knocked out cold, when she found you on the bathroom floor. Blood all over your head, sick on the mat, the poor woman was a mess on the phone." Her dad informed her.

"Mrs Adams?" Nancy asked in confusion.

"Yes," Her mum replied, "thank God she phoned an ambulance when she did, they said you would have died of hypothermia if you'd have stayed on that cold floor all night. She saved your life!"

Nancy pushed her head back into her pillow. She didn't even remember seeing Mrs Adams.

"You're absolutely fine though." Kim chimed in. "We ran all the tests and scanned your head. Your cut and the bruising are just superficial. Obviously, we still need to observe you tonight, but if all is well, you won't miss Christmas tomorrow, so don't worry." She placed the jug and cup on the tray table that floated over the end of the bed. "Do you want to see your face?" She asked pulling the mirror out from under her arm.

Nancy nodded.

Her mum got off the bed, to let Kim stand beside her with the mirror. She held it up in front of her face and Nancy squirmed in shock at the sight of the bruising that surrounded the cut. She then noticed, the deep, black mascara smeared around her eyes and the track marks her tears had left before she had gotten into the bath. She remembered pulling the small vanity mirror down from the windowsill in the bathroom and staring into her eyes looking for hope. She had found none. However, now staring at herself, she felt an overwhelming sense of it. The contrast of the dark makeup that dirtied her face, against the light of the life in her eyes was undeniable, it was as if she had been reconnected with her soul. For the first time in a long time, she was awake.

"Doesn't look too bad, does it?" Kim smiled.

"No." Nancy mumbled.

Kim nodded, "Right, I'll leave you all to it. If you need anything, just press the button."

"Thank you!" Nancy replied.

"Yes, thank you so much!" Nancy's parents said in sloppy unison.

"My pleasure!" Kim responded, ducking back out of the curtains.

Her mum sat back down on the bed next to her. "Thank God you're okay!" She said, pulling her glasses down from her head to take a closer look at Nancy's cut.

"Do you remember falling?" Her dad asked.

Nancy smiled, "I think my bath water was a bit hot and it made me a little light headed."

Her dad shook his head. "What were you even doing home so early, I thought you finished at six?"

"Oh. What time is it now?"

He looked at his watch. "Just gone eight? They brought you in at about six. It took them a while to contact us; Mrs Adams didn't have our new number."

Nancy nodded while listening, but none of it made sense. Not only did she not remember Mrs Adams coming to her rescue, but the whole timeline was wrong. Tonight, had already happened, how was it only eight o'clock? She had got dressed after the bath, sat down, had cereal, watched TV, gone with Lena. She couldn't understand it, so, maybe, it hadn't happened at all.

"Why were you home so early my darling?" Her mum asked.

Nancy sheepishly looked at her parents. She knew they'd be disappointed with her answer, so she hesitated, then mumbled, "I walked out!"

Her dad immediately put his hand to his forehead and smoothed his fingers across it. Nancy could see he was trying to compose himself.

"Ah Nancy! Why this time?" Her mum sighed sarcastically.

Nancy shrugged.

"Come on Nance, what is going on with you?" Her dad snapped in frustration. "This is your eighth or nineth, or however many, I've lost count." He moved his hand back down from his head and looked at her mum. "We went to your apartment too, to get you some clothes before we got here."

Her parents both looked awkwardly at her. "We don't understand." Her mum shook her head, "It was a real shock to see where you've been living for the past few years. You had such a beautiful place before. I mean, it was so cold and bare. You could fit all your belongings into one bag."

"I don't need anything fancy." Nancy argued defensively.

"That's not what we're saying!" Her dad interjected.

"We're asking what is going on with you?" Her mum croaked.

Nancy looked down at her mum's hand holding hers, she could feel the warmth radiating from her rough chapped skin, the result of years of using cleaning products without gloves. Her parents had always worked so hard and given her so much, she didn't want them to feel as though she wasn't capable of the same.

"Do you take drugs?" Her dad whispered.

Her mum quickly glared at him, telling him to keep his mouth shut.

"No!" Nancy protested, surprised by the question. "Of course I don't!"

"We just wondered that's all." Her mum justified. "You hear stories about high flyers getting addicted to cocaine, don't you? And, Lena's mother has been telling us about some of the unsavoury people she's been hanging round with lately."

"No! My God. No!" Nancy snapped.

"Then what?" Her mum pleaded. "Please Nancy, what?"

Nancy could see the tears forming in her mum's eyes. She didn't want to hurt her parents with the truth, that was the last thing she wanted, but that's exactly what she was doing by not telling them. Nancy exhaled loudly at her sad realisation and closed her eyes. It was time. She had to come clean and tell them everything; how she felt, what had happened, she had to bare her soul – even if it terrified her. She needed help, but what if they got on their high horse? She wrestled with her thoughts for a few moments, until, she realised it didn't matter anymore. Here they were in tears at her hospital bedside. They'd come because they loved her. No matter what their reaction would be, helpful or critical, it would be out of their love for her.

"No more running!" She thought, they deserved an explanation and it was time to be brave.

She opened her eyes and looked at them. "I almost killed myself tonight." She began, with an unemotional frankness, "Accidentally at first, but I chose not to save myself."

Her parents silently stared at her in disbelief, as her admission washed over them.

"No!" Her mum whispered.

Nancy nodded in confirmation.

Her mum lunged at her and held her tightly, "Oh, my baby!" She sobbed.

Her dad grabbed her hand and held it tightly in his. His face furrowed in sadness; her news had winded him. "Why Nancy?" He muttered softly.

It killed her to see them so upset, but now she had begun to tell the truth, she had to continue. She took another deep breath, "Because I was tired of living."

Her mum let go of her and shuffled back straight. She sniffed and wiped steaming tears from her face, as she asked, "But why?"

"I'd just given up. It started years ago really."

"Years!" Her dad repeated.

"Yeah," She uncomfortably mumbled, "Before I qualified. I just didn't want to be there. It wasn't for me."

"But you did so well!" Her mum frowned.

"Because I wanted to make you both proud. But when I started my first job, it got a lot worse."

"Nancy if you didn't want to do it, you should have just said." Her dad snapped.

"No. I was sick of being the joke of the family. Everyone always laughing at me, saying I'm away with the fairies. I wanted to prove myself."

"You didn't have to prove anything."

"Yes, I did."

Her dad shook his head, looked away and tutted.

"That's how I felt!" Nancy added, but he didn't respond.

"Go on Nance, why did it get worse?" Her mum quickly prompted.

Nancy smirked, "There were so many crazy things going on in that office, like everyone tried to get an ace card on you, to keep you in their pocket. So many things didn't sit right with me, so not only did it make me really paranoid, but it ate away at me, having to always turn a blind eye and I just began to hate people. I dreaded every morning so much, that I'd throw up in a bag in my car before I walked in. It became my morning ritual. I was so happy to finally leave after my training, but the next place was pretty much the same."

"You stayed in the second place for years though."

"I did, because I'd dedicated so much time and jumped through so many hoops to get there. I kept being told how it was rare for someone of my age to have climbed to that position so quickly, plus, I had it engrained in me that jumping from place to place wouldn't be good for my long-term career goals. So, I stayed until I couldn't do it any longer."

"Did something happen?" Her mum asked.

"Yeah, one day one of the bosses came flying into my office, screaming at me. He threw a booklet hard at my face, telling me to fix something that I didn't even have anything to do with. The corner got me and I actually had a mark on my cheek from it."

"What?" Her dad quickly became animated.

"Yeah." Nancy snorted, "He did later apologise when he realised that it wasn't me, but that didn't excuse what he did and what made it worse, was I found out that one of the other girls had actually set me up!"

"The bitch!" Her mum seethed.

"I know, so I stayed until I couldn't bare it any longer and it was such a huge relief when I left, I actually felt excited about my life again, but everyone else thought I was crazy."

"You didn't tell us any of this though. We thought you loved it, that's why we gave you a hard time because we were shocked. If you'd have just told us!"

"Let me finish." Nancy interrupted her dad, "I'm not blaming you! I didn't tell you, because I just wanted to close the door on that part of my life entirely."

"When I get my hands on that little weasel!" Her dad grumbled.

"Exactly! That's why I kept my mouth shut and I didn't want you to think that I was weak for not standing up for myself. It just wasn't worth it; everything always gets manipulated and these people always have cronies to back them."

"We would have backed you!" Her mum chimed in.

"Just, let me finish!" Nancy sighed, "As you know, since then I still haven't been able to settle, nothing has felt right. My hate for everything has just grown, because all of these superficial things that people stress about don't matter to me, they never have and I just feel like an alien." She snorted, "But as much as I've wanted to be away from people, I've hated being alone too and started to hate being me – I'm a disappointment."

"We've never made you feel that way!" Her dad fiercely denied.

"No! No, you haven't, I'm saying that I felt that way about myself and put that pressure on myself. That is what you both need to understand. This isn't about what either of you did or didn't do, it's nothing on either of you. This is about how I made myself feel." She paused, exhaled loudly, then continued, "Anyway, to make things worse in this last job, I had a relationship with the manager. I fell for him before I worked there, that's how I got the job. I knew he had a girlfriend, but I let him tag me along too." She huffed to herself.

"Nancy!" Her mum scolded.

"I know, I know. You don't need to say anything, neither of you do, I don't need a lecture or for anyone to tell me it was wrong, I know I shouldn't have let it happen. But I walked out today, because he really excelled at being an arsehole. Then, when I got home, the realisation hit me; I'd have to stand in front of both of you tomorrow, the two people that I love the most in this world and disappoint you again." She paused and gulped trying to hold back her tears, "I love you both so much and I have never wanted to hurt you, but I'm so lonely and feel very lost."

"Oh Nance! My darling!" Her dad wrapped his arms around her and gently kissed the top of her head.

Her mum propped her glasses back up onto her head and dried her face with a tissue from her pocket. Then pulled out another clean tissue to wipe the two silent streams now running down Nancy's cheeks.

"Come on! Don't cry my baby!" Her mum wept.

"I'm sorry! So sorry!" She sobbed.

"Don't be silly. But I just don't understand why didn't you come to us sooner?" Her dad asked, leaning back to sit at her side.

"I was too proud!" Nancy spluttered.

He shook his head. "You're coming back home Nance and I won't take no for an answer."

"Yes!" Her mum agreed.

"No. I don't want to be a burden."

"A burden?" Her dad cried, "How could you ever think that?"

"It's just, you and mum should be enjoying your time together, now you'll be at the restaurant less."

"Are you serious? Nancy that's like a knife through my heart, you thinking that you would ever be a burden!"

"Sorry Dad but –"

"You should be! Now you're coming home and that's the end of it!"

"Thank you." Nancy nodded, "That would be lovely!"

"Where does this manager live?"

Nancy snorted, "He doesn't even matter anymore, honestly. For too long I've been blaming him. The problem was me; I should have told him where to go a lot sooner. I've needed to be stronger and braver in so many aspects of my life. I've wasted so much time."

"It's like you've had an epiphany." Her mum smiled.

"I feel like I have! I had this really weird dream about Lena, she –"

"Lena!" Her dad cut in, "Yes, before I forget, Francesco called us when we arrived here, he wanted to come and see you tonight. He also said Lena wants you to go and see her tomorrow if you're up for it?"

Nancy suddenly remembered. She'd escaped from the ambulance, run to Lena's house, almost bulldozed Francesco off his feet and he had confirmed that Lena was okay. She cringed for a second in embarrassment, but her body quickly relaxed in relief. Lena was okay.

"Nancy did you hear that?" Her mum asked.

Nancy pulled her face into a smile, "Yes! Typical Lena; I'm the one in hospital and I have to make the effort to go and see her, rather than her come to me!"

"I didn't know you two were speaking again."

"We weren't." Nancy replied slowly in confusion.

"Do you want Francesco to come and see you then?" Her dad asked.

"Oh no! Not like this." Nancy shook her head.

"Nance, he's been one of your good friends for years. If you want to change, do it now. Your friend is asking to see you."

"Fine, okay, but don't tell him anything I just told you. I don't want anyone else to know. Just say I slipped!" She grumbled.

Her dad smiled, patted her knee, then stood up.

"Don't go and phone him now! We all need to talk!" Her mum hissed.

"I just need a minute." He said moving to the end of the bed. He turned and smiled at Nancy, then disappeared through the split in the curtain.

Her mum looked back at her and rolled her eyes at his departure.

"Dad's really upset, isn't he?"

"Well, you've taken the wind out of both of our sails."

"I'm really sorry Mum!"

"I know, I know," Her mum sighed, "so, what now then my angel?" The level of concern etched on her mum's face aged her.

"I honestly don't know." Nancy shrugged, "I just need a little bit of time to think."

"The nurse said you bolted out of the ambulance and they had to track you down. Then Francesco told us you went to see him."

Nancy nodded. "I didn't have my gown tied Mum; I literally flashed the whole world running through the streets."

"Oh God! Nancy! Why did you run?"

"I thought, well, I thought Lena had died."

Her mum's face contorted in confusion. "What on earth made you think that?"

"I don't remember hitting my head in the bathroom. I remember getting dry, dressed, eating cereal, watching TV and then Lena appearing in my apartment with a hole in her side, telling me she'd been in a car accident."

"Really?"

"Yeah! When I woke up on the bathroom floor, I couldn't remember anything, then in the ambulance, when the paramedic tried to take my blood, it all came flooding back and I had to go and save her."

"Nancy that is bizarre."

"I know! But it was all so real to me Mum."

"Oh, my baby! You've had a nightmare of a night." She forced a sad smile.

Nancy looked down at the bed.

"Did you see any pearly gates in this dream?"

"No!" Nancy chuckled, "I saw a cliff edge and a huge wolf."

Her mum tutted, "That says a lot about what's going on in here!" She moved her hand to gently touch Nancy's head, then moved her hair out of her face and fixed it behind her ear. "You know why you didn't see the gates, don't you, my angel?"

"I'm not good enough?" Nancy shrugged.

"No!" Her mum tapped her hand, "You didn't see them, because it's not your time. You have more life to live."

Nancy hugged her mum tightly.

"Promise me my darling! That you'll stop all this overthinking now and just live it! Talk to us, stop living in your head."

Nancy moved out of her mum's embrace, looked down at the bed and faintly nodded, "I won't do anything like this again. I promise."

Her mum gave her three hard kisses on her cheek. "Don't make me worry!" She whispered.

Both women, then drew their attention back to the curtains, as they heard her dad's low voice approaching from behind them. They watched as he reappeared.

"Francesco is on his way." He smiled.

"Thanks Dad!"

He shuffled to resume his position on the bed next to her, "Now do we have to keep you on suicide watch or have you got it out of your system?" He darkly joked.

"Raphael!" Her mum cried.

Her dad always used dark humour when he was uncomfortable or upset, like Nancy, it was his coping mechanism.

"It's out of my system." Nancy confirmed.

"Thank God for that!" He smiled, "Well in other news we've got all sorts for dinner tomorrow –"

"Raph! Our daughter has just tried to kill herself, don't pretend like everything is okay!"

"I'm not, I'm just giving her something to look forward to; trying to keep her from jumping out of the window tonight." He sniggered.

Nancy laughed, but she could see her mum wasn't amused.

"Well, it's nice to see you're both taking this seriously!" She grumbled.

"Mum, I'm not going to do it again. If anything, it was a huge wake-up call! Please don't worry."

"Don't worry!" Her mum frowned, "You are sitting in a hospital bed on Christmas Eve with a slice across your forehead, telling us you meant to do it!"

Nancy sighed. "I know, but –"

"I just don't understand why you let it get to this point Nancy!"

"Oh, for God's sake Carmela, she's just told you why!" Her dad interjected, "Our poor girl has had a few rough years and she's a proud, independent, young woman, who didn't want to come crawling back to us. I respect that!"

"What?" Her mum cried.

"Let me finish! But, while I respect that, it was foolish. As much as you say it wasn't anything to do with us, what I'll never forgive myself for, is watching you spiral. I knew you hadn't been yourself for a long time. We both knew!" He looked over at her mum, who sadly nodded in agreeance, "But we didn't help. The first time we get to see our daughter in weeks and she's sitting in a hospital bed after a failed suicide attempt." He paused and looked to the ceiling trying to conceal his tears. "It breaks my heart!"

171

Nancy burst into tears and hugged him. "I'm really sorry Dad. I am!" She sniffed.

"No." He said, pushing out of her embrace, "*I'm* sorry my angel, if you'd have succeeded tonight, I just, well, I just, I don't know. Thank God you didn't." He took a tissue from her mum and wiped Nancy's face, "Now enough, enough of these tears, we put all of this to bed for tonight! Tomorrow is a new day, you come back to live with us and we'll figure everything out together. Okay?"

Nancy nodded and gave a snotty smile in response.

"Okay good. And your mum has made a tiramisu for tomorrow, so don't be going anywhere tonight."

Her mum playfully hit him in the arm and shook her head.

"Is Uncle Pete still coming tomorrow?" Nancy asked looking at her mum.

"Yes, we haven't told anyone, we rushed straight here, but we can cancel if you *really* want?" She replied.

Nancy thought about it for a few moments and pursed her lips.

"He's an arse wipe isn't he Nance." Her dad piped up.

Nancy laughed.

"That's my brother you're talking about!" Her mum snapped defensively.

"He's such a prick Mum!"

"Erm, language!" Her mum scolded.

Her dad laughed loudly and Nancy rolled her eyes.

"He's family!" Her mum said sternly.

"Family!" Her dad scoffed, "He's always boasting about his houses, his cars, his boat and whatever else, the guy is a multi-millionaire, but every family occasion that tight bastard sits there, eating my food without a sniff of a contribution."

"Because they're our guests!" Her mum protested.

"I don't care; I'm going to tell him tomorrow to put his hand in his pocket!"

"Don't you dare!" Her mum cried.

"And don't get me started on his sly insults!"

Nancy sat there and watched them bicker for a good ten minutes; Uncle Pete was always a sore subject. Her dad didn't approve of how rude and obnoxious he was to her and her mum, but for the simple reason he was family, her mum seemed to tolerate it.

They continued on and on, until, finally, they were interrupted by a hand popping through the curtains and waving at them. A deep strong voice followed, "Is she decent?"

Her parents fell silent, while Nancy replied to the hand, "Yes, I'm dressed."

Francesco stepped through the curtain with a nervous grin on his face and her parents jumped up to greet him. Her dad shook his hand and her mum hugged and kissed him on both cheeks.

"How've you been lad?" Her dad asked, "We haven't seen you in ages!"

"I've been so busy with work!" He replied, "And I've nearly finished renovating the houses too. The first has taken years!"

"They needed a lot doing then?"

"Not all of them, I span three of them round quite quickly, but the first one I bought, needed completely gutting! It's been a nightmare, just not enough hours in the day."

"You're moving into the first one, aren't you?"

"Yes, I've put so much into it and I really love it there. It's so peaceful and the garden is huge."

"Your dad was saying the other day that we should come and see what you've done."

"Yeah course, anytime, just give me a call and I'll meet you up there."

"Will do. It's so good to see you again lad!" Her dad shook his hand again, then turned to Nancy, "Right Suicidal Sal, we've got a dinner to prepare, we'll leave you with Francesco, but we'll pick you up in the morning. Just give us a call, when you've been released back into society."

Nancy sniggered, "Okay. Thank you."

"Wait, we've just got here, we can't just leave her!" Her mum argued.

"Carmela! She's fine! She wants a nice dinner tomorrow, as do we all."

"No! This is more important!"

"Does she really want you pecking her poor head all night?" Her dad grinned and all three turned to look at her.

Nancy smiled. "I love you both so much, but yeah, I'm fine. Go!"

Her mum walked back to give her a hug and kissed her on her cheek. "I love you so, so much my baby, I want to stay with you!

"No, honestly Mum, please. I swear I'm okay."

Her mum huffed as she let go of her, "Well we'll talk tomorrow then?"

Nancy smiled and nodded.

"You just call us straight away if anything changes, or you need us, no matter what time it is!"

"Yes, I will."

"Promise me!"

"I promise!"

"Bloody hell Carmela, come on!" Her dad hurried her impatiently.

"Don't rush me, Raphael!"

Nancy chuckled to herself; they were like a double act. They loved each other very much and we're happily married, but they never stopped bickering, (on the rare occasion they did, you knew they'd fallen out.)

"Bye Mum, bye Dad!

"Bye both." They said as they disappeared out of the curtains.

17

Do you love me?

Francesco watched them leave, then turned and raised his eyebrows at Nancy, "That was a quick exit!"

Nancy rolled her eyes and grinned.

They make me laugh!" He smiled. "What did your dad call you? Suicidal Sal?"

"Yeah," she squirmed, "you know him and his sense of humour. Just a joke!"

Francesco grinned in agreeance, as he walked over to sit on the bed at her side.

"Can I sit on here?" He asked.

"Yeah, course." She pushed herself up to give him more space.

"Look at the state of your head!" He marvelled at the cut, "I've got to say Nance, you really had me worried. Your dad told me that you slipped getting out of the bath and knocked yourself out!"

"I did!" She awkwardly confirmed.

"What was all that about though, escaping from the ambulance and running to our house?"

"I just had this horrible feeling that Lena had —" She paused.

"Had what?" He prompted.

"It doesn't matter."

"No, go on, had what?"

"Had died." She whispered.

Francesco smiled, "My little bitch of a sister is most definitely alive!"

"I know! Thank God! My mum said she wants me to come and see her tomorrow. It made me laugh, I've been rushed into hospital and she wants me to make the effort to see her."

"Well, that's Lena, isn't it? All she's missing is a crown."

Nancy chuckled.

"What made you think she'd died?"

"I had a horrible dream when I was unconscious."

"What happened in it?"

"I'd rather not go into it right now. Listen Francesco, I'm really glad you're here, it's so lovely to see you, but it's Christmas Eve, shouldn't you be with your girlfriend?"

Francesco pursed his lips, shook his head and sheepishly averted his eyes down to Nancy's hand resting next to his.

"What does that mean?" Nancy asked.

"It means," He began, lifting his head to look over at the heart rate monitor, "That I broke up with her."

"What?" Nancy cried, "Oh come on, that's cold! You can't do that on Christmas Eve!"

"I know, I know, it sounds shitty!" He sighed, now looking into Nancy's eyes.

"It's cruel!"

"Yeah, but you don't know why?"

"Why then?"

"Well after we saw you, we got into an argument. I asked the paramedics if I could ride along with you in the ambulance and Grace said that it was disrespectful to her if I went with you."

"Well yeah, I agree. You don't just ditch your girlfriend for some half naked, crazy person."

Francesco laughed, "I explained to her that we're good friends and I wanted to make sure that you were okay, but she still said no. So, I said, come with me then, we'll drive behind the ambulance and again she refused. She said she wasn't spending her Christmas Eve babysitting some strange girl."

"Which is understandable." Nancy interjected.

"It is, but then I said —" He paused and looked uncomfortably back down at her hand.

"What? You said what?"

"I said, she's not a strange girl, she's the love of my life!" He looked back up into Nancy's eyes; his face taught with nerves in anticipation of her rejection.

"Oh shit! You never!"

"I did." He reaffirmed, wincing in embarrassment.

Nancy stared at him open mouthed. His beautiful blue eyes sparkled in the fluorescence of the light and his soft, plump lips stretched into an uneasy smile. Beep, beep, beep. The alarm on her heart rate monitor began to sound and nurse Kim came flying through the curtains.

"Everything okay Nancy?" She asked, shuffling quickly to her side, trying to examine Nancy and the machine at the same time.

"Yes, fine!" Nancy grumbled, annoyed with her racing heart. "He's just too beautiful to look at." She added in her head.

Francesco smirked at Nancy's obvious embarrassment.

"Can you turn that on silent or off for a moment please." She asked Kim.

Kim grinned, "Not really no, you're still under observation."

"Please, just for a moment." Nancy begged.

Kim deliberated her request for a few seconds then said, "Okay, seeing as you're not alone, but just give me a shout when your visitor leaves and I'll turn it back on."

"Thank you!"

Kim flicked the switch and shuffled back to the end of the bed.

Francesco and Nancy watched her leave, then he turned back to her, "Say something then Nance, the suspense is killing me here!"

"Why did you say that to her?" She whispered.

"Because it's true. I hadn't seen you for so long, but I did think about you all the time and if I'm honest, I've missed you a lot. Then seeing you tonight, just how scared and confused you were, it broke my heart. I'd never seen you so vulnerable and I wanted to protect you; I needed to help you." He paused to admire, the happy tears that glazed Nancy's eyes and softly wiped a droplet from her cheek with his thumb. He then gently took hold of her hand and sniggered to himself, "And, when I saw your naked behind walking away from me, I realised that I didn't want any other man to see that bare arse, but me."

Nancy laughed and pulled him into her. She put her arms around his neck and hugged him tightly.

"You silly bastard!" She sniffed.

"Why am I?"

179

"You've given up miss perfect for me! You do realise that, don't you? You're trading in Barbie for Morticia Addams."

Francesco pulled out of her embrace, but leant in closer, putting his hands at either side of her legs to balance himself, "Would it be really cringy if I clicked my fingers."

"What do you mean?"

"You know, like The Addams Family!"

"Oh my God. Don't. I'll cringe to death!" She put her hands on his to stop him.

He laughed, "I do mean it though Nance. If you'll have me, I want to be with you."

"I just want you to be sure though. I mean, she cooked, she was successful, she went to the gym! I'm, well, I'm, I'm, I'm me!"

"How do you know so much about her?" He grinned.

Nancy paused. It was Lena that had told her about Grace in her dream, but she couldn't tell him that. She quickly scrambled for an answer, "Erm, I just know of her," She lied.

"Oh, okay. Well, anyway, you said you loved me! Is that true?"

"It is! I do love you!" She beamed.

"That's all I want. I don't want weird protein shakes or to constantly be on a strict diet. I don't want to be told how I should dress or be pushed to buy more properties for her benefit, so she can brag to her friends and family about how many I own. Without sounding clichéd Nance, I just want to be loved."

Nancy chuckled, "You are dressed like a pretentious prick!"

Francesco snorted at her insult. "I am!" He looked down at his clothes.

"Did she buy them for you?"

He gave an embarrassed half smile.

"Oh, dear Lord! How many houses did she persuade you to buy?"

He held up three fingers.

"Oh Francesco! Could you even afford them?"

"Not really no, it has been a bit of a worry over the last few months, but by some miracle I've gotten by, thank God. I've actually just sold them and made decent money. I'm going to live in the fourth, you know, the one I originally bought before I met her."

Nancy shook her head. "What a man will do for a pair of boobs!"

Francesco sniggered, "They were pretty big boobs to be fair!"

Nancy hit him playfully in his shoulder.

"You haven't said yes to me yet Nance?"

"I think you should sleep on it."

"No, I've waited for too long already. You said you loved me!"

"I do. I love you so much."

Francesco softly kissed her lips. The electricity felt like she'd just been plugged into the mains.

"Thank God Kim had turned the heart rate monitor off, she would have been back through those curtains like a shot." She thought.

He moved back a little and looked lovingly into her eyes.

It took a few seconds for Nancy to recompose herself, but then she grinned and snorted at him, "You're such a creep."

"Why?" He laughed

"You've just split up with one woman and now you're sitting on another's hospital bed kissing her."

"You'll be the last woman I ever kiss."

"Oh my God! Stop!"

He laughed.

"You and your cheesy lines. I can't cope."

"That's what women like don't they?"

"No! Well not me anyway."

He leant in and kissed her again, but their lips lingered for longer this time, until she gently pushed him away. "You do realise that you have to take me out properly though, on a proper date before all this business!"

"I actually have one planned."

"Go on."

"I have a little snowy cabin booked for a few days. It's in such a beautiful setting."

"Did you just re-gift me your ex-girlfriend's Christmas present?"

He squirmed, "I did, but it's honestly beautiful and – non-refundable."

"Are you joking?" Nancy exclaimed, "Did she know she was going?"

"No and no, which makes it like it was never hers."

Nancy shook her head. "No, it doesn't, you tight sod!"

"Come on Nance it'll be beautiful. I promise. We'll sleep in separate beds if you want."

"You just said it was a little cabin, how many beds does it have?"

"Well just one. But it'll be that cold that you'll need to snuggle into me to keep warm."

Nancy cackled.

"It's not like I'm a stranger though, is it? Come on, it'll be fun!"

Nancy shook her head.

"Don't make me beg." He cracked out his best effort at a movie star like smoulder. It was more Zoolander than Brad Pitt, but it worked. She couldn't say no to that face.

"Fine!" She sighed, "I'll come with you."

"Yes!" He leant in and kissed her again. "In that case I have a little present for you now too." He reached into his pocket and pulled out a wrapped gift, with a little name tag hanging off the underside of it. He handed it to her and she immediately flipped it over to read the tag.

"Oh shit." He fumbled quickly trying to pull the gift back out of her hands, "I forgot to pull that off."

Nancy pushed his hands away. "Oh, for God's sake Francesco!" She groaned, as she read the small piece of card, "Another bloody re-gift."

"I was supposed to pull that off."

"You're such a slimeball." She said throwing it back at him.

"They're thermal socks for the trip." He stuffed them back into his pocket.

"I don't need your ex's socks!"

"I know, I know. Just a shame for them to go to waste too."

"They're socks!" She shrugged.

"I'll give them to my mum." He smiled.

Nancy slid down in the bed and pulled the covers up over her head.

"I'm sorry Nance. I was just trying to make you laugh."

"No, you weren't, you were trying to get your monies worth."

"That is partially true, yeah, but I do really want you to come with me. This is the first time I've actually been excited about it."

"If you didn't want to go, then why did you book it?"

"It was going to be the decision maker for me. I've been thinking about ending things with her for a while and I thought if she was still an uptight bitch in such a beautiful, peaceful setting, it would confirm things for me. Then all of sudden, as if by some miracle, you run naked into my arms." Francesco heard Nancy faintly laugh from underneath the covers. "We're meant to be, you and I."

"If you liked me so much, why didn't you find me and ask me out. Why did you wait till after you saw me naked?"

"I didn't want to commit to anything, until I'd seen what I was getting."

Nancy threw down the covers from her face and glared at him.

"I'm joking, I'm joking. Put that death stare back under there." He pulled the covers back up over her face. "I don't know is the honest answer. I guess I was too worried about ruining our friendship if things turned sour, but, then you turning up out of the blue and telling me that you loved me, I took it as a sign. So, I acted on it."

Nancy let Francesco stew for a few moments, then slowly pulled the covers back down from her face. "I'll go with that." She grinned wryly.

"I'll even buy you your own socks to sweeten the deal."

"Good!"

He quickly kissed her lips again. "Good." He smiled, then began to laugh. "Look at all your makeup smeared over your face! You look like a panda that's been in a fight."

"I've had a very traumatic evening thank you very much!" She grinned, pushing herself back up in the bed.

"I know." He gently held the side of her face and once more studied the cut above her eyebrow. His jovial demeanour seemed to calm and his face became sombre. "I know I've been joking round, but I am so relieved you're okay. If no one had found you Nance, I just, well, I just can't bear to even think about it."

She quickly looked away, "I know." She grumbled.

"I'm so glad you're here." He hugged her tightly and kissed her hair. "You mean so much to me." He then let her go and looked into her eyes. "And even sitting here, right now, looking like the panda that you do, you're the most beautiful woman I've ever seen."

"Oh, Jesus!" She spat at his compliment.

"No, that's not me being cheesy! I genuinely mean that. You're beautiful."

"I know!" She blushed, "You're not too bad yourself either."

He smiled. "I could honestly sit here all night and talk with you, but I'm sure you want to rest. Right?"

"I do actually, sorry! My head is pounding!"

"Oh sorry!"

"No, no, don't be silly! I'm really glad you came."

"I'll get you a proper gift for tomorrow, I promise. One that's your very own."

"No, I was only joking, you don't have to do that!"

"I do! That's what boyfriends do, don't they?"

"Oh, so you're my boyfriend now, are you?"

"Course I am! I mean I'm practically your husband!"

Nancy laughed. "Honestly though, don't get me anything, because I can't get you anything!"

"Steal me a bed pan, so I don't have to walk all the way to the bathroom in the middle of the night."

"You're disgusting!"

"You obviously love it!"

Nancy paused for a few seconds, admiring him. "I do." She smiled. She then put her hands on his face and pulled him in towards her, kissing him more confidently and much harder this time. His aftershave was beautiful and he tasted of mint.

He rocked back and looked surprised at her, "With kisses like that, I'll quite happily stay here with you tonight."

She laughed. "No, you will not. Go!"

He sighed in playful disappointment, "If I must. Call me when you get home and settled though, okay? I'll come see you."

"I will."

"Promise?"

"I promise!"

He kissed her once more. "I love you Morticia Addams!"

Nancy smiled, "I love you too."

"Right then!" He stood up and shimmied to the split in the curtains. "God, I'm so relieved you're okay!"

"I'm glad I ran into you!"

He laughed. "Oh wait. I forgot to mention one more thing before I leave. A funny thing actually. Remember all those drawings you did for me?"

Nancy nodded.

"Well, I kept them all in this little folder thing, but anyways, before I saw you at my house, it was randomly out on my bed. I think Evangeline must have got it out, but what are the odds."

Nancy's face dropped in astonishment. First, she knew all about Grace and now this. *She* had left it out on his bed, not Evangeline.

"Are you okay Nance?"

"Yeah," she whispered, then cleared her throat, "yes, sorry. I just had a sharp pain in my head."

"I'll call someone."

"No, no. It's fine. Are you sure Lena is okay, like you've actually spoken to her?"

"Yes, I told her that you came looking for her, she wants to see you tomorrow remember?"

"Oh yeah course." She smiled awkwardly, "I'll stop talking now."

"You get some rest! I'll go find the nurse to switch your machine back on."

"Thank you!"

"See you nice and early."

"Yes. Goodnight!" She waved.

"Night Nance."

As soon as he disappeared, she threw her arms over her face. "Ouch!" She moaned, as she caught her forehead. She was so confused; she knew she had left it out on Francesco's bed, but how could she of, if she'd never left her bathroom floor. "But Lena." She whispered to herself. Lena said she wasn't going home, yet Francesco confirmed she was alive and well at home. Nothing added up. Maybe Evangeline had just been snooping through his things and it was a strange coincidence. She looked around her bed to see if her phone was on any of the surfaces, but it wasn't, so calling Lena was out of the question. "I'll ask her tomorrow." She mumbled. It was probably for the best. It would be the first time she'd spoken to Lena in a long time and if she started blabbering on about some elaborate dream, "Lena will probably just put the phone down." She thought.

She reached for the control of the bed and lowered her head a little, trying to find a comfier position to sleep. A huge grin spread across her face, as she pictured herself kissing Francesco. She had waited so long to kiss those beautiful lips and now she finally had. It was better than she could have ever imagined, (except for the setting and the circumstances) but it was a slice of heaven in her chaos.

Just then nurse Kim appeared again. "Time for more painkillers." She smiled.

Nancy looked up and grinned, "Thank God for that!"

"I can imagine you've got a headache." She said, handing Nancy a small paper cup containing two pills.

"It's horrendous." Nancy grumbled, sitting up to take them. Kim passed her a glass of water to help her swallow them, then flicked the monitor back on.

"I assume it's safe to put this back on, now your handsome guest has left?"

Nancy snorted into her water. "Yes! Thank you."

Kim chuckled, "Now, try and rest as best you can. I'm sure you don't want to stay in here longer than you have to, especially if he's waiting for you on the outside!"

Nancy responded with a shy smirk.

"I'll come and check on you every now and then, but just press the button if you need me doll."

"I will, thanks."

After Kim left, Nancy lay back and closed her eyes. Waiting for the painkillers to kick in, she began thinking about going to the cabin to take her mind away from the pain, then slowly, she fell to sleep.

18

The Ride Home

Nancy woke to faint mutterings and machines purring in the distance. She slowly opened her eyes to find a new nurse and a doctor at the end of her bed.

"Morning!" The nurse said flatly.

"Morning!" Nancy grumbled.

The doctor said nothing, he was looking down studying a blue clipboard.

"What time is it?" Nancy asked.

"Just gone six thirty."

"a.m. or p.m.?" She squinted.

"a.m. Don't worry."

Nancy stared at the ceiling for a few moments, then reached for the remote to heighten the head of the bed. "Can I go home now then?" She asked, as she sat up.

"I'm just going to take one more look at you." The doctor stated without lifting his head.

Nancy frowned at his arrogance. He put down the clip board, brushed past the nurse, quickly pulled a torch from his pocket and shone it straight into Nancy's eyes.

"Look at me." He instructed, as Nancy squinted out of the light.

"That's a bit bright for this early in the morning." She smiled.

But the doctor ignored Nancy's attempt at humour and continued blinding her with his torch. Her face quickly relaxed from its smile and she opened her eyes as wide as she could. He put his hand to her head, gently felt around her wound and with a little pressure stretched the skin around the cut.

"Ouch! That hurts!" She protested.

The doctor sighed and looked over at the nurse. "It's already started to heal; pupils are fine and her reactions are fine. She can go." He then walked away and pushed out of the curtain.

"Arrogant prick!" Nancy mumbled under her breath.

"What was that?" The nurse asked.

Nancy didn't repeat herself. "Can you call my parents now please?"

"Yes. I'm just going on a tea break hon, then I'll call them, okay?"

"How long is your tea break?"

"Fifteen minutes hon."

"Well, is there a phone I can use now please. They'll be here within fifteen minutes."

"No sorry hon!" She grinned and quickly pushed out of the curtain.

"Helpful!" Nancy huffed to herself.

She sat up and slid the blankets down to her knees. She pulled her feet out of them, then turned to dangle them out over the edge of the bed. It immediately made her think of being out on the cliff edge with Lena. She tried to remember the words from the passage on the paper, then laughed to herself remembering how Lena had called them 'a load of shit'. She pushed herself off the edge and stood up, but the floor was freezing, so she immediately jumped back up onto the bed. "Lena's cold hands." She thought, that's who she remembered being saved by, not Mrs Adams. It was all still so vivid in her mind, every minute detail.

She then noticed a small black sports bag on the floor. She jumped down and unzipped it. It was her clothes; she vaguely remembered seeing her mum with a bag. She emptied it onto the bed and got dressed in a bobbled, beige sweatshirt and a pair of tired, black leggings. She pulled on her socks and pushed on her dirty, chequerboard, Vans slip-ons. It felt so good to be dressed in her own clothes, even if they were borderline rags.

She briefly sat back on the bed and looked down at her beaten-up shoes. She thought about how her Converse had magically appeared on her feet and how she'd banged on the door screaming for Mrs Adams. She shivered at the thought of it, so turned her thoughts to something a little calmer; the excitement of moving back home. Her parents had recently taken a step back from the restaurant, with a new manager having taken over, so they had more free time. "It'll be nice to spend some time with them." She thought.

To Nancy's surprise Francesco's voice suddenly came from behind the curtain "Are you decent?"

"Yes!" Nancy joyfully replied.

"That's a shame." He said poking his head through the parting.

"What are you doing here?"

"I called a while ago to see if you were ready to be picked up. They said you were waiting to see a doctor, so I just drove here anyway. I told your mum and dad last night that I'd come for you."

"Eager."

"Well, I thought the longer you stayed in here, the more time you'd have to sit and stew over whether you'd made the right decision, telling me that you loved me."

"I don't remember saying that!" Nancy protested, squinting at him in confusion.

"Oh!" Francesco looked crestfallen.

"I'm joking." She quickly reassured him.

He put his hand to his heart and shook his head pretending she'd winded him. Nancy walked quickly towards him and threw her arms out to hug him. He caught her by her lips and kissed her, while wrapping his arms around her waist.

"Good morning!" He whispered.

"Morning." Nancy replied, but she quickly pulled out of his embrace, "Can we get going, you smell so fresh and I desperately need to brush my teeth and get a shower!"

"You're not chancing a bath again then?" He teased.

Nancy grinned at him and walked back to get her bag, then both left through the curtains.

They signed out at the ward's front desk, before making their way to the car park. Nancy had no coat, so when they got outside it was like walking into a freezer. Francesco quickly took off his warm, fleece lined, lumberjack jacket and put it around her shoulders. It buried her, but it felt like someone had just switched on a radiator.

"Only minus one today." He smiled.

193

Stood in just his thin cotton top, she could see how much he was suppressing the urge to shiver. "Have your jacket back!" She offered.

"No. The car's just here, we'll whack the heating on."

It was a nice car, Nancy had no idea of the make or model, she had no interest in cars, but it looked expensive.

"Is this yours or a lease?" She asked.

"Mine!" He beamed proudly, taking her bag from her and opening the door to put it on the back seat.

She happily climbed into the front passenger seat. He got in next to her, turned the heating on high, then pulled off.

"Is that okay?" He asked, beginning to navigate the car park.

"Yes. Oh my God, I can't believe it's so cold."

"It's meant to snow again tonight."

Nancy laughed.

"What are you laughing at?"

"Us, talking about the weather!"

He snorted. "Merry Christmas!"

"Merry Christmas." She smiled, putting her hand on the back of his neck and playing with his hair.

"Ah, so glad you're here Nance!"

She turned her head to look out of the window. It was surreal that she *was* here, she thought.

Francesco left her in a contemplative silence for a few moments, then said, "You're very quiet."

"Sorry," she removed her hand and turned to flash him a reassuring smile, then put her hand on top of his as he held the gear stick. "My head is a bit all over the place to be honest."

"Don't apologise! Do you want to talk about it?"

"Not really."

"Just tell me one thing." He paused.

"What?"

"Did you really just slip getting out of the bath?"

Nancy sighed and looked back out of the window, but kept her hand on his. "I don't know what happened to my head. I have no recollection of hitting it." She half lied, "What I do remember though, is the water being too hot, so I'm guessing I just passed out." She kept it as uninteresting as possible, to prevent further questioning.

"The water must have been boiling for you to pass out, why didn't you get out sooner?"

"I don't know." She mumbled. "Can we not talk about it please."

"Yeah, course, sorry." He nodded. "Well, in other news, I went to pick up my dad and a few of his friends from the pub last night, a couple of hours after I'd left you and guess who came over to chat to me?"

Nancy shrugged, "Who?"

"Joel."

Nancy immediately coiled in her chair; her heart dropped at hearing his name. She gave a slight "Oh."

"He told me you walked out of your job yesterday and said you gave him a piece of your mind."

"I did." She proudly confirmed.

"He said you were very dramatic and he messaged you to come out for a drink, to smooth things over."

"He's vile!" Nancy huffed.

Francesco chuckled to himself. "I'm glad that's how you feel about him. I can't believe you went anywhere near him!"

"Oh, Francesco please! I don't want to talk about him or see him ever again."

"That's music to my ears, but the only reason I'm telling you, is because I told him that you were now my girlfriend and to be honest, he was a real jealous arsehole about it."

Nancy's ears suddenly pricked up, "Why? What did he say?"

"Nothing repeatable."

Nancy squirmed, "I hate him!"

"He apparently likes you in his own twisted way."

"Oh God. Stop! I don't want to know."

"I know, I know, that's not why I'm telling you. I'm bringing it up because he attacked me!"

"What?" Nancy cried.

"Yeah! Basically. He was drunk and obviously, you being the topic of conversation it quickly went south, so I gave him a piece of my mind. Then I turned to walk away and he tried to hit me in the back of the head with his glass."

"Oh my God!"

"Yeah. Luckily though, he missed and got me on my shoulder. So, I turned back to face him and he grabbed my jacket and cocked his arm back to punch me, but before he could throw it, I got him, right in his mouth. I knocked his two front teeth clean out and sent him to the ground."

"Oh shit!" Nancy cried. "Are you okay?"

Francesco laughed, "Yes, I had a padded denim jacket on, so it didn't go through. The silly bastard!"

Nancy now noticed Francesco's grazed knuckles. "Are you going to get into trouble?"

"No!" He smiled, "I called the police as soon as it happened. I had about 20 witnesses, all in my favour and the police watched the CCTV, which clearly showed him approach me, then hit me when I moved away. They took him and his teeth to A&E and asked if I wanted to press charges, to which I said no."

"Why?"

"I have no time for that nonsense."

Nancy let out an excited squeal. "Oh God! His teeth!" She grinned, holding her hands up to her cheeks. "Oh, he'll be livid!"

Francesco glanced at her. "That's put a smile on your face!"

"I just can't believe it! Someone finally hit him in his smart mouth!" She wrapped her arms around Francesco's arm and put her head on his shoulder. "Thank you!" She whispered.

"You're welcome. It was actually a pleasure."

Nancy laughed. "What did your dad say?"

"Oh God, when he hit the ground, my dad and his friends were shouting for me to finish him off!" Francesco shook his head in embarrassment. "But I just helped him back to his feet and I got one of the lads there to bring a chair over for him, while we waited for the police."

"You helped him? What if he had tried to hurt you again?"

"I think he knew better at that point!"

"I just can't believe it!" She chuckled, but then quickly became concerned, "Do you think he'll try to sue you for his teeth!"

"No!" Francesco scoffed, "Oh, wait, am I taking you back to your apartment or straight to your mum and dad's?"

"Oh." Nancy paused to think. "Do you have a few minutes to spare or do you need to rush home?"

"No. I can stay as long as you want. Evangeline opened all of her presents at five this morning, so we just all kind of hang around and wait for dinner now."

Nancy smiled, "Five! Aw, I remember being that excited. What did she get?"

"Everything!" Francesco chuckled. "Kind of need to know where you want taking though."

"Oh, yeah, well, can you please help me get my things from my apartment. I don't have much, but I don't want to go back there alone and I'd rather get it out of the way now, so it's done."

"Yeah course, but will someone be up this early to let you in?"

Nancy chuckled to herself, as she thought of Mrs Adams poised by the front door, waiting for her to knock. "Yeah, someone will be up."

"Okay, yeah, just direct me then."

"It's literally just left at these lights, then right and right again."

"I'm looking forward to seeing it. Casa Nancy!"

"I think you'll actually be quite shocked at how basic it is."

"Is it a tent in a field?" He laughed.

"It's not much bigger." She huffed. "Okay, it's that grey building just there, you can park straight in front of it."

Francesco did as she instructed and stopped just outside of the three-story building.

"Brace yourself for Mrs Adams."

"Who's that?"

"My landlady. She's a miserable cow."

"Isn't she the one who saved you?"

"She is, which she'll probably complain about, so get ready!"

They both got out of the car and walked over to the front door. Nancy rang Mrs Adams on the old intercom to the side of it.

"Hello?" Mrs Adams answered.

Nancy took a deep breath, then said, "Hi Mrs Adams, it's Nancy, I –"

Mrs Adams, cut her off.

Nancy dropped her head and stared at the floor.

"I told you she was hard work." She sighed turning to Francesco, but the front door quickly swung open behind her. Nancy span round and there in all her cigarette ash glory was Mrs Adams.

"You stupid girl!" She cried.

"What have I done?" Nancy asked.

"You could have died!"

"It wasn't intentional!"

"It was stupidity!" She looked behind Nancy at Francesco and began to reel off her story. "I had just sat down with a cup of tea, when I heard a loud bang that came from her flat above me, then silence. I usually hear her tip toeing about, but nothing like that. So, I went upstairs, I'm banging on her door, no answer, nothing. I let myself in and I'm shouting her, but still nothing. So, I open the door to the bathroom and the amount of steam that came billowing out of there was ridiculous. I looked down and there she was, unconscious, lying naked on the floor, there's blood all over her head, sick on the mat beneath her, it was a horrible mess. I couldn't see a phone anywhere, so I ran back down the stairs and called for an ambulance. When they were on their way, I ran back up to stay with her and put some towels over her to keep her warm. I don't know why but I pulled the plug out of the bath and the water even then was too hot!" She looked back at Nancy and shouted, "It was too hot, you silly girl!"

"I was so cold!" Nancy protested.

"Oh no, don't you give me that! Do you know how horrible it was for me to find you like that?" She stared sharply waiting for an apology.

Nancy held up her hands in defeat and gave her what she wanted. "I'm sorry Mrs Adams."

"Sorry, sorry! Is that it? And then you just turn back up here this morning, like everything's okay?"

"No, it's not okay. I came to collect all my belongings."

"Beat you to it." Mrs Adams, turned and wheeled out a suitcase that was hiding behind the door. She then reached behind the door again and pulled out a lamp. "Consider this your eviction."

"Wait, what? You can't just go and pack all my belongings?"

"I can and I have. Your mother gave me permission!"

"But —" Nancy was about to protest, when she heard a hoarse, breathless voice to the side of her shout, "Hey you!"

Nancy knew that voice, she reluctantly glanced to her side to confirm her fear. It was Mrs Jones, aka 'The Beast'.

"Fuck's sake!" Nancy mumbled, as she speedily rode towards them on her mobility scooter.

"Heard you got the boot!" Mrs Jones grinned.

"I walked out actually!" Nancy informed her.

"Not what I heard."

"What's this?" Mrs Adams cut in.

"This one," Mrs Jones began, pointing at Nancy, "She got fired yesterday for her lack of customer service."

Mrs Adams looked unsurprised at Nancy and tutted, "Well there you go, you wouldn't have been able to keep up with the rent anyway, would you?" She pushed the lamp into Nancy's arms.

"Nothing like a Christmas morning eviction." Mrs Jones smiled.

Nancy's patience quickly disintegrated. "What is it with you two miserable bitches. Why do you hate me?" She shot both of them a wide-eyed glare, demanding an answer.

The two women just cackled. "Oh, don't be so dramatic!" Mrs Adams began, "We just have no time for you."

"Why though? I haven't done anything to either of you!" Nancy spat.

Mrs Adams smirked at Mrs Jones who shook her head, then looked back at Nancy.

"You're just such a bloody wet blanket." Mrs Adams began, "Nancy, it's like I've had a ghost living above me. Three years you've been here, three years and every time I'd try to speak to you, you were just cold and vacant. Never have I seen you have a friend over, or even a male friend for that matter." She nodded at Francesco, who had now moved back to the car, giving the three women their space. "For so long I've wanted to give you a bloody good shake and wake you up! I've never seen such a young girl so miserable."

"Well, you didn't need to be so blunt with me all the time!"

"I *was* nice when you first arrived!"

Nancy paused for a second to cast her mind back, but before she could respond The Beast cut in.

"No male visitors? That is a surprise!"

Nancy turned to face her, "Why is that a surprise to you, you don't even know me!"

"I've known you a good while!" She barked, "I've seen you in action with that manager of yours. Oh sorry, my mistake – ex-manager." She chuckled.

"You don't know anything!" Nancy hissed.

"Oh, I do. You're like his little lap dog."

Nancy seethed, "For your information, I am not his lap dog and it was me who told that bastard to stick his job, I was not fired."

Mrs Jones smirked at Mrs Adams, then both began to patronisingly applaud her.

"Why are you clapping?"

"Well done! Finally," Mrs Jones said, "you've found your back bone."

Nancy immediately turned away from them and headed for the car. "I'm done with this. Francesco let's go." She handed him the lamp, then dramatically snatched up her suitcase handle and yanked it through the air. Francesco clicked the button on his keys to open the boot and it slowly began to rise. Mrs Jones and Mrs Adams still both stood watching her, she could feel their eyes on her back.

She patiently waited for the door to rise high enough, then clutched her case with both hands to throw it inside. Francesco quickly intervened and caught it mid-air, "Watch the car please darling."

"Oh, sorry." She whispered.

"So, who's this one now?" Mrs Jones goaded.

"None of your business." Nancy retorted and made her way to the passenger door, but in the corner of her eye, she saw Mrs Jones look at Mrs Adams for an answer.

"She spent last night in the hospital, then turned up here with him." Mrs Adams shrugged.

"You move on quickly." Mrs Jones sniggered.

Nancy stopped in her tracks, slammed the car door shut and marched back over to her, stopping just in front of her front wheel.

"What the fuck is your problem?" She hissed through clenched teeth.

Francesco uncomfortably watched on, as he now stood in the road by the driver-side door, shivering, "Just get in the car Nancy. Leave them!" He shouted.

"No. I want to know why this woman is such a vile bitch! Not just to me. But everyone!"

"Get your little whore arse out of the way or I'll run you over!" Mrs Jones snapped.

Nancy stood firmly, "No. Come on. Tell us!"

Mrs Jones' face turned red with rage and she jolted her scooted forward, trying to encourage Nancy to move, but this didn't deter her.

Nancy put her hands on the handle bars and leant in closer, "Tell me." She repeated.

"Nancy, just leave it now. Let her be." Mrs Adams cut in, "That's enough from both of you!"

Nancy looked over her shoulder at the disappointment on Mrs Adams' face and did as she was told. She removed her hands, shot both women an angry glare and once more moved towards the car.

"Do you think I like being known as The Beast." Mrs Jones snarled.

Nancy stopped and once again turned back to her, "I think it's the perfect name to describe you." She smiled.

"I didn't always look like this you know."

"I don't think it's about the way you look. I think it's because you're such a bitch with everyone."

"Because no one is nice to me!"

"I've always been nice to you! Always!" Nancy cried.

"Don't tell lies! Whenever I come into that pharmacy, you're like a robot. It's a fight all the time to get what I need and nobody cares. Do you give me a second thought when I leave?"

"No." Nancy shrugged.

"Exactly. No one does. You either tell me it's not ready or send me to speak to the receptionist at the doctors; which is like pulling teeth. If you'd have just taken a moment to actually help me instead of flirting with that manager, maybe I'd have a little respect for you."

Nancy had no comeback. She'd never thought about it like that before. She looked hard at the woman sitting in the chair. "You're horrible with everyone though."

"Because no one has time for me! I've tried so hard to keep some independence since my accident, but it's so difficult when no one will help me."

"Why aren't your meds right?"

"Because the doctor is useless! I know I can only have some things once a month, but there are others I need sooner and there's no consistency."

"Why don't you just go private?"

Mrs Jones looked at Nancy in disbelief and snorted. "Like that's even an option for someone like me! This is the real-world girl! I don't have the money for that."

This startling revelation of Mrs Jones' sadness, intrigued Nancy. "What happened to you?" She asked bluntly.

"I fell down the stairs in the shopping centre. There was a spilt drink on them. I fell from the top to the bottom, cracked my head open and broke my back in four places."

Nancy winced at the thought of the pain.

"Now I'm on God knows how many tablets and I've blown up like a bloody balloon."

As much as this was a very unfortunate tale, in Nancy's mind it still didn't completely excuse her behaviour, "People don't call you The Beast because of how you look though, it's your attitude!"

"My attitude!" She scoffed, "I can't get into most shops in the high street because either the isles are too narrow for my scooter or there's a big step by the front door and the retail park is quite a distance away. So, I knock on the shop windows for help, but I get told that I have to pre-order online." She sarcastically began to chuckle, "Pre-order milk and bread! The arseholes can't just put those two things through the till for me. Or they helpfully inform me that they deliver, just like you so helpfully informed me. I don't want to be cooped up getting everything delivered and I don't want to go online; I want to be like everyone else and just nip to my local shop when I need to."

The layers of The Beast were unravelling. This woman was so vulgar because of years of being neglected by society.

Nancy suddenly felt sick and averted her gaze. She had only been defending herself from this woman's rage, but she now knew that her rage was very well justified. Nancy hadn't been helpful; she had simply gone through the motions of doing the bare minimum, to get this unpleasant woman to leave as quickly as possible and after she left, Nancy never gave her a second thought. Mrs Jones was simply fighting to be heard; she was fighting to regain the precious normality that had been taken from her.

"You're right." Nancy mumbled as she looked remorsefully back at Mrs Jones, "I'm sorry!"

"Too late now." She snapped, "You would never have been sorry if I hadn't explained myself, would you?"

"No." Nancy sighed.

"No. Exactly. I'd just be another lazy, fat woman to you. So, do me a favour, move yourself out of the way, so I can park my scooter."

"Park it?" Nancy repeated in surprise.

"Yes, I'm spending Christmas day with my sister."

"Oh." Nancy moved to the side. She didn't know of any other women that lived in her building. There was a strange guy in the basement flat, then Mrs Adams and herself in the attic.

Nancy watched as Mrs Adams left the doorway and helped Mrs Jones disembark her chariot. The penny dropped. That's why Mrs Adams was always so cold with her, because Mrs Jones was her sister. Nancy recoiled in embarrassment. She felt like a complete idiot, all this time she had been riding the band wagon so proudly condemning The Beast, when in truth, Mrs Jones was simply a woman pleading for help. She felt so disappointed in herself. If Mrs Jones hadn't shared her story, Nancy would have never seen her for the real person she was, rather than the person she was forced to be. She had been so wrapped up in the war going on in her own mind, that she'd been oblivious to others battling a war in their lives. When Mrs Jones had called her useless, it wasn't an insult, it was simply the truth.

Now watching Mrs Jones hobble towards the front door, guided by her sister, she couldn't just leave with Francesco and put this woman to the back of her mind, she had to help her.

"I would never have guessed that you two were sisters." She said, "You know with the different surnames."

"We have both been married!" Mrs Adams replied without looking at her.

Nancy sighed, "Look Mrs Jones, I'm sorry, truly I am, for everything. I don't expect you to accept my apology, but I do want you to know that I realise now how unhelpful I've been and I have no excuse for it."

At this point Mrs Adams turned round, "Oh Nancy! I've explained to my sister time and time again that you're vacant. I've known for a long time that there's been something going on with you. Obviously, this has been no help to her, but you can't be of help to anyone in that state."

Nancy closed her eyes, raised her eyebrows, then squinted hard trying to hold back her tears. Mrs Adams looked sympathetically at her, while Mrs Jones still scowled.

"It's still no excuse." Nancy whispered.

Unexpectedly, Mrs Adams, with her free arm, put it around her and hugged her tightly. "Welcome back!" She smiled.

"I am so sorry." Nancy sobbed.

"I know you are and I was absolutely devastated when I found you last night, but in all honesty, I wasn't surprised."

"I'd just given up!"

Mrs Adams rubbed her arm comfortingly, "I'm so glad you're still here!"

"Thank you so much for saving me!"

"Well, me being a nosy, old cow finally came in useful, didn't it?"

Nancy snorted "I'm just so thankful!" She moved back out of Mrs Adams' embrace and looked at an unusually quiet Mrs Jones. "I know I don't work there anymore, but I want to help you." She began, "I passed my courses, I sort of know about medication, I'll come with you to the doctors to make sure it's right and then the pharmacy. I'll give you my number and I promise I won't let them fob you off, we won't leave until it's right!"

Mrs Jones' stern face cracked into a half smile, "No. It's fine."

"No, please, let me help you."

"I don't want to put you through the embarrassment of having to go back there."

"I'm not embarrassed. I'm actually proud of the way I left, you did me a favour," Nancy stepped to the side, so the two women could see a very patient and very frozen Francesco still waiting by the car, "and Francesco here, he punched the manager's two front teeth out last night."

Mrs Jones erupted into an excited cackle. "You did?"

Francesco uncomfortably nodded in confirmation.

"About time someone did!" She cried, "Good for you!"

Nancy turned back to the two women. "Please let me help you!"

Mrs Jones took a moment to think, then begrudgingly nodded. "My sister has your number I assume."

"I do." Mrs Adams confirmed.

"Thank you, Mrs Jones!" Nancy smiled.

"It's fine!" She sighed, "Now go. We don't want to be hanging round in the cold all day talking to you!"

Nancy smiled and turned to make her way back to the passenger side of the car. "Merry Christmas." She said looking over her shoulder at them.

"Merry Christmas both!" They replied, already having moved into the doorway.

Nancy and Francesco got into the car and Nancy waved goodbye to the two women, as they set off for her parents' house.

19

The Break-Up

"Well, I wasn't expecting that!" Francesco chuckled.

"Neither was I." Nancy sighed, "I am glad it happened like that though."

"I didn't know you were so low Nance."

"No." She muttered, then paused, "No one did."

"You could have told me!"

Nancy looked quizzically at him, "I'm not going to call you out of the blue and be like, hey Francesco, we haven't seen each other in a while, but I'm feeling a little suicidal can we hang out?"

"Suicidal?" He squinted in shock.

"Well no." Nancy quickly tried to withdraw the comment.

"That's a strong word Nance."

She didn't answer, but she knew that if she was going to make this relationship work, she had to be honest with him too.

"Are you telling me, that last night was a suicide attempt?"

"It wasn't planned and I didn't know it would kill me, but I didn't try to stop it from happening either."

Francesco took a long sharp intake of breath, then slowly and steadily exhaled. He remained silent for a few moments, which Nancy took as his grave disapproval. She awkwardly turned her attention out of the window, waiting for him to say something, but he didn't. She gave him a few minutes more to digest her admission, then turned back to him, "Are you okay?" She whispered.

"Not really no." He bluntly answered.

"Francesco please."

"I just don't have the words." He replied shaking his head. "I don't understand."

"I know, I know."

"You know, but you still did it."

"I wouldn't do it again though."

"What's so different about last night and now. You can't lie to me like that."

"I'm not lying!" She cried. "Everything is different!"

"Just like that?"

"Yes!"

"No, it doesn't happen just like that."

"It has for me!"

Francesco put his hand across his face, slid it down to his chin and rubbed his beard in thought.

"What are you thinking?" Nancy demanded.

"That, I'm just so disappointed in you!"

"Disappointed?"

"Yes! I mean, that's not the woman I know. You're not like that."

"Like what?"

"Aw, Nance, you know."

"No, I don't know, like what?"

"One of those, that you know, can't handle stuff."

"One of those. It can happen to anyone Francesco."

"I know, but you just, you just have to get on with it, instead of sitting around feeling sorry for yourself."

Nancy shook her head. She couldn't believe what she was hearing, "Well, I'm sorry for being weak!" She snapped.

"That's not what I'm saying."

"That's exactly what you're saying. Pull over."

"Oh, don't be like that, I'm allowed to be disappointed, aren't I."

"You're allowed to be however you want to be, but I don't need a lecture from someone like you!"

"Someone like me?"

"Yes. Now pull over."

Francesco did as she commanded and slowly came to a stop. She threw open the door, pulled off his jacket and threw it onto the passenger seat.

"Don't be ridiculous! You can't walk home like that. You're over reacting."

"No. I am not!" She cried, pointing furiously at him, "You know what your problem is?"

"Go on, what?"

"You're so high up on that horse and think you're some kind of oracle of good advice, telling me what I should be doing, telling Lena what she should be doing."

"What do you mean telling Lena what she should be doing?" He interrupted, "We're not talking about Lena."

"It's the same thing! It was the best decision of her life to have that beautiful child, but do you make it easy for her?"

"Lena is a trainwreck!"

"No!" Nancy screamed, "No she is not. She doesn't want to spend time in that house because of how you all treat her!"

"What, buying her food and taking care of her daughter? Yeah, she's got a tough life."

"How dare you think it's that shallow. All you do is pick fault with her, make snide remarks, you push her to go out, and why does she surround herself with these losers, because they don't care about anything but having a good time. That's all she wants, to escape and have a good time. Do you know how much it hurts her when you all jump to criticise her mothering skills, or criticise anything that she does for that matter? Yes, she can't afford her own place, or afford all the things that you can provide for Evangeline, but that woman loves that child more than anything."

"So that's her shitty excuse for why she spends her time with drug addicts in bars, rather than being at home with her daughter?"

"She needs to escape from you all to stay sane for her daughter! Maybe if you were all a little more considerate of her feelings, she'd stay home."

"You don't know anything Nancy. You're obviously as much of a mess as she is and I guess that's why you two are friends."

Nancy trembled with rage, she couldn't argue with him anymore, he'd shown his true colours. He was just like all of her men before him. She slammed the car door shut and stormed off into the cold.

He beeped his horn for her attention, but she didn't turn back, this only infuriated her more, who did he think he was beeping at her? She began jogging to quickly distance herself from his car.

Unusually, he still hadn't driven past her by the time she'd made it up the street to the crossing. She wanted to look over her shoulder to see if he was still parked up or had turned round, but she resisted the temptation.

She hit the button and waited for the crossing signal. After one near death experience, she didn't want to tempt fate and run across, even if the road was quiet.

A single car pulled up to the red light. It was him, he'd planned it and she knew he was looking at her, but she refused to meet his gaze.

"Fuck's sake!" She mumbled to herself waiting for the signal. The two of them stayed in an uncomfortable deadlock for mere seconds, but to Nancy it felt like forever. Finally, the light flashed for her to go and she ignored him as she walked past the front of his car. She held her head high pretending the cold didn't bother her, to prove him wrong about that too. She reached the other side, walked a few paces, then felt the air rumble, as he put his foot down and sped away. Nancy shook her head, "Pathetic!" She seethed. She waited until he was out of sight, then quickly crossed her arms around her body in an attempt at heat preservation and increased her pace to a brisk walk.

Luckily, her parents' house wasn't too far, only a few short streets away.

"What a cold prick!" She thought to herself. She had heard things from Lena, but she'd never seen that side of him for herself. It was a surprise to see him being so unsympathetic and judgmental. As much as she loved him, she wasn't going to be made to feel weak by anyone. Not anymore.

20

The Lost Phone

When she arrived at her parents' front door, she pulled down the handle and walked straight in. She felt an overwhelming sense of relief as the heat hit her and the smell of beautiful food filled the air.

"Hello." She shouted.

Her mum came running out of the kitchen and pounced on her, hugging her tightly. "Merry Christmas!" She sang.

"Merry Christmas." Nancy chuckled, hugging her back.

"Oh my God, you're frozen! Where's Francesco?" Her mum dropped her arms and looked behind Nancy to the door.

"He had to go and get ready." She lied.

"Oh, I told him I'd made breakfast for you both."

Nancy just grinned.

"Oh well, more for you." She smiled.

"Where's Dad?"

"Outside, chopping logs for the fire so he doesn't have to do it later."

Her mum grabbed her hand and led her into the kitchen, "Come on, it'll still be warm."

When her mum said 'breakfast', this was breakfast on another level. A full spread was laid out on the kitchen table. Bacon, sausages, smoked salmon, poached eggs, scrambled eggs with peppers and spring onions, toast and every type of condiment imaginable. It was a buffet for ten people, never mind four.

"Bloody hell mum!"

"Well, I couldn't decide what to make you, so I made everything."

Nancy laughed. "This could feed a family of ten!"

"We're celebrating!"

"Yeah, I suppose it is Christmas."

"No. Not Christmas! We're celebrating you coming home."

Nancy laughed and hugged her. "Thank you!" She whispered.

"I'm just so glad you're still here my angel. We didn't sleep a wink thinking about what you said last night. It honestly broke our hearts." She let go of her daughter, "But you're here and you're well and that's all that matters. I promise things are going to change, it's all downhill from here!"

"Uphill, you mean!" Her dad corrected her appearing in the kitchen doorway.

"No, it's downhill. It's easier to walk downhill, isn't it?"

Her dad shook his head, "When someone's health deteriorates, you say they've gone downhill."

Her mum thought about it for a few seconds, "Well, whatever it bloody is, you know what I mean. Now just sit down both of you and eat."

Nancy and her dad sniggered.

"Morning sweetheart." He said putting his arm around her shoulders and pulling her into him to kiss her forehead. "How was your night with the sick and the sad?"

"Raph!" Her mum cried.

"What?" He grumbled, "You're not in hospital if you're well and happy, are you? I'm just stating facts." He took his seat at the table.

Nancy laughed and sat next to him. "It was okay actually, I just slept."

"Where's Francesco?" He mumbled, with his mouth already full of egg and bacon.

"He had to go home." She lied again.

"Oh, shame." He grumbled. "So, how are you feeling today my darling?"

"I feel really good actually. I went to pick up my belongings from the flat, Mrs Adams had already packed it all for me."

"She said the room was spotless, so she's going to send you back your deposit." Her mum informed her, "She said the only dirt was some black sand on the floor by the sofa, but she thinks the ambulance crew brought that in."

"Black sand?" Nancy said, tucking into her breakfast.

"Yes, she said it was nothing, she just hoovered it up."

Nancy stopped. "Black sand?" She repeated again.

"Yes! A small mound by the sofa."

"Shit!" Nancy choked on her egg.

Her mum quickly hit her on the back, "Are you okay?"

"Yeah. I'm good, I'm good." She gulped down what was in her mouth and looked at her parents in horror, "Did you see my phone anywhere when you went to get my clothes?"

"No." Her parents shook their heads.

"Oh." Nancy went pale.

"Are you okay? Have you lost it?" Her mum asked.

217

She didn't answer. The last time she'd seen her phone; it had disintegrated into black sand and slipped through her fingers onto the floor next to her sofa.

"Nancy, have you lost it?" Her mum repeated.

"Yes," She spluttered, "Do you have Mrs Adams' number?"

"I wrote it down last night, it's on the piece of paper by the phone."

She quickly got up from the table. Her dad didn't look up from his breakfast.

"What's the matter?" Her mum called after her.

"I just need to ask her if she's seen it."

"You can do that after breakfast."

"No, I need to know now." Nancy insisted, abruptly leaving the room to use the phone in the hall. She quickly grabbed it and dialled the number on the paper. It only rang once before Mrs Adams picked up.

"Hello?" She answered.

"Hi, Mrs Adams, it's Nancy again."

"Again!" She sighed.

"I know, sorry to bother you, but I just wanted to ask really quickly if you'd seen my phone when you packed my things? I think I may have lost it walking home from work last night."

"No, there was no phone." She replied, "I even moved the cushions from the sofa when I was hoovering."

"Yes. My mum told me about some sort of black sand?"

"I told your mum that it was nothing and I'll send you back your deposit."

"Yes, she told me, thank you for that. Okay, no worries, I'll leave you to it. Sorry to bother you again. Goodbye."

"Bye Nancy."

Nancy ended the call and dropped her hand to her side. She stared in silence at the wall in front of her. First of all, she knew about Francesco's girlfriend Grace, then, Francesco mentioned the book of drawings, then, there was sand where her phone had disintegrated, but Lena was alive.

"Nancy?" Her mum shouted from the kitchen, "Nancy did she find it?"

"No." Nancy responded quietly.

"What was that?"

"No." She repeated louder.

"Are you coming back to eat breakfast then?"

Nancy placed the phone back on its hook. She had suddenly lost her appetite. She needed to know the truth and the only person who possibly knew that, was Lena. She grabbed her mum's coat and hat from the coat rack.

"I'm just going to re-trace my steps." She shouted from the hall, "See if I can find it." She heard a chair in the kitchen screech across the tiled floor, so she turned, to find her mum standing in the doorway of the kitchen, her brows slopped with concern.

"Can you not eat breakfast first?"

"No. I won't be long. Just save me some please."

"Why do you need it so much?"

"It's just a rigmarole to have to cancel things and then try and get a new one over Christmas. If it's gone, it's gone, but I just want to check."

"I think you should at least wipe your face first!"

Nancy looked at herself in the mirror by the stairs. Her face was still smeared with makeup and she still hadn't brushed her hair. She didn't have time though, she needed to know now.

"No one is going to see me! I ran through the streets naked last night, so I'm actually well-dressed compared to that." She chuckled.

Her mum closed her eyes, shook her head and exhaled loudly in disapproval.

"Don't be like that Mum. I won't be long! I promise." She walked back to her mum, kissed her on the cheek, then quickly turned to open the front door and pulled her mum's hat onto her head.

"Don't be long!" Her mum huffed behind her.

"I won't." She repeated and quickly shut the door.

21

Did it Happen?

Although she desperately wanted to know the truth, her brisk walk slowed, as the warmth of the morning sun calmed her. She was filled with an overwhelming sense of contentment. To now be stood admiringly in the flood of its grace, was a stark contrast from being rattled with fear in the dark of the previous night. She was alive and she felt it. She noticed everything. The minutia of the day; the rumble of a car in the neighbouring street, the distant bark of a dog and the loud bird chorus as she walked past the bare trees of the park. She stopped as she saw a small robin on a fence post ahead of her. It sang so beautifully, proudly puffing out its chest, then sucking it back in, as it breathed through notes. It was something she would never normally take the time to even register, but today she marvelled at its vivacious spirit. She smiled to herself in thought; like sleeping beauty she had been awoken, but not by true love's kiss, no, she had been awoken by a kick up the arse from Lena.

Finally, she reached the foot of Lena's driveway. She had now acclimatised to the cold and felt quite at home being outside. Like a child, she watched the small clouds of steam float from her mouth, thinking that the last time she stood in this spot, her world had fallen apart as she sobbed and begged for Lena not to leave her. Now, she had the freedom to find enjoyment in simply breathing. Then, it suddenly occurred to her, did she really need to know the truth? If it was real or not, did it matter? There was something magical about how she felt today, regardless. She walked up the driveway and stood on the doorstep trying to decide whether to ring the bell or walk away. "No!" She whispered to herself, she did want to know if Lena had been there. She pushed the door bell and turned to look out onto the street while, she waited for someone to answer. She noticed Francesco's car wasn't in the driveway, "Thank God!" She mumbled to herself. She hadn't even thought about what she might say or how she'd act if she saw him.

The door flew open, Nancy quickly turned her head at the sound and there standing in her pyjamas, with a very unimpressed look on her face was Lena. Her face immediately changed to surprise when she saw it was Nancy.

The two stood in silence for a few moments, staring awkwardly at one another, until Nancy dove in and hugged her tightly. "It's so good to see you!" She cried.

Lena quickly stood out of her embrace and frowned in disgust at Nancy's appearance, "You look like shit!"

"I *have* just got out of hospital!" Nancy chuckled, wiping happy tears from her eyes.

Lena shook her head and grinned, "Come in then!" She moved to the side of the doorframe, so Nancy could enter. "Hurry up! It's bloody freezing!"

"Where's your mum and dad?" Nancy asked.

"Francesco's gone to pick them up from church. My dad had too much to drink last night so couldn't drive."

Lena led them down the hallway into the kitchen and there sat at the table was Evangeline finishing her breakfast. The little girl looked up at Nancy and smiled.

"Merry Christmas Evangeline." Nancy greeted her.

The little girl mumbled back shyly.

"Did Santa bring you lots of toys?"

Evangeline nodded, then looked at her mum.

"This is Nancy." Lena began, "She would be Auntie Nancy, but she's been absent for…how many years is it now?" Lena stared at Nancy, frostily awaiting a response. Evangeline looked back at Nancy too in confusion, to which Nancy comically rolled her eyes and shrugged.

Evangeline then picked up her bowl and showed her mum it was empty. "I've finished."

"Good girl!" Lena praised her loudly, "You can go and play with your toys now." The little girl jumped down from her chair and flew past Nancy into the living room across the hall.

"Tea? Coffee?" Lena asked.

"Coffee please!"

"Well sit down then!" Lena snapped impatiently, gesturing to the table.

Nancy pulled out a chair and slid into it quietly. Lena appeared quite cold and irritated, in fact, Nancy felt a little unwelcome, so she sat in silence waiting for Lena's que to talk.

Lena flicked on the kettle, then turned to reach up for the coffee mugs on the top shelf of one of the kitchen cupboards and as she reached up, her pyjama top rose to reveal severe bruising on her ribs.

"Oh my God! It's true!" Nancy cried. She didn't know what she was more shocked by, the evidence of last night being real or the severity of Lena's bruising. Lena quickly snatched the mugs down and pulled down her top to conceal the healing wound. She placed the cups on the sideboard, paused, then continued to make the drinks, deliberately ignoring Nancy's revelation.

"Lena! It was real!" Nancy exclaimed.

Lena carefully placed the teaspoon into the sink, then put her head against the high cupboard and dropped her shoulders.

"Lena?" Nancy prompted.

Lena sighed, then looked over her shoulder, "Well, we both know I'm not bruised from you throwing that pathetic cushion at me!" She turned to face Nancy and her face beamed into a mischievous smile.

Nancy dropped her head into her hands and burst into tears. It was true, it was real!

Lena walked over to her and held her tightly. "Don't cry Nance. You already look a sight, don't make it worse!"

"You're alive!" Nancy croaked holding Lena's arm tightly.

"Shush. Keep your voice down!" She hissed.

"Sorry, I'm just so happy!" Nancy sniffed. "You made it home!"

Lena kissed Nancy on top of her head, then let go of her to bring the coffees to the table. She gently placed the white matching mugs down and sat next to Nancy, while reaching to hold her hand.

"I'm so sorry Lena!" Nancy whispered trying to compose herself.

Lena sat back in her chair and shook her head, "It's not your fault and I never should have insinuated that last night. You didn't put me in that car; it was nothing to do with you *or* my family. I was blaming everyone else because I felt so guilty and I just couldn't accept what had happened."

Nancy sniffed and smiled, "I love you."

"I love you too! I'm so glad you made it back Nance!"

"What happened to us?"

Lena put her hand back on Nancy's, then turned slightly and looked to the kitchen window. A strong beam of light illuminated her face, making the tears in her eyes sparkle. It was as if Nancy was glimpsing the remnants of the angel she had journeyed with.

"We fell apart!" Lena choked.

Nancy squoze Lena's hand.

"You were such a pathetic mess!" Lena chuckled, turning back to her friend and wiping her eyes.

"I can't believe it," Nancy whispered, "it was real?"

Lena nodded in confirmation, then took a sip of her coffee.

"What happened to you when you left me then?"

"It was insane." Lena whispered, "I went back to the crash site and saw my body still stuck in the car. Honestly Nance, it was horrifying. Like, I don't think that image will ever leave me!"

"Oh God!" Nancy grimaced.

"Anyway, I was told to sit back in the car, then stand back out, which took me a while because I was terrified. I eventually did it though, but it was bizarre, when I looked back, the tree branch had still skewered the passenger seat but my body wasn't there anymore and there wasn't even a spec of blood on the seat!"

"What?" Nancy mouthed.

"I know. Then I was told to not look back and walk home."

"Were you in pain?"

"I was! My adrenaline numbed it a little, but what happened next was even weirder. As I walked out of the trees, I tried to look under my t-shirt, but it was too dark. So, I waited till I got back out onto the street and oh my God Nance, it was disgusting. Like it actually made me gag."

"Oh my God, don't tell me!"

"There was a hole, like literally a *Death Becomes Her* hole!"

"I said don't tell me!" Nancy grimaced at the thought.

"I could see my actual ribs."

"Lena!" Nancy protested.

The colour drained from Lena's face and she pushed her coffee away.

"What did you do?" Nancy asked.

"I fucking panicked! But I had to do something, so I walked home."

"Why didn't you go to the hospital?"

"I was alive walking round with a fucking big hole right through me! What do you think they would have said at the hospital?"

"So, what then?"

"As soon as I got in, I grabbed the first aid kit and my mum's sewing tin, ran upstairs and locked myself in the bathroom."

"What the hell were you going to do with the sewing tin?"

"Sew myself back up, obviously."

Nancy threw her hand up to cover her mouth and winced at Lena behind it. "Please tell me you never sewed it up!"

"No." She smiled with relief. "I didn't have to, thankfully! Can you imagine?"

Nancy shook her head and frowned in disgust.

"When I looked at it again in the bathroom, there was still lots of blood, but the hole had pretty much closed up. So, I jumped in the shower to wash all the blood away and it kind of washed away with the blood. It's completely gone, not even a pin prick or scar left, like it just disappeared. Obviously, I'm bruised to hell as you can see," She lifted her top to show Nancy, "but Nance, honestly, I swear, it was a huge hole!"

Nancy grimaced again and uncomfortably rubbed her lips at what she was seeing and hearing.

"Did you hear anything else? Like, the person that had been talking to you?"

Lena dropped her top back down. "No, gone and I didn't know what to make of it all. I thought maybe because the crash was traumatic, I'd imagined the hole and the whole night. But then Francesco came through the door, saying you had run half naked through the streets, covered in blood, with an ambulance chasing you to see if I was alive." She laughed.

Nancy's face tightened in embarrassment, "I did!" She moaned, "but I just had to know if you were okay."

"I appreciate that!" Lena smiled.

"Do you think there's a catch to what happened then, or is that it?"

"I think we'd be silly to throw away the second chance we've been given, put it that way!"

"No, I know that, but has it come at a cost, like, is there a price. I mean, how often does this happen?"

"I don't know, but even if it did happen to people, they're not going to say anything are they?"

"No, that's true. But why us? Out of all the millions of people in the world who deserve to live, why us?"

"I don't know and I'm not going to question it! I get to stay here with Evangeline, that's all that matters to me."

"It just doesn't make any sense though."

"Or maybe it makes perfect sense. We've been given this epiphany, this gift. We're awake now."

Nancy laughed, "When did you become so profound?"

"When I lay dying in the woods with a tree branch stuck through my body." She frowned.

Nancy exhaled and pushed back to rock on the two back legs of her chair.

"I tell Evangeline off for doing that, don't rock on your chair."

"Oh, sorry." Nancy quickly put the chair back on all fours.

"We just need to appreciate what we've been given." Lena looked sternly at her, awaiting her compliance.

"No, I agree, I do. It's just crazy."

"I think getting mauled by that pissing wolf was crazy!" Lena grinned.

"Oh my God that was horrendous! I —"

"Wait, how did you get home?" Lena interrupted.

"I followed you, but I woke up on my bathroom floor surrounded by paramedics. They said I'd hit my head on the radiator, but I hit it on the ground, didn't I? You know, when it was windy by the cliff?"

"Yeah, it wasn't in the bathroom."

"Thank you for pulling me out the bath by the way!"

"You were so bloody heavy. You literally dropped to the floor like a fat fish, flapping back and forth."

Nancy chuckled, "I was in so much pain!"

Lena squoze her hand tightly, "Joking aside Nance, I was so upset to see you like that under the water. You were just floating, really still."

Nancy looked down at the table and her face fell into deep regret.

"Promise me you'll never let yourself get that low again!"

Nancy didn't raise her head.

"Nancy, promise me!"

She kept her gaze on the table, "I promise." She muttered.

"That's not convincing!"

"No, I do, I promise. I just feel embarrassed and guilty, having you and Mrs Adams find me like that."

"Mrs Adams?"

"Yeah, my landlady."

"Well don't be embarrassed! We need to keep talking, but maybe some other time. It's all a bit raw and heavy today."

Nancy looked up and half-heartedly smiled. "I agree. What shall we talk about instead then?"

"You and my brother?"

"Oh God no." Nancy squirmed and looked back down into her coffee, "I had an argument with him."

"Already?" Lena laughed.

But before Nancy could continue, the sound of the front door being pushed open echoed down the hallway and into the kitchen. They both turned to greet the new arrivals. Lena's mother was the first to enter the room, quickly followed by her father.

"Nancy!" They exclaimed in unison, "Merry Christmas!"

"Merry Christmas!" She responded, standing to hug them.

"Oh God, look at the state of your head! And your face for that matter! Are you okay my darling?" Mrs Ferrara hugged her tightly once again and kissed her cheek.

"I'm fine!" She smiled.

"Fancied a Christmas Eve streak last night, did you?" Mr Ferrara chuckled.

"I did!" Nancy cringed.

He put his arm around her smirking and pulled her into him to kiss the top of her head. "It was a very interesting night on the whole. I wonder if Santa put your friend's two front teeth back in?"

Nancy laughed.

"What friend?" Mrs Ferrara asked.

"No one you know." He slyly winked at Nancy, then left the kitchen.

Nancy shot Lena an embarrassed look.

"I heard the universe rewarded Joel!" She smiled.

"Who's Joel?" Mrs Ferrara asked looking at Nancy.

"I'll tell you later Mum!" Lena replied, saving Nancy the explanation.

Mrs Ferrara rolled her eyes. "Francesco was strange in the car before. He's in such a short mood, how was he with you this morning?"

"Fine!" Nancy lied.

"Maybe Grace is giving him a hard time again!" Lena interjected.

Mrs Ferrara tutted, as she hung her coat on the back of one of the chairs, "Yeah, probably. I'm not fussed on that snobby bitch.".

When her back was turned, Lena quickly mouthed to Nancy, "She doesn't know about you two."

"Oh." Nancy mouthed back.

"Did Lena tell you about what happened to her prince charming last night?" Mrs Ferrara interrupted. She flicked on the kettle, then sat at the table to join them. It was just like old times, Mrs Ferrara loved a bit of gossip and drama, which was probably why nobody told her anything.

"No!" Nancy shook her head, then looked at Lena in fake surprise.

Lena rolled her eyes.

"Go on Lena, tell her!"

"He crashed his car into a tree!" Lena sighed.

"Oh God! Was he okay?" Nancy asked.

"He was fine!" Lena replied quickly.

Mrs Ferrara tutted under her breath, "Nancy, if Lena was in that car last night, she wouldn't be here! The whole passenger side was like a pin cushion; it had that many tree branches through it! She would have been killed instantly!"

Nancy looked awkwardly at Lena, who had pulled her coffee back to her and was now looking down into it.

"He was drunk!" Mrs Ferrara continued, "Fled the scene! Luckily, Mrs Blackwell told me in church that they'd found and arrested him!" Her words appeared to be followed by an awkward stand-off between mother and daughter. Lena grinned at Nancy, while Mrs Ferrara glared at Lena.

"Well, thank God no one was hurt!" Nancy cut in.

Lena didn't respond, but Mrs Ferrara looked at Nancy and dramatically huffed, "What am I going to do with this girl?"

Nancy smiled and quickly changed the subject, "Where's Francesco?"

"He's gone to his house. You'll see him later. Your mother and father have invited us this evening."

"Oh, right." Nancy nodded. She could feel the dread creep into her stomach. It was going to be awkward being with Francesco in front of everyone.

"I'm not sure if he's bringing Grace. I think they had an argument about him coming to visit you last night."

Lena sniggered as she pushed herself up from the table and moved to stand in the doorway of the kitchen.

Mrs Ferrara frowned, "Why are you laughing?"

Lena ignored her question and changed the subject, "It's good that we're coming over later, Evangeline has a Lego Princess castle that isn't going to build itself! I'll bring it for you to do for her."

Nancy snorted, "Already dishing out your orders!"

Lena smiled and moved just outside of the doorway.

"Making up for lost time aren't I." She grinned, "Anyway, as wonderful as it's been to see you, I'm going to get ready now and if I were you, I'd do the same. Do us all a favour and get a bloody shower! You look like shit and smell like hospital!" With these words she disappeared and began to climb the stairs.

"That girl!" Mrs Ferrara whispered shaking her head.

Nancy laughed; she had missed how straight-talking Lena was. It was one of the things she had missed most about her, because more often than not it was what she needed. "She's definitely one of a kind."

"Do you want another coffee?" Mrs Ferrara asked.

"No, no thank you, I better go see my mum and dad! *And* get a shower."

"I'll see you out!"

Both got up and moved into the hall.

"See you both later." Nancy shouted into the living room.

"Bye Nance! See you later." Mr Ferrara shouted back.

As Nancy opened the front door Mrs Ferrara threw her arms around her and hugged her tightly! "I'm so glad you're okay my beautiful girl!" She sniffed, "I didn't want to make a big thing about it in front of Lena. Your parents told me about what happened last night and how your landlady found you. I was in bits! You know I love you so much!"

"I love you too!" Nancy replied, hugging her tightly.

She sniffed loudly in Nancy's ear.

"Don't cry!" Nancy chuckled, moving out of her embrace. She held her hand to comfort her. "Everything is okay!"

"We could have lost you both last night!"

"But you didn't!" Nancy smiled, "She wasn't in that car!"

Mrs Ferrara couldn't respond she was too choked with tears, so Nancy hugged her tightly once more. "Come on. Please don't cry!" She whispered.

"I'm okay. I'm okay. I'm so glad Francesco came to see you last night and he didn't listen to that bitch Grace. He put my mind at rest when he came home and told me you were in good spirits. He was so happy to see you!" Mrs Ferrara stood back and dabbed her eyes with a clean tissue she pulled out of her sleeve. A relieved smile crept slowly across her face. "I couldn't have asked for anything more precious than to have both my girls come back to me. I've missed you so much!"

Nancy smiled, "We'll have a good catch up about everything later!"

"Yes! I'll look forward to it."

"I do have so much to tell you!"

"I can't wait!"

"I'll see you later then!"

"Yes, yes, you go. See you later my darling!" Mrs Ferrara smiled.

Nancy walked down the driveway, silently waved another goodbye and walked out onto the street.

22

Uncle Pete

Back at her parents' house she'd finally had a shower, the dark makeup smears were no more and her hair was clean. Luckily, her parents had bought her new clothes as a Christmas present, seeing as Francesco was still MIA with all her belongings. She used some of her mum's face cream to smooth her dark eyebrows into place, but didn't bother with any other makeup, she couldn't be bothered, she felt exhausted.

As she sat upstairs in her room alone, just taking a moment to collect her thoughts, she was overjoyed to have finally rid herself of the impersonator that had been inhabiting her body. Not only had she physically come home; she was now back home in her heart and was going to do everything in her power to keep it that way. She knew the value of her precious time, the significance of controlling her fear and the importance of being less critical of herself. Her search for perfection or her version of utopia had disconnected her from reality, so much so, that she had become blinkered to everything but its aspirational siren song.

She lay on her bed and looked at the ceiling. "I'm going to write!" She whispered to herself. "That's what I can do. That's what I'm good at!"

She jumped off her bed and went out onto the landing where there stood a rustic, wooden dresser. She knew there would be paper and a pen in one of the drawers. She rustled through them and found an empty note pad and a black biro, but just as she slid the drawer shut, she heard the front door open and got *the* call from downstairs.

"Nancy, the family are here!" Her mum shouted.

She fell dramatically against the dresser with dread.

"Nancy? Are you coming?" Her mum called again.

"Just give me a minute." She shouted back. She went back into her room and put the pad and pen on her bed, then turned to look at herself in her full-length mirror. She liked her new clothes, blue, high-waisted jeans and a cropped, white sweatshirt. She walked closer to the mirror to examine her cut and debated whether to quickly hide some of the bruising with her mum's makeup, to lessen her arsehole of an uncle's focus on it. She felt gently around it. It would be too sore to clean the make-up off afterwards, she thought, so she decided she'd let him see it in all its gory glory.

She left the room and began to descend the stairs. "Here we go!" She sighed. When she reached the bottom step, she looked into the mirror opposite, forced her face into a fake, exaggerated smile and held it. "Hi everyone!" She mumbled, as she entered the living room.

Her two cousins immediately turned and smiled. They both greeted her with a "Merry Christmas Nance," and stood to give her a one-armed loose robotic embrace. Her uncle, however, didn't look up and remained in conversation with her dad, whilst his wife, her step-aunt Sue, stayed slouched in a chair in the corner. She gave her a half smile; it was obvious she was already drunk.

"Your dad has just been telling us about you slipping in the bathroom last night Nance. Looks like a nasty bump you've got there." One of her cousins said.

"Glad you're okay!" The other added.

Their comments immediately caught her uncles' attention and with his cold, grey eyes, he looked up at her. He was an odd shaped man, like an upside-down pear, with grey, receding hair and a thin slither of a mouth. His clothes were all designer, tailored to an inch of their life and he had a sharp nasal quality to his voice.

"Yeah," Nancy replied nervously, "wasn't an ideal way to spend Christmas Eve." She chuckled.

"What a mess!" Her uncle blurted from across the room, "Trust you to make Christmas Eve dramatic."

This comment although mild, infuriated her. If it was from another member of her family, she'd have laughed it off, but she couldn't tolerate this arse wipe's sly jibes. She reluctantly grimaced at him in response.

"As long as you didn't keep your mum from cooking my dinner, I'll let you off!" He added.

"He'll let me off?" Nancy thought, "He'll let me off!" She looked at her dad and flared her nostrils, but her dad closed his eyes and slightly shook his head, signalling for her to stand down. She did as she was told, she obediently turned and walked out of the room into the kitchen to cool off.

She found her mum plating up the food onto an array of dishes.

"There she is!" Her mum smiled at her appearance, "You look beautiful my angel. Your clothes fit lovely." She dropped what she was doing to walk over and give her yet another hug and kiss. "Have you said hello?" She asked.

"Yes." Nancy grumbled rolling her eyes.

"Just ignore him, he won't be here that long." She whispered.

Nancy pulled a face of disapproval at her mum, then moved over to the prepared dishes. "Shall I start taking them through to the table?" She asked.

"Yes. Everything else is set up."

Nancy picked up the Brussels sprout masterpiece, along with a gravy boat and walked through the kitchen into the adjoining dining room. She put them down on the table and admired all her parents' hard work. The table was a festive treat, it looked like a feast table from some medieval castle, the only thing that was missing was a boar's head with an apple in its mouth. Her dad was right, there had been so much effort put into this meal, that it would have been selfish of Nancy to spoil it by confronting her uncle. She could grin and bear him for the sake of her mum.

Her mum then appeared behind her with a tray of the last few dishes and condiments. "There!" She said, "What do you think?"

"It looks amazing mum!"

"You take a seat and get started; I'll go and tell the others to come through."

Nancy sat down and quickly began to fill her plate with everything she wanted, so she wouldn't have to ask anyone to pass her anything. She couldn't be bothered making any more conversation than she needed to. Then, just as she began pouring the gravy over her meal, she heard her uncle gasp from behind her.

"How rude, starting without us!" He roared.

"I wasn't starting, I was just making up my plate." She snapped back.

"Well, you should have waited." He said scornfully, moving to sit at the head of the table.

"It's her house!" Her dad chimed in, grinning at his brother-in-law and moving to sit opposite him.

Nancy smiled at her dad, then scowled at her uncle, but he appeared to totally ignore her dad's comment and was now too engrossed in collecting all the food he could, mounting it onto his plate. Her mum sat down next to her and her cousins and step aunt sat opposite, leaving an empty space next to Nancy. There was silence as everyone gathered their food, other than polite requests to pass certain things around the table, there was no other conversation. Nancy glanced over at her step-aunt's sparse plate of two or three roast potatoes and a small piece of boiled ham. She was sat back nursing a tumbler of whiskey staring at it. She was either building up the courage to eat it, or she was scared to put her drink down, in case someone took it from her.

"How's your businesses going Sue?" Nancy asked.

This question seemed to please her, she looked up from her plate and smiled, "Really well thank you. We've got two more clinics opening soon and another store, so it will be three clinics and eight stores all together. It's so much work, such a headache, but I'm so proud." She beamed.

"Amazing!" Nancy smiled, but that was the end of the conversation. Sue's head immediately dropped back down and her dry, brown hair framed her staring competition with her meal.

"I'm really proud of her." Her uncle cut in, "She works so hard."

"She hits the bottle pretty hard too," Nancy thought to herself, "but anyone would if they had to live with you."

"We're all hard workers in our family and we reap the rewards." He continued.

Nancy didn't look up; she kicked herself for speaking. She knew where this was going and she wasn't going to let him antagonise her. Head down, she silently continued to enjoy her food.

"John here has just bought himself a holiday home in Canada and Tom has just bought majority shares in a beautiful vineyard in California. I've just expanded my business too, so we're all climbing the ladder."

Nancy raised her head to watch him grin at her mum and unfortunately, he caught her eye, "What are you doing with yourself these days Nancy?" She was about to answer, but he quickly cut her off by adding, "Besides attention seeking trips to A&E."

"I slipped in the bathroom," she hissed, "how is that attention seeking?"

"I'm only joking." He chuckled, as her mum glared at him.

"I'm a writer now actually and I've just written my first novel." She lied, hoping it would deaden the conversation before she snapped.

"Oh, anything worth reading?" He sniped.

"Obviously," she frowned, "or I wouldn't have bothered writing about it, would I?"

"Do you want some gravy, Sue?" Her mum cut in trying to redirect the conversation.

Sue, shook her head and mouthed back, "No thank you."

"No, what I mean is, are you any good at writing? You know, or is this just another one of your pointless ventures?"

Her mum slammed her cutlery down on the table and knocked her chair flying backwards, as she jumped to her feet. "Enough!" She cried, "Enough! I will not have you sit here, eating our food and drinking our wine, while you take swipes at our daughter."

"Carmela I was just —"

"No. Now you listen to me. For too long I have sat back and watched you do it, since she was little you've belittled her. You've always done the same to me, but brother or no brother, I'm telling you now, it stops."

"No, I have not!"

"I'm not going back and forth over this with you! I'm telling you now; it stops!"

"Well, I'm sorry you feel that way, but someone has to give her a reality check, maybe if you gave her a few home truths every now and then, she wouldn't be back living at home at her age."

Her mum pursed her lips and looked over at her husband, who was poised ready to support his wife and daughter. She nodded at him, finally giving him the permission he so desperately wanted, to say, "I think it's best if you all leave."

Her mum smiled at him. "I do too. I really do. We're not having another Christmas listening to your bullshit."

"Excuse me? You're telling *me* to leave?" Her uncle spluttered.

"Yes!" Her mum snapped. "I'm telling you to leave! Stop eating and please go."

"Don't be ridiculous Carmela!"

"I'm not! I've had enough and I'm telling you to leave!"

"It's just tough love! That's probably why Nancy is so overly sensitive, she gets it from you." He laughed.

Her mum looked down at her food and closed her eyes. "Get out!" She hissed.

"Oh, come on!"

At this point Nancy's dad jumped to his feet. "Pete, enough is enough. You heard my wife, please leave."

Her uncle huffed in astonishment and jumped to his feet. "Tom, John, Sue." He individually pointed at them commanding them to join him. All immediately put down their cutlery and begrudgingly, got up and shuffled round the table to the door with Sue still cradling her whiskey.

"Last chance Carmela!" He warned.

"Apologise to my daughter and you can finish your meal!"

"Apologise for what?" He shrugged.

"Get out Pete! Just piss off!" She shouted.

Her uncle glared at Nancy, "Let's go!" He snarled.

Her cousins and Sue kept their eyes to the floor in embarrassment and silently followed his lead.

Nancy and her parents remained at the table and patiently listened for the sound of the front door to confirm their departure. When they heard it slam shut, her mum pulled her chair back to the table and sat down. She put her head in her hands and sighed, as she rubbed her forehead in thought.

Nancy sheepishly looked at her dad, who had now moved into the empty seat next to her and relocated his meal and drink. He put his arm around her shoulders and comfortingly pulled her into him. He then let go of her and continued to eat, motioning for Nancy to do the same.

"I'm sorry Mum!" She whispered.

"You've got nothing to be sorry for." Her mum quickly reassured her, looking up from her hands and smiling. "I will not sit here and listen to that man bully you anymore. I just can't believe it's taken me thirty years to finally call him out for it. I'm the one who should be saying sorry."

Nancy put her head on her mum's shoulder and her mum rested her head against her daughter's.

"Now, come on, let's just eat and enjoy our day!" Her mum smiled.

Nancy lifted her head and all three tucked into their meals. The heavy atmosphere had lightened, the wine tasted sweeter and every mouthful of food was more satisfying. Nancy could relax, as once more, it felt good to be home.

23

The Apology

After dinner, all three helped to clear the table and fill all shapes and sizes of Tupperware with leftovers. Once the dishwasher had been filled, her mum washed the remaining pots and pans in the sink, with Nancy and her dad on drying duty.

There was a knock at the front door and they all stopped to look at the clock.

"What time is everyone coming?" Nancy asked.

"Not for another hour!" Her mum shrugged.

"Maybe it's Sue asking for a refill in the tumbler she took!" Her dad joked.

Nancy laughed, but her mum wasn't amused. "I'll go and answer it." Nancy grinned.

She walked out into the hallway and cautiously opened the front door, readying herself to deal with an unwanted family member, who had either forgotten something or in Sue's case was returning something. However, to her surprise, it was neither. Standing there before her, was Francesco. Her heart began to race, no matter how disappointed she was in him, he was just too beautiful! Especially today, in his shirt.

"What are you doing here?" She asked coolly, stepping outside and closing the door behind her, to prevent her parents from prying.

He fumbled for his words. "You look beautiful!" He eventually managed to say.

Nancy squinted at him in annoyance. "So earlier I was a trainwreck and now I'm beautiful! I don't have time for your mood swings Francesco!" She turned her back on him and reached for the doorhandle to go back inside.

"No, wait!" He said, gently catching her free hand. Nancy glared at him over her shoulder, so he quickly dropped her hand and took a step back.

"I-I just came to apologise." He stuttered.

Nancy let go of the handle and turned to look at him. "Go on!"

"I was out of order before! Completely out of order!"

"You were!" Nancy agreed.

"It was just so upsetting to hear," he continued, "I was really disappointed in you for doing something like that!"

"Francesco, you have no right to be disappointed in me!"

"Yes, I do." He cried, grabbing her hand once more, "Nancy, I love you. You don't realise how much I love you and to think that you were so low that you didn't want to be here anymore, well, I took it personally. It hurts me so much that I can't even think about it!" He quickly looked away and bit his bottom lip.

Nancy could see his eyes glaze. She pulled his hand to her lips and kissed it, causing him to quickly move his other hand to pinch the bridge of his nose, trying to block his tears ducts with his fingers. Once back in control, he removed his hand and looked at her. "You were right!"

"About what?" She asked.

"About me being horrible with Lena. I spoke to her; she broke down and clung to me God bless her. I didn't mean to be cruel; I was so cold with her because I thought I was just making it crystal clear how much I disagreed with how she was living, to encourage her to stop. Not for one minute did I ever think I was pushing her to be that way."

Nancy half smiled, in acceptance of his admission.

"She actually opened up to me. I haven't spoken to my sister like that in years. I even cried! I've missed her so much! My little sister has needed me for so long and I've been so cruel!"

"No! Don't say that!" Nancy interrupted.

"No, it's true. I was cruel to her, just like I was cruel to you before."

"Francesco, there is nothing about you that's cruel. You may say the wrong thing, but you just care, that's all, if you didn't care then you wouldn't be so hard on us!"

"I do care. So much!" He let go of Nancy's hand and threw his head back, wiping his eyes with the back of his hands, "Argh!" He groaned, "I don't want to cry again." He tried to chuckle.

Nancy wrapped her arms around him. "I love you, Francesco!" She squoze him tightly, as he put his arms around her and rested his chin on top of her head, "That before wasn't me, I swear it wasn't Nance."

"I know."

"Please let me make it up to you. You know me! You know I'm better than that."

Nancy didn't even have to think about it. Even though she'd not seen that cold side of him before, she knew he cared and he had always been a little empathetically reserved, as anyone would be if they'd grown up with Lena. She was that dramatic, he'd become desensitised to certain levels of hysteria.

Nancy tilted her head back to look up at him and smiled. His beautiful blue eyes made her body melt against his. "I suppose I'll let you off." She quipped.

He leant down and passionately kissed her lips hard. Again, he smelt amazing and his lips were beautifully soft. She moved her hands up to the sides of his face and he slid his down to squeeze her bum, then briskly scooped her up, so she could wrap her arms around his neck and her legs around his waist. He pulled his lips away, just for a moment, to look into her eyes, she mischievously pouted at him, then parted her lips for another kiss, when, the door behind them swung open and they heard a voice say, "Oh, sorry!"

It was her mum. Francesco dropped her and both immediately removed their hands, quickly side stepping away from each other, like two naughty teenagers.

"Francesco was just dropping my things off." Nancy smirked.

"Oh, are your parents still coming too?" Her mum asked, she was clearly more embarrassed than they were.

"Yes, just going to get them now. I thought I'd free up the boot first, my mum is bringing some presents for you all."

"Oh, what is she like? I told her not to."

"You know her, she loves it." He smiled.

Her mum stared at them for a few moments, as if giving them the opportunity to explain themselves, but they didn't.

"So, what's all this then?" She probed.

"Nothing." Nancy shrugged.

"Doesn't look like nothing?"

Neither knew what to say. It felt so awkward because everyone knew each other so well. Nancy and Francesco shyly glimpsed at each other, then Francesco beamed, "I've got a new girlfriend, Mrs Costa."

Nancy grinned at her mum and nodded in confirmation.

"Well, finally! You two have been sniffing round each other for years!" She turned back into the house, "Raph, get the champagne, you've got a new son-in-law."

"Mum!" Nancy cried in embarrassment.

Her dad came to the door, "What are you shouting about woman?" He looked outside and saw Francesco. "Oh, hi lad, where's your family?"

"I'm just going to get them now." He replied, beginning to turn and walk back to his car.

"No, wait." Her mum shouted. "Go on tell your dad." She winked at Nancy.

"Mum, you're killing me!" She squirmed.

Her dad looked puzzled at them both, "What? You're not pregnant already, are you?"

"What?" Nancy cried.

Nancy's mum hit him in the arm and shook her head.

Her dad laughed. "Well, what?" He asked.

"They're together." Her mum yelled.

Her dad smiled, "Yeah, I know, tell me something new."

"What do you mean you know?"

"Why do you think he wanted to pick her up? That's why I invited him for breakfast."

"Oh."

"Keep up baby!"

"Wait. He knew!" Her mum snapped looking back at Nancy.

"I didn't tell him!" Nancy deflected.

Her parents both looked at Francesco, who quickly looked guiltily at Nancy, "I told him this morning. Sorry Mrs Costa!"

"And you never told me!" She shouted at her husband.

They began to bicker. Nancy sighed and walked over to them, while stressfully gesturing for them to disappear back inside. They obediently moved back into the house, giving her just enough room to shut the front door behind them. She exhaled and turned back to Francesco, grimacing. He laughed and held out his hand to her. She walked back to him and he pulled her sharply into his chest and hugged her tightly.

"Have you told your mum and dad yet?" She asked.

"No." He chuckled, "Well, I think my dad knows, but I'll go tell my mum now before she gets here. She still thinks I'm with Grace!"

"Oh shit!"

"I know.

"Have you heard from Grace?"

"I have actually. She wasted no time either to be honest. She came to get her belongings before, with her ex-boyfriend!"

"Oh God!" Nancy snorted, pushing out of his embrace to look up at his face.

"I know. Her ex did all the decorating in my houses, where she spent most of her time 'overseeing'. She happily confessed everything, how they'd started seeing each other again and had been for a few months, so it now makes sense why she never slept with me."

"What? Not once?"

"No! Not once, she told me she was religious, so I obviously respected that, but no, she was just sleeping with him instead. I don't know why she strung me along to be honest, it's weird."

"You did meet her at the gym!" Nancy huffed.

Francesco playfully rolled his eyes, let go of her and began to walk to his car, "What does that mean?"

Nancy laughed, "Nothing. You better let your membership expire now that you're with me!"

"Don't you want me to look good!"

"Not better than me, no!"

He laughed. "Do you still want your suitcase?" He joked.

"I do please!" She playfully pouted, now standing next to his car.

He opened the boot and pulled out her suitcase and lamp. "You know this lamp would look really good in my bedroom, in my new house."

"You can have it!" She smiled.

"I'd rather you come with the lamp!"

Nancy laughed loudly, "You haven't even taken me out on a date yet, never mind your bedroom!"

"I'll take you for a McDonald's breakfast in the morning?"

Nancy snorted and playfully hit him. "No. I want a proper date!"

"Nando's before then?"

Nancy raised her eyebrows and stared hard at him, jokingly unimpressed by his offers.

"Fine, I'll take you somewhere nice."

"A proper date!" Nancy insisted.

"Yes, a proper date!" He sighed in defeat.

He put his hands on her waist and pulled her into him. He went to grab her bum again, but she pushed him away and laughed, "Bugger off now!"

"Why?" He protested.

"I told you; I want a proper date!"

He playfully grabbed her waist and pulled her into him again. "But I love you!" He smiled.

"I love you too, but no!" She laughed, kissing him.

He leant against his car and sighed, "I can't be bothered with my parents and all their questions now." He winced.

"I know." Nancy sighed.

"I know what I'd rather be doing, than spending the afternoon with them."

"Oh my God, stop and get in your car!" She laughed.

"Are you sure?"

"Positive! Go!"

Francesco let go of her waist, shut the boot and moved reluctantly to his car door, he then stopped and jokingly winked over his shoulder.

"Francesco, bugger off and go get your parents!" She laughed.

"Fine!" He smiled, climbing into his seat.

Nancy shut the car door for him and ushered with her hands for him to leave, giggling at his persistence. He smiled at her through his window, then put the car into gear and drove away. She stayed by the curb and watched until he turned out of the street.

She grabbed her suitcase, then realised her lamp was missing. "Crafty sod!" She chuckled to herself.

It felt magical to finally be with him, she couldn't believe her luck. As pathetic as it was, the second he pulled out of the street; she began to miss him. She pulled her suitcase up the driveway and went back inside.

She could hear her parents still playfully bickering in the kitchen, as they continued to clean up after dinner.

"I'm just going to take my things upstairs." She shouted into the kitchen.

"Do you need help carrying it up?" Her dad replied.

She looked down at the small case, "No, I can manage thanks."

She carried it up the stairs, into her room, then dropped it next to her bed. She was about to leave the room, but stopped and walked back over to it. She knelt down, unzipped it and there it was, her blood stained, snot riddled dressing gown. "How!" Nancy whispered, as she slowly pulled it out in awe, then she cuddled it tightly. She didn't know whether to wash it or frame it. She deliberated what to do for a few moments, then thought about her parents' reaction to her framing a dirty, old dressing gown and how she'd fail to explain it. She dropped it to her side and created a washing pile.

When the case was empty, she picked up the pile and went out onto the landing to drop it into the laundry basket. She flicked open the lid and put them in, but pulled back her dressing gown to check her pockets. The first was empty, however, when she put her hand into the second, there it was. The note that she'd kept from the chair teetering on the cliff edge. She excitedly opened the envelope and unfolded the paper to read it;

Imagine there are three states of being, past, present and future. Every moment of our lives is captured in time, carved into the stone of time. If I moved into the past, I couldn't change it because it's nothing more than a memory, a shadow of time. If I moved into the future, I still couldn't change it, because the stones of the present are continually being laid. So, it is right here and only here in the present that I can make change. The past shapes us, but it can't dictate the future. It offers only an advisory notice. Therefore, you shouldn't fear the future, because right here in the present is where we are in control of our universe.

She had been too distracted to give these words any real attention when they were first read to her, but now she understood. The passage was simply an instruction, advising her to focus on only what she could control. If she had listened, the night probably wouldn't have unfolded as dramatically as it did. She smiled, then held it to her chest, "Thank you!" She whispered.

She went back into her bedroom, picked up her small, leopard print make-up bag and walked over to sit on the floor in front of her mirror. She'd decided to put some make-up on before Francesco came back, even though she felt comfortable without any in front of him, she felt a little more herself with it on. She symmetrically, winged her eyeliner, loaded her long eyelashes with mascara, tidied her eyebrows, then lined her full lips with nude liner to exaggerate her thick pout. Finally, she defined her beauty spot just above the corner of her top lip with a brown pencil, and did her best toothy Marilyn Monroe smile. Her white teeth sparkled. She was back!

24

The Approval

There was a loud knock at the front door, it echoed up the stairs into her room and her heart sang.

"They're here!" Her mum called from the bottom of the stairs.

Nancy couldn't wait to be with Francesco again. She sailed down the stairs, but, "What if his parents don't approve?" She thought. Immediately, her happiness was yet again smothered, as she began hypothesizing the worst. She positioned herself near the back of the hallway, behind her parents. From there she'd judge their body language as they entered.

"Merry Christmas!" Francesco's parents sang.

"Merry Christmas!" Her parents sang back.

They hugged one another, while briefly mentioning the cold outside. They appeared jovial enough, no obvious signs of unease or reluctance. They moved further inside still chatting, as they made way for Lena and Evangeline to enter behind them. Lena greeted Nancy's parents, then immediately smirked at Nancy as if to say 'they know', to which Nancy gave an uneasy grin.

"Nancy!" Francesco's mother shouted, now clocking her at the back of the hallway.

Nancy grinned back at her nervously.

"Evidently, your Christmas Eve streak caught my son's attention!"

Nancy squirmed; for the first time in her life, she couldn't read her. Was she joking or about to dive into a lecture? "Apparently so." Nancy replied. Where was Francesco? Why hadn't he come through the door? She couldn't see him. Had their disapproval scared him off?

"I was the last to know as usual." She looked at Lena and her husband who began to laugh. Then turned back to Nancy, "Why the secrecy?"

"It wasn't a secret," Nancy replied, "I just didn't know how to tell you."

"Well, I'm disappointed!"

Nancy's heart stopped beating. "Disappointed?" She thought.

She wanted to run away and cry, until, "Oh Mum, stop it now," Lena cut in, "she's just got out of hospital for God's sake. What did you want her to do, call you from her hospital bed?"

"It could have been mentioned before, that's all I'm saying."

Lena huffed and rolled her eyes.

"You're disappointed?" Nancy croaked.

Mrs Ferrara turned back to see the sadness on Nancy's face, "No," She quickly reassured her, "no, I'm not disappointed that it's you Nancy! My God no! I'm disappointed that nobody told me sooner." She turned to Nancy's mum, "They don't tell me anything Carmela. No one does."

Carmela pouted in agreeance, "Nobody told me either and I don't think they would have. I caught them at it, out in the front."

"Mum!" Nancy cried.

Mrs Ferrara laughed and turned back to Nancy. She took one of her hands and held it between hers, "I honestly couldn't be happier my darling! Finally! You both took your time!" She smiled and hugged her tightly.

Nancy exhaled in relief, "I was so nervous!"

"Why?" Mr Ferrara asked also coming over to hug her, "I'm not going to lie, it was a shock!" He added.

"It was!" His wife agreed, "We still thought he was with Grace!" She looked wide eyed at Nancy's parents and shrugged.

"Good riddance to her!" Mr Ferrara grinned.

"Why?" Mrs Ferrara asked.

Mr Ferrara didn't answer; he just winked and smiled at Nancy. "We're very happy it's you Nance!"

"Thank you!" Nancy smiled back, "Where is he though?"

"Oh, he's just getting the presents out of the car," Mrs Ferrara motioned with her hand to the open front door, "and Evangeline's princess castle."

Nancy looked over at Evangeline, "Are you going to help me put it together?"

Evangeline shook her head, "No. I can't be bothered. Mum said you'll just build it for me!"

Nancy snorted and looked up at Lena.

Lena smiled proudly.

Mrs Ferrara tutted. Then turned her attention back to Nancy, "So when's the wedding?"

Nancy nervously clenched her teeth and shrugged.

"I'm joking, but I think we should at least toast the happy new couple."

Nancy cringed. She flashed Lena an uneasy glance.

"Yes!" Carmela agreed, "Everyone go into the living room and I'll get us all a drink. What does everyone want?"

Lena ushered her mother into the living room, while Nancy stayed in the hallway. She quietly exhaled in relief and put her cold hands against her embarrassed cheeks to cool them. As much as she loved them, they were sometimes a bit full on.

Finally, Francesco came through the door. He held a sack of gifts in one hand and a large box of Lego under his opposite arm.

"Oh my God, I didn't know it was that big!" Nancy cried at seeing the size of the box.

"What can I say, I'm blessed." He smirked.

Nancy shook her head and laughed, "I meant the box!"

He beamed and walked over to kiss her. "Look at you!"

"Thought I'd make an effort."

"I love you without anything on." He cheekily winked at her.

She laughed and took the box from him. "Your parents seemed okay with us?" She whispered.

"Yeah, they are. It took them a little by surprise, just because of the whole girlfriend to girlfriend transition, but yeah, they weren't surprised about it being you."

"Why?"

"I think they've always known I had a thing for you."

Nancy laughed.

"Were you honestly worried?" He asked.

"Yes!"

"Why?"

"I don't know, I just panic about everything."

"Don't!" He kissed her again. "This castle is going to take you all night by the way. I've had a quick look at the instructions; they go on and on."

"Oh God!" Nancy sighed studying the side of the box. "It's a bit old for her, isn't it? Who bought it?"

"Me!"

"Obviously! Couldn't you have just got her a ready-made one?"

"No. This is the one she asked for."

"Oh!" Nancy chuckled. "Oh, yeah, before I forget too, my lamp, you took it!"

Francesco smiled, "Yes, I'm putting it in my bedroom remember?"

"Honestly?"

"Yeah. You offered. That's your Christmas present to me. You can come visit it later if you like?"

Nancy shook her head and playfully raised her eyebrows at him.

He laughed, "In all seriousness though, I would like to take you out tomorrow. On a proper date!"

"Where?" She asked.

"It's a surprise."

"No, go on, tell me!"

"No, you'll love it though. I promise."

"I don't trust you!"

"Well, that's a good start to a healthy relationship."

Nancy laughed, "I mean, I just know there's going to be some angle to it."

"The only angle is you'll have to be up really early in the morning!"

Nancy grumbled, "How early?"

"We'll leave at six."

She grumbled again.

"If you don't want to get up too early, you can always stay at mine to save time?"

She put her free arm around his neck, leant in to his lips and whispered, "No!"

"Fine." He groaned, "Suit yourself. Just make sure you're ready for six then, okay?"

"Fine!"

"I mean it. I know you. Not six-thirty, not seven, six on the dot."

"*Okay*! I'll be ready."

"Good. Now come on, move it, let's go and make a start on this castle."

He nodded towards the living room for Nancy to lead the way and the two entered the room.

Everyone was now in deep conversation thank God, so they slipped in without drawing any attention. They sat near Evangeline on the floor and placed the box down between them.

"I've got your presents here Nancy!" Mrs Ferrara said, reaching for Francesco to hand her the sack. Their families always bought each other Christmas gifts, even when Lena and Nancy weren't speaking.

"You shouldn't have gotten me anything!" Nancy replied.

His mum rummaged through the gifts, squinting at the name tags as she dished them out. "Oh, they're just little bits." She said, as she handed Nancy hers.

Nancy carefully unwrapped the three small packages; perfume, bed socks and lipstick. "I love this perfume and this lipstick! Thank you!"

"You're welcome! I know you like your cosy socks too."

"I do!"

"Francesco, got me these ones." She wiggled her toes, proudly showing Nancy her new socks.

Nancy smiled to herself and looked at Francesco, who immediately looked down at the Lego, confirming Nancy's suspicion that they were in fact the regift.

"Francesco said you're going away?" Lena asked.

"Are we?" Nancy looked surprised at him.

"A cabin or something wasn't it?" Lena added.

Nancy squinted at Francesco.

"I said we were thinking about it!" He corrected his sister.

Nancy went to speak, but Lena quickly interrupted. "Never mind just making plans with him, what are *we* going to do?"

It felt so good to have her best friend ask her that question. She was so excited to start this new chapter with her. "Whatever you want." Nancy shrugged.

"Let's go out next weekend, we could –"

Nancy rolled her eyes and cut in, "I'm not going out drinking!"

"Let me finish!" Lena scolded, "We could take Evangeline out, to spend her Christmas money."

Evangeline's little face lit up at the thought of the trip.

"Yeah course, let's go!" Nancy smiled at Evangeline.

"When do you go to the cabin though?" Lena asked.

"It's booked for next week! Wednesday to Friday." Francesco mumbled quietly.

"Was it cheaper mid-week?" Nancy chuckled.

"She wasn't worth the weekend prices," he quietly replied, "I'd move it to the weekend for you though – If you wanted to come and you're free, that is?"

Nancy stared at him, as he shyly looked back down to continue sorting the small coloured bricks into piles. She couldn't believe her luck. To be here with her beautiful extended family, all of them happy to be in her presence, wanting to make plans with her.

Francesco looked up, anxiously prompting for an answer.

"I'm free mid-week!" She smiled.

They laughed, ate and drank till around eight o'clock. Evangeline at this point was snuggled into Lena's side on the grey armchair. Nancy and Francesco chuckled as they watched her little eyes continuously close, then pop back open, as she desperately fought to stay awake. Lena looked down at her, "I think it's time for you to go to bed."

"No!" Evangeline protested, "My castle isn't ready!"

"It is." Lena laughed, "Come on." She shuffled to the end of the seat, then scooped her baby up into her arms.

"Ah, bless her. Time to go." Mrs Ferrara smiled watching her cling to her mum. She held onto the arm of the sofa, and tipsily stood up.

"You okay there, Mum?" Lena sniggered.

"I'm fine." She snapped.

Lena laughed and wrinkled her nose at Nancy, then they all filtered into the hall, while Nancy and Francesco stayed behind in the living room.

He looked down at the castle and scratched his beard. "How am I going to get this back without breaking it?"

"God knows!"

He smiled, then stood and helped her up with him. He pulled her in close and kissed her. He tasted so sweet after nearly devouring a whole box of After-eights. "You taste nice." She smiled.

"I can't stop when I get going on those things." He frowned, looking down at the box, "Are you still up for tomorrow?"

"Definitely."

"Six o'clock on the dot."

"Yes!" She groaned, "I'll be ready!"

"Good."

"Francesco! Come on!" Lena shouted from the hall.

"I'm coming! I'm just trying to pick up this castle."

He kissed Nancy again. Neither wanted to pull away. His hands slid down to her bum, she put her arms around his neck and they held each other tightly. Eventually, he released her and chuckled, "I've messed up your lips." He tried to gently rub it back into neat lines.

"Francesco! I swear to God, if you don't open this car right now —" Lena shrieked.

He sighed and shook his head at her impatience, "Hang on!" He shouted back, then quickly knelt down to carefully manipulate the Lego castle onto the cardboard lid of the box. "There. Easy-peasy." He nervously grinned, slowly rising.

"Francesco!" Lena shrieked again.

"I'm coming!" He yelled back. He looked at Nancy in annoyance and she quietly sniggered. She followed him into the hallway and his parents smirked at his emergence.

"What?" Francesco innocently asked.

Mrs Ferrara raised her eyebrows at Carmela, "He took his time trying to pick up that castle!"

"I didn't want to break it!" Francesco protested.

Mrs Ferrara moved outside with her daughter and husband. He walked to the door, then looked in the mirror at the bottom of the stairs to find Nancy's lip liner stains around his mouth. "Oh." He laughed.

Francesco turned back and smiled at her, "See *you* in the morning."

"You will."

He moved through the doorway and headed for the car.

"Night everyone." Her mum shouted after them.

They waved them off, then went back inside.

"That was lovely!" Her mum yawned.

"It was." Her dad agreed moving to kiss her mum.

Nancy turned to begin climbing the stairs, "Where are you going?" Her dad asked.

"I was just going to get ready for bed, I'm really tired."

"No. Come on Nance! Watch a film with your old dad." He put his arm around her shoulders.

"Okay." She nodded. They walked into the living room.

"Does anyone want a drink?" Her mum shouted after them, "I'm going to make myself a hot chocolate."

"I'll have one Mum."

"Not for me!" Her dad responded, "I'm still finishing my beer."

Her dad sat in his seat at the farthest end of the sofa, while Nancy picked up what was left of the After-eights and sat next to him.

"What do you want to watch?" He asked picking up the remote.

"Anything, just see what's on."

He scrolled for a few moments, then spotted their family favourite, the film that Nancy had watched all alone, crying into her cereal, after the bath, "Oh, look, here we go, *It's a Wonderful Life*; I haven't watched it yet this year."

Nancy's eyes immediately filled with tears, but she desperately fought to contain them, "Me neither." She lied.

She rested her head on his arm and after a few moments her mum appeared with their mugs of hot chocolate. She handed one to Nancy and sat down next to her.

"Your dad and I were saying only last night, how we haven't watched this yet. Have you?"

"No." She lied again.

"There we go then." Her mum smiled, "All together." She snuggled into her daughter.

"Yeah," Nancy whispered as her lip quivered and her heart burst, "back together."

25

The Date

Five-fifty-seven the next morning, Nancy stood out in the dark on the curb waiting for Francesco. She was so excited for their first date, she'd got up extra early to wave her hair and put on a full face of make-up, even though he'd told her to just put on warm scruffs. Finally, she saw two headlights in the distance. She faintly waved and grinned as he came closer, but he rolled a little further past her. She walked to the car and opened the door, "Why did you drive past me?"

"I didn't recognise you; you look stunning!" He joked.

She got into the car and playfully hit him in the arm.

"I actually can't believe you're on time." He jibed.

"It's going to be my new year's resolution."

"That's not going to last." He snorted.

She glared at him, "Shut up, you! Where are you taking me anyway?"

He put the car into gear and pulled away. "It's a surprise."

"The fact that I'm in scruffs, I'm guessing a walk somewhere?"

"Correct."

"Are you honestly not going to tell me?"

"Nope."

Nancy groaned; she had always been too impatient for surprises. "That was lovely yesterday with everyone, wasn't it?"

"I loved it. I'm so glad you and Lena are speaking again; it's been weird not spending as much time with your family."

"I've missed Lena so much!"

He cleared his throat, "What about me?"

"I forgot about you to be honest."

He laughed, "I know you did, you had them all lined up, didn't you."

She playfully hit him again.

"I'm joking, I'm joking."

"Does Evangeline like her castle?"

"She's literally been up since five playing with it."

Nancy laughed, "I bet Lena loved getting up that early."

"She was sat with pretty much a fish bowl of coffee in her lap and grunted at me when I said bye."

Nancy laughed again. "I'll go and see them later, *if* I survive this first date."

"What do you mean first? We've been out loads of times?"

"Yeah, but not like this. You didn't flirt with me or anything before."

"No, that's true. I did almost kiss you when we went bowling that time."

"I knew it! I thought you were about to, but then you just turned and sat down."

He started laughing and put his hand on her knee, "I bet you were devastated!"

She sarcastically huffed, "Not really, I had all the others lined up remember."

He jokingly squoze her knee hard and she burst into laughter, pulling his hand away, "Get off and watch the road."

He then reached back over and put his hand on her thigh, "I'm so glad we're here together now though."

She put her hand on top of his, "Me too, as long as you don't blank me when I go to kiss you again."

"That's not going to happen."

They drove for a few more miles, talking and laughing together, then reached a busy car park in the middle of a wood.

"We're going to watch the sunrise at the top of Mount Arthur, aren't we?"

"Yes, we are."

"Since when have you been romantic?"

"Just today. This is pretty much the peak for me, so I wouldn't expect much in the future."

She chuckled.

He undid his seatbelt, "I'll just go get a ticket for the car."

Nancy got out too and pulled her hat on. She looked up at the mountain to see a trail of lights moving like a snake up towards the top.

"I didn't realise it was so popular!" She said as Francesco returned.

"Neither did I to be honest. I thought we'd have it to ourselves with the fresh snow."

She walked over to him, put her arms around his waist and leant into him, "It's still going to be beautiful."

He leant down and kissed her, then slowly pulled away and smiled, "It will be if you get your arse up there in time."

She laughed, "You'll have to carry me."

"No, if you fall behind, you're on your own."

He moved to the back of the car, with her following and opened the boot, where he pulled out a rucksack.

"My lamp!" She cried, spotting it in the corner.

"You mean *my* lamp!" He corrected her.

She smiled. "What's in the bag?"

"I have hot chocolate and cinnamon swirls."

"I love cinnamon swirls."

"I know, that's why I brought them."

"Where the hell did you buy them? Everywhere was closed yesterday."

He looked up at the peak, ignoring her.

"They're stale leftovers, aren't they?"

"No!" He shook his head, "They're very fresh actually."

"Where did you get them from then?"

He hesitated, then mumbled, "I got Lena to make them yesterday afternoon, as a peace offering to you, but forgot them when I came to say sorry."

"You make me sick!" Nancy frowned.

"Why?" He laughed.

"You're just creepy thoughtful."

"I'll leave them here then."

She grabbed his hands as he went to put the bag back, "No, no, I'll eat your creepy swirls."

He playfully scowled at her, as he put the bag on his back and locked the car, "Just focus on getting yourself to the top, you."

She smiled sweetly at him and his scowl melted. He put his hands on her shoulders and marched her forward a few paces.

"Well, this is a first. I've never walked with a guy like this on date before."

He moved closer behind her, threw his arms around her, pulled her into him and kissed her neck, "Is this better?"

"Much better."

The climb was hard work, the path was steep and the ice under the fresh snow made it that slippery, Nancy spent more time on the ground than upright.

"I'm glad you said old clothes." She said looking down at her knees caked in mud.

"I knew you'd be all the over the place." He joked.

"Say's you?" She pulled up his arm and pointed to the thick dirt on his left side.

He laughed, "I honestly didn't think it was going to be this hard."

"It'll be worth it though."

"It will. We're nearly there."

Nancy grabbed his hand and gently pulled him, while he panted hard. "And you go to the gym?" She sniggered.

"Do you want to carry this rucksack?"

"It's only a drink and cakes!"

He huffed and shook his head as she pretended to start jogging, "I think if you were in that hospital gown walking in front of me, I'd move a lot faster."

She laughed, "It's a bit too cold for that up here."

Finally, they made it to the top and found a spot just away from the crowd. Francesco pulled a waterproof picnic blanket out of the rucksack. "It's still going to be cold, but at least it's something dry to sit on."

"It's perfect." Nancy said, sitting down before the wind whipped it away.

He pulled out a tall thermos and the cinnamon swirls wrapped in foil. "Just hold these a minute please." He handed them over to her and sat down.

She unscrewed the cup from the top and handed it to him, then undid the valve and poured it, while he held it still. He continued to rummage with his other hand in the rucksack.

"This is such a beautiful idea." Nancy beamed.

"I'm glad you like it. I was honestly racking my brain, then I remembered about this."

"You didn't bring Grace here, did you?"

He laughed, "No. She would never have done this with me. If it wasn't shopping or a vegan meal, she wasn't interested."

"What did you two even talk about?"

"Not much really. It was either drama between her and her friends or her weird diet shit."

"Riveting." Nancy sniggered.

"Oh, bloody hell!" He tutted.

"What's the matter?"

"I've only brought one cup."

"You've literally just had your tongue in my mouth; I don't mind sharing."

"That's true."

271

They unwrapped the cinnamon swirls, and sipped the hot chocolate as the sun began to peak over the horizon.

"Here we go!" Francesco smiled.

"Thank God. I can't feel my toes."

"Sit here." Francesco opened his legs for Nancy to sit in-between them. She rested her back against his chest and he put his arms around her. "Is that a little warmer?"

"A little, thank you."

"Tell Lena the swirls were delicious by the way."

He tutted, "You weren't meant to ask where they'd come from."

"Can you bake?" She asked.

"Simple things. What about you?"

"It's not really one of my talents."

"Do you still draw?"

"I haven't in ages. I think that's my happy place though, just headphones on, sketching away."

"You'll have to draw me, like he does on Titanic; what does she say to him?"

"Draw me like one of your French girls?"

"Yes!" Francesco laughed.

"I'll have to make sure the pencil is super sharp to draw your tiny details."

"Cheeky bitch!" He laughed.

"I am going to start again."

"There's an outbuilding at my new house, I'll turn it into an art studio for you, if you like?"

"Really?"

"Yeah. I'm not putting any heating in there after your 'tiny' comment though."

Nancy laughed.

"You can bloody freeze!" He sniggered.

She put her head back, slid down a little and looked up at him, pouting.

"Fine!" He smiled looking into her dark eyes, "You can have a hot water bottle."

She kissed him, then snuggled back into his chest.

They sat contently watching the sun rise higher; the beautiful red aura setting the hills ablaze, as it hit the white snow.

"It's magical." Nancy whispered.

"It is out of this world." He clenched and released his fists, then wiggled his fingers attempting to warm them.

"Are you okay?" Nancy asked.

"I am absolutely frozen!"

"Me too, but I didn't want to seem ungrateful and ask to leave."

Francesco motioned with his head for her to get up, "Let's go!"

Nancy jumped up, grabbed the rucksack and quickly shoved the thermos and foil back inside.

Francesco laughed, "I love that you'd risk frostbite to save my feelings."

She smiled, "What more do you want!"

He rolled up the picnic blanket and walked over to her to kiss her, but she jokingly pushed him away, "I'll kiss you when we're at the bottom. My lips are literally stuck to my teeth."

He grabbed her hand tightly, guided her quickly to the path and they began sliding down it.

Back in the car, soggy and cold, Francesco threw the rucksack onto the backseat, put the key in the ignition and turned the heating on high.

"Thank God for that!" Nancy sighed, slouching in her seat. "Don't get me wrong, I loved it."

"It was fantastic," he interrupted, "but no, I agree, it's nice to be back in the car. Did you bring spare clothes?" He asked, noticing her bag in the passenger footwell.

"I did." She smiled.

"Do you want to come back to my new house quickly then; I don't want to take you home just yet."

Nancy didn't hesitate, "I don't want go home yet."

He smiled at her.

"I'm dying to see this house of yours."

"You'll love it and it will be warm, don't worry."

He put the car into gear and they drove off.

"Do you have much left to do?"

"Just decorating really and I already have some furniture set up. I've stayed over some nights, while I've been working on it."

"I'm excited."

He glanced at her uncomfortably.

"What?" She chuckled.

"Nothing."

"No go on, what's that weird face for?"

"No honestly it's nothing."

"Tell me now!" She tutted.

He smiled, focusing ahead, "Well, I don't want this to sound creepy," he rolled his eyes, "or forward," he continued, "but I bought it when we started getting to know each other didn't I?"

"You did."

"Well, now here we are together, it's just like it was meant to be." He reached for her hand and pulled it to his lips to kiss it, "I'm so excited for you to finally be there with me."

Nancy was taken back by such a beautiful thought. "You said in the hospital that I was the love of your life. When did you fall in love with me?" She asked.

He burst into laughter, "I actually vividly remember the exact moment."

"Go on." She prompted.

"Well obviously we went out together and stuff, but it was after that, when we'd drifted. You were out and Lena saw you."

"When Lena and I weren't speaking?"

"Yes, she called me to come and get you because she could tell that you'd had way too much to drink and saw Joel hanging around. Do you remember?"

"I remember you taking me home, but I didn't know Lena had called you. I thought you were just there."

"No. I drove in especially for you." Francesco glanced at her adoringly.

Nancy smiled and pushed his face to focus on the road, "Carry on then."

"Well, you were the happiest drunk I'd ever seen in my life!"

"Why?" She chuckled.

"On the way to the car, you were just rambling on about really random shit."

"Like what?"

"How you didn't trust woodlice because they drank from their bum."

Nancy erupted into laughter, "I still feel really disturbed whenever I see one. Is that when you fell in love?"

"No, not just yet. When you first got into the car you sang to every song at the top of your lungs."

Nancy winced in embarrassment.

"But then as we got closer to your parents' house, you suddenly hit the wall and just wanted to sleep."

"Oh God!" She cringed.

He laughed, "You kept batting me away when I tried to wake you, so I just picked you up in the end."

Nancy snorted.

"Anyway, your dad was out, so your mum asked if I could carry you up the stairs. So, I did. While she went to find you a bowl in case you were sick, it's at this point that I fell in love."

"Why what did I do?"

"As I lay you down on your bed, you put your arms around my neck, opened your eyes, smirked, then kissed me."

"That did not happen!" Nancy cut-in.

"It did I swear!"

"Did you kiss me back?"

"No, course not, you literally just pecked me on the lips."

She looked at him dubiously.

"Honestly that's what you did."

"I know you carried me up the stairs, because I got a lecture the next morning from my mum about being in control, but other than getting into your car, I don't remember anything after that."

"Well, that's what honestly happened!"

"And you did nothing about it the next day?"

"I thought it was just the drink and you didn't mention it, so I never."

"I called you the next day to say thank you though. We could have been together ages ago, if you'd have just told me how you felt."

"I know, but maybe it just wasn't the right time."

Nancy huffed and sat straight in her seat. She then put her hand on the back of his neck and stretched her fingers up into his hair, "Maybe, you could have saved me from the whole Joel experience."

Francesco sighed, "Yeah probably. When did you know you loved me?"

"Really quickly actually. We'd just started speaking, when I was working in the restaurant."

He laughed, "What did it for you?"

"You were just different."

He smiled and put his hand on her thigh, "How so?"

"You're a creepy weirdo."

He laughed, "You have a type then?"

"Apparently so!" She chuckled.

They pulled onto a rural street, with large houses scattered along it; each hidden behind neat hedges and mature trees.

"Here it is!" Francesco beamed proudly as he turned into the driveway.

"Oh wow! Bloody hell Francesco! I wasn't expecting this!"

"Looks good doesn't it!"

The tall Victorian house stood at the top of a long lawned front garden, thick with snow. Cherry, sycamore, cob nut and pine trees guarded the perimeter, "It's definitely private." Nancy said, admiring them.

"Yeah, I was going to cut them at one point, but they don't affect the sun, so I'm just going to leave them.

He took his key from the ignition and stepped out of the car, "Come on, I'll show you inside."

Nancy picked up her bag and followed him to the sage front door. "I love the door."

"It's original. I've tried to salvage as many things as possible. All I did was give it a fresh coat of paint."

He put the key in the lock and opened it, revealing a generous porchway, which opened onto a hallway. Every wall was freshly plastered, waiting to be painted and there was a rich, warm parquet floor.

Nancy walked ahead of him into the hallway, "I'll come and help you paint, now your decorator has run off with your ex-girlfriend."

He walked over to her and held her with one arm, while he gently poked her with his knuckle up and down her ribs, tickling her, "Stop!" She shouted, squirming in a fit of laughter, trying to free herself.

He let go and smiled, "I'd appreciate your help."

"I don't come cheap though!"

"I'll get you more cinnamon swirls, shop bought this time though! From the self-serve at the bakery, with a nice glaze of germs on them."

She flicked her middle finger up at him and walked ahead into the living room. It had a sofa and TV in the centre covered in dust sheets. "This is a big room." She commented.

"Yeah, there's another across the hall about the same size, then a kitchen and utility at the end."

He led them back into the hall and walked towards the kitchen, but Nancy stopped to admire the tall window above the staircase. "That's beautiful." The light bathed the dark, stained wood of the banister, giving the whole stairwell a soft glow. Even though the house was bare and unfinished, it had a warm, welcoming, homely feel to it.

Francesco walked back to her, "It is, isn't it. That's my second favourite part."

"What's your first?"

"Come with me." He led her into an empty kitchen, which ended in a wall of glass and through it lay a large mature garden.

"Oh my God, it's huge!"

"I know! Amazing isn't it."

"Can we go out?"

"Yeah course."

He led out into the garden and she admired the large fenced space, magically frosted in a pristine white blanket. She noticed the row of outhouses to the far left, then a pretty little structure in the opposite corner.

"What's that?"

"A kids' playhouse. It was left here, so I fixed it. Evangeline will love it."

She turned back to look at the house. "How many bedrooms does it have?"

"Four."

She paused suddenly feeling very nervous, "It's a beautiful *family* home." She pouted and raised her eyebrows as she turned back to him.

Francesco uncomfortably sniggered, "Well, yeah, I wanted a *family* home. I'm thirty-five Nance, nearly thirty-six. It would be nice to be a dad, before I get too old."

Nancy pursed her lips and silently nodded as she looked back at the house. She stood in deep thought analysing the architecture.

"What are you thinking?" He anxiously asked.

She gently shrugged, "How could I be a mother?" She thought. She couldn't look after herself, never mind take care of something as precious as a child. Her head began to spin and she looked back at him, to find his usual strong, calm face awash with nervous panic; his clear uncertainty in what he'd basically just asked of her melted her heart. She was overcome with love.

Knowing all that he did about her, it was bizarre to Nancy how much he still wanted her. He embraced her craziness and looked past her eccentric, dark walls to the good at her core, wanting to not only share his life with her, but for her to be the mother of his children. Never had she felt this way before and in that moment, she realised that she'd found what she'd been looking for.

She broke into a mischievous smirk, moved over to him, put her hands on the waistband of his sweatpants, pulled him towards her and slipped her fingertips just inside the top of them so they rested against his skin.

He leant down and kissed her, then broke into an uneasy smile, "Go on, please, tell me what you're thinking?"

She sharply inhaled, again looked at the house, then slowly exhaled, as she looked back up into his beautiful eyes, "I'm thinking, that you should show me the bedroom that we're going to put our lamp in."

Epilogue

Several years passed, Nancy lay snuggled in her bed too excited to sleep. The anticipation was killing her, until, finally, she heard the pitter patter of tiny feet sprinting wildly across the wooden floor of her room. Francesco lying next to her, groaned in pain as their three children leapt onto the bed shouting, "He's been! Santa's been!"

Three weeks after Nancy and Francesco had returned from their snowy cabin trip, Nancy found out she was pregnant. This news was swiftly followed by a quick wedding before she gave birth to a son, followed two years later by another son and three years later by a daughter. Her life was now absolute chaos, but she loved it. Thriving in the beauty of normality, she never had a second to overthink anything. From time to time, she would cast her mind back to that dark night, but only in gratitude, to have been saved and to now belong in this beautiful second life. Life still wasn't all rainbows and roses, but when the clouds rolled in, she could deal with them, because no longer did they catch her sleeping. This was a woman who loved and trusted herself.

She also dedicated a lot of her time to helping others who felt disenchanted with their own lives. She wanted to give them hope, that the dark will clear if you take it upon yourself to shine a light through it. She wanted others to know, that waiting for the guidance of a lighthouse in a storm isn't practical. The lighthouse keeper may have taken the night off or the light may be down for repairs. There are too many variables and too much reliance on others to prevent self-progression. The rescue boat has to be launched from within, by containing the fear to do it and keeping tight control of the ship.

Printed in Dunstable, United Kingdom

75972339R00163